A Taste of Honey

ROCKY BARILLA

Rosquete
Press

Cover and book design by Eileen Jurkovich © 2014

Library of Congress Control Number: 2014912348

ISBN: 978-0-9904851-0-0

Upcoming works by Rocky Barilla:

Ay to Zi

The Devil's Disciple

Published by Rosquete Press
All works are or will be available as Kindle or
CreateSpace Editions on Amazon.com

DEDICATIONS

This book is dedicated to my wife, Dolores,
who always raises an eyebrow
to each of my latest endeavors,
but supports me anyway.

"In the long history of humankind (and animal kind, too)
those who have learned to collaborate
and improvise most effectively,
have prevailed."

Charles Darwin (1809 - 1882)

CONTENTS

	Acknowledgements	i
CHAPTER 1	Returning Home	1
CHAPTER 2	A Cold Beer	9
CHAPTER 3	Big Red	20
CHAPTER 4	The Bed	30
CHAPTER 5	The Penguins	37
CHAPTER 6	Clean Sheets	44
CHAPTER 7	The Lunch	51
CHAPTER 8	Smoke	61
CHAPTER 9	The View	66
CHAPTER 10	El Sombrerón	72
CHAPTER 11	The Wake	78
CHAPTER 12	The Burial	82
CHAPTER 13	Water	90
CHAPTER 14	Dirty Laundry	95
CHAPTER 15	Delirium	101
CHAPTER 16	Clean Bedding	105
CHAPTER 17	Strawberries	110
CHAPTER 18	Mental	116
CHAPTER 19	The Poem	120
CHAPTER 20	The Picnic	128
CHAPTER 21	Mother Superior	134
CHAPTER 22	The Sonnet	138
CHAPTER 23	Looking for Mangoes	142

CHAPTER 24	The Dinner	147
CHAPTER 25	Subterranean	153
CHAPTER 26	Father Rivoli	158
CHAPTER 27	Dirty Clothes	164
CHAPTER 28	Drunkenness	169
CHAPTER 29	Transformation	178
CHAPTER 30	Duped	186
CHAPTER 31	Warning	192
CHAPTER 32	Magic Mushrooms	200
CHAPTER 33	Tears	208
CHAPTER 34	Mistrust	215
CHAPTER 35	Captured	221
CHAPTER 36	Inferno	226
CHAPTER 37	Exodus	232
CHAPTER 38	Successor	240
CHAPTER 39	The Shelter	244
CHAPTER 40	Mother Superior	250
CHAPTER 41	Deluged	255
CHAPTER 42	Marcia's Tale	262
CHAPTER 43	Dilemma	265
CHAPTER 44	Attack	268
CHAPTER 45	Lavender	275
CHAPTER 46	Long Live the Queen!	282
	About the Author	285

ACKNOWLEDGMENTS

I want to thank all my family, friends, and colleagues who afforded me tremendous support and love while I wrote my books. This is especially true for my wife, Dolores, who is my teammate and partner in everything we do. The heavy duty editing was done by the smart one in the family, our daughter Carmen Cave (Ph.D. Stanford) who remarked that my writing sometimes resembles the speech patterns of Yoda, the Jedi knight: "Patience, I must have." Additional editing was done by my special friend, Sherril Smith Scharf who is Ms. Happy.

The wonderful cover and formatting was done by a special friend, Eileen Jurkovich. People who drink caffè affogatos rock.

Muchísimas gracias to my wonderful mentor and advocate, the brilliant Chicana writer, Denise Chavez, who has given me inspiration and guidance in the sharing of creativity and all things good and beautiful.

And lastly, a special tribute to Eddie Cano (Lincoln High School '44) and Herb Alpert & The Tijuana Brass for their inspirational renditions of "A Taste of Honey".

CHAPTER 1

RETURNING HOME

Wednesday, May 17, 1974, Somewhere in the Jungles of Guatemala. The portable cassette player was blasting "Oye Como Va" from the passenger seat of the Jeep. The driver was doing his best Carlos Santana impression in a high-pitched rendition. He was bouncing and bopping up and down to the sound of the music. Then the first raindrop pinged the windshield like a tiny pebble. This was followed by another watery pellet. Then came a third, a fourth, . . . In a few moments, the olive green Jeep was being pelted by thousands of wet missiles. The bombardment pelted the vehicle mercilessly. His jaws started to tense up. He gripped the steering wheel tightly until he felt his fingernails pricking his palms. His hands in turn started to feel wet with sweat.

Alejandro quickly turned on the windshield wipers to the three-dot position, maximum speed. He reached over and turned the cassette player off. *I'm tired of this damn rain!*

The darkness of the moonless night had been tolerable up to this point, but the sudden onslaught of the tropical storm had made the visibility barely manageable. His vision was reduced to less than twenty meters in front of the vehicle. He flipped the headlights to high beam and shifted into second gear in a seamless coordinated motion. While he was nervous, he did not panic. The Jeep veered a little to the right. Alejandro kept command. The torrential rains created a floor of red clay where the road should have been.

The windows were starting to fog up. Alejandro jammed the fan knob on the defroster to High. He could almost feel the brown hair on top of his head frizzing. The humidity seemed to be rising.

He stole a quick look at his wristwatch. It was 9:07. The stars, that had given him guidance as the night had begun, had now disappeared. Dark clouds cloaked the skies. The wind started to pick up and the night was getting blacker.

Suddenly, discerning a dark form on the road in front of him, he stomped on the brake pedal with both feet, bringing the Jeep into a muddy slide.

৵

The previous night Alejandro had stayed in a pueblo at the base of the Sierra de Cuchumatan cordillera. A few weeks before, his best friend from law school had convinced him to take the scenic route from Costa Rica to his home in Mexico City. Alejandro thought that he could use a few days of diversion before starting his new job. Besides, he wanted to test his two-year old, slightly used 1972 Jeep that his father had bought for him a few months prior.

Since Monday, two days earlier, he had battled the hundreds of black billowing semi-trailer trucks, the overflowing buses, and innumerable road detours. It had poured rain intermittently for extended periods and he was fatigued from the eternal vigilance of his defensive driving.

The sunrise is awesome, he thought, as he greeted that Tuesday dawn. The heliotrope skies had pulled the sun up over the saddle of the nearest mountain range. He washed his face and reddish-brown beard in the cracked white basin in the communal bathroom of a roadside inn to the clucking sounds of the chickens pecking the earth in the garden behind. He also decided to give his beard a little trim.

As Alejandro changed into the lime green guayabera that his mother had given him the prior Christmas, he grimaced slightly. His nose detected that the shirt was a little ripe from being worn two days in a row, but then again, he would be returning home in a few days. The trip from San José was not supposed to take more than five days. He should be in Mexico City no later than Saturday.

He would have a few weeks to spend with his family before starting his new job at the Banco Comercial. He knew that his family wanted him to continue living with them in the Colonia Las Lomas. However, Alejandro was almost 22 years old and he knew that he had to venture out and become independent. Of course, he would stay close to his family.

And besides, he wanted to watch the upcoming World Cup that was being hosted in West Germany. There was family dissension on which team to support. His father, Señor Rubí, was a West Germany aficionado while Alejandro and his little brother cheered for Brazil who had won the title four years before in 1970. There would be shouting and screaming in the household for days.

Alejandro had succeeded in graduating from the Facultad de Derecho in San José, Costa Rica. He had earned good grades in his final semesters, after a less than stellar performance in his first year of law school. His father, Alberto Rubí, had pulled many strings to have his son enrolled in this law school. Señor Rubí was the owner of an automobile parts manufacturing enterprise that exported headlights, windshield wipers, and spark plugs throughout Central and South America. He had business and political connections everywhere.

The Facultad de Derecho had a first rate reputation for turning out excellent Latin-American international business law practitioners. The summer prior to his graduation, Alejandro was hired to work as an intern at the Banco Comercial in the San Ángel district of Mexico City. The president of the bank just happened to be a fellow Coyoacan Lions Club member with Señor Rubí. His father had always reminded him that, *"It isn't what you know, but whom you know."*

ဢ

Earlier that Wednesday morning Alejandro had left the pueblo after a breakfast of soft-boiled eggs, warm bolillos, and a large cafe con leche. His stomach felt full and satisfied. He threw his blue duffel bag along with a liter water bottle into the passenger side of the Jeep.

On this day three of his journey, he had stopped at a rustic highway food stand and purchased a few items. A group of locals who were jammed into the back of a pickup truck stared at the newly arrived stranger. The bald, toothless food vendor treated him curtly because Alejandro had paid him in Costa Rican currency. He felt bad, but he didn't have any other type of money. He frowned at the dirty looks. *He probably overcharged me anyway,* Alejandro thought.

He continued to drive up the mountains along precipitously curving roads. It took over an hour to safely pass the diesel-belching bus with boxes piled precariously on the rooftop that was trudging along to the next village. Alejandro kept a respectful distance from the smoking beast lest he choke on the fumes. He fiddled with the car radio with little success except for an earful of static. He needed to change the run-down batteries on his cassette player that was making Celia Cruz sound garbled. He whistled a few boleros from the latest Trio Los Panchos album that he had heard back in San José. His body was in a relaxed state as he gazed at the countryside. The slow crawl kept him in second gear most of the time. Unfortunately, the poorly paved highway had been too narrow to allow him to pass without the threat of a head-on collision. Additionally, the bus driver made no attempt to accommodate Alejandro and the other vehicles behind him.

After the bus turned right at an intersection, Alejandro made good time and stopped around midday in a village next to Las Lágrimas de la Señora River. He inhaled his lunch of bread, cheese, and red grapes. His fingers felt sticky from the juice of the grapes. Three buzzards soared in circles above his head. His eyelids felt heavy. He decided to take a half hour siesta in the Jeep before resuming his journey. He did remember to replace the batteries on his cassette player before he fell asleep.

During the afternoon drive, the air conditioning seemed to be straining. At times it emitted hot air rather than cold. There was a high-pitched whining sound. Alejandro had set it to Maximum for most of the trip. The outside humidity and heat had been stifling.

At dusk Alejandro had refueled his Jeep in another pueblito and grabbed a cup of coffee that burned his hand. After a brief pause for thought, he decided to press onward in his journey. The caffeine had stimulated his entire body. His blood pulsed with warm spurts of energy. He was wired. He was determined to press on under the canopy of stars. Again the road became unpaved and more difficult to navigate as he drove on. There was a dearth of signs. The vehicle shook as it went over the ruts. The old man with the straw hat at the fuel station had advised him to follow the highway to the right.

The man probably had never ventured outside of his pueblito, Alejandro surmised.

Alejandro took out his red BIC lighter and lit a cigarette. The Jeep's cigarette lighter had shorted out a month earlier. The stars disappeared as the evening progressed. He inhaled. He felt the smoke tickle his lungs and smother any signs of tiredness. The wind was howling like a pack of coyotes. The Jeep was being pushed and pulled by the gale. The tall palm trees on both sides of the road were bending over like bows prepped to shoot their arrow fronds into the skies. *I probably should have stayed at the last town like the old man advised.* He squinted and looked at the road. *I can't see anything.*

The skies kept getting more and more ominous.

Alejandro missed the ashtray as he tried to flick his cigarette. *Oh, well, the Jeep was a mess anyway. I should stop at the next town.*

᨞

Both feet hit the brakes. Alejandro's body lurched forward, restrained only by the seatbelt. His knees buckled. The sudden stop had wrenched his back. The Jeep fishtailed to the left halting only a few meters short of the fallen palm tree.

Crap!

The blown-over palm tree looked too heavy to move. He rolled down the window a little and threw the cigarette butt out. He rolled the window back up and shifted the gearbox into first gear. Because his vehicle had skidded sideways toward the fallen tree, he had to maneuver the Jeep in order to orient his tires for the proper approach angle. He gingerly nudged the vehicle forward until the front tires made contact with the tree trunk. Slowly he pressed the accelerator with his foot. The engine sputtered in protest. The front tires raised themselves up and then stopped. The back wheels spun in the mud. The front tires slid back down from the palm trunk and the Jeep bounced when it hit the road.

Holy Crap! His facial muscles drew taut.

The rain kept coming down in buckets. Once again, Alejandro gunned the Jeep into reverse, trying to give himself enough room for a running start. He squinted in order to try to examine the fallen tree. He decided to pick the narrower part of the tree trunk. He shifted back into second gear. It was difficult to locate to see much. The storm continued to howl around him. He wiped his brow that was now moist from apprehension. He repeated the maneuver. It resulted in the identical unfortunate result.

I don't want to be stranded here overnight, he worried.

The downpour kept on. Once again Alejandro put the Jeep into reverse. He paused and exhaled deeply. Then he popped it into second and eased forward, approaching the tree diagonally. The left front tire bounced upwards as the Jeep started to climb the tree. The other front tire lifted up. The Jeep started to slide to the right. He gunned the engine and jerked the steering wheel to the left. The Jeep leaped forward and the front tires went over the trunk. The left rear tire hit the tree and the Jeep bounced up again. The underside of the Jeep dragged on the palm making a scraping sound.

What the f__k! He was starting to panic. His breaths were shallow and fast.

The Jeep was impaled on the tree. Alejandro slammed it into reverse and slowly edged the vehicle back about a meter. The rear axle creaked. He straightened out the steering wheel and went forward. The rear back tire started to rise. He carefully increased the pressure on the accelerator. The wheels caught. The Jeep lurched forward and bounced hard over the trunk.

Crap! I hope my oil pan didn't crack.

He checked his oil pressure gauge. The needle was near the top end. Alejandro was sweating profusely. He was swearing aloud. He was now tired and irritable.

Off into the pelting rain he fled, slipping the Jeep into third gear. The gale continued to pummel the vehicle. The road widened. He started to pick up speed. He figured that he would be approaching a pueblo some time soon. Alejandro lit another cigarette and began to relax. He exhaled a grayish-white cloud of smoke. He craned his neck from side to side looking for any visible signs to the nearest pueblo.

Alejandro slowed down as he approached a crossroad. At first he gave himself a smile, but then a thousand thoughts zoomed through his mind ricocheting off his brain. *Which way should I go? There are no signs. I don't have a map. I think that I should go straight. But the man at the fuel station advised me to stay right. Crap! I had better turn to the right.*

It was now almost eleven o'clock. He steered to the right. At least the road now seemed much better than that by which he had traversed the country all day.

He shifted into fourth gear. The torrential storm started to wane. There were patches of night skies once again piercing through the veil of clouds.

The Jeep rounded a curve. In the next instant Alejandro felt his left shoulder and head slamming into the driver's window as the right side of the Jeep started to rise.

CHAPTER 2

A COLD BEER

Alejandro was dazed. He tried to move. Hot liquid dripped down into the left eye from the top of his head. Glass from the front windshield had been dispersed everywhere like a shower of glittering diamonds. His ears were ringing. It was almost pitch black outside. His headlights could hardly penetrate the jungle in front.

Holy crap! What happened? His head ached. His forehead frowned to remember. The last thing he recalled was that three quarters of the road had disappeared. The Jeep had fallen and slid off the remnants of the eroded road. The vehicle had become almost airborne as it started to roll over. As it tumbled, Alejandro was being suspended in the air by his seatbelt.

The Jeep had turned a full revolution before it hit the grove of small palm trees and bounced onto the driver's side. Mud and branches engulfed the windows. The vehicle came to rest partially leaning against a host of clinging vines and bamboo.

My frigging head! He kept blinking his eyes. *Try to stay calm. Let's see . . . the engine is still running. Try to stay cool . . . Take a deep breath.* He inhaled, but it was painful. *Good, now another. Turn the engine off. Oh, I can't move. I can't move! What the f__k! Am I frigging paralyzed? Oh, my God! No one will ever find me in this hellhole.* He was trying to bounce his body forward, but couldn't. The frustration within his senses started to build.

The Jeep suddenly lurched forward a half meter. Vegetation had crept into the space once occupied by the windshield. He thought he heard a creak, but his ears were still drumming. Instinctively, Alejandro tried to brace himself with his elbows and feet.

His left arm was tingling with numbness and pinpricks of pain. Alejandro could barely move it. Inside the back of his head, a wave of heat was pushing itself forward. His brains were getting warmer. He slowly reached over the steering wheel and turned the ignition key counter clockwise. The engine sounds ceased. He tried to turn the headlights off, but to no avail. As he reached for the light switch, a pain shot through his left shoulder causing him to fall into unconsciousness.

The mosquitoes were buzzing by his ear. The crickets and frogs were serenading one another. Hopelessly, still in a daze, he tried to swat at the invisible demons. He missed and a sharp twinge shot through his left arm. His right hand grabbed his left. The shoulder was swollen and throbbed.

The cabin of the Jeep was soaking wet and permeated a musty odor. Slowly, he regained his awareness.

Crap! What happened? Where am I?

There was a steamy mist surrounding the Jeep in the predawn hours. The rain had completely ceased. The headlights weakly punctured the misty haze in front. Slowly, Alejandro reached over and pushed in the headlight switch to turn them off. It took a few moments for his eyes to adjust to the dimness. He could barely make out the dark green jungle. He closed his eyes. He inhaled slowly, but deep enough to feel the extent of his pain. He tried to gauge what hurt the most and what parts of his body were still of use.

What am I going to do? I'm totally screwed. Throughout the early morning, he kept falling asleep, only to be aroused by shooting pains throughout his body. The rain began to fall again. Pitter-patter. Pitter-patter. Finally, he woke up. The birds were chirping. His whole body ached. The early morning light fell upon the cabin of the Jeep. The rain had ceased again. His throat felt parched. *I'm so frigging thirsty.* With great difficulty, Alejandro tried to twist his body onto his right side in order to reach into the backseat. However, he was constrained by the seat belt. Gingerly, he unfastened it. With great care and much pain, he slowly maneuvered backwards.

F__k! It hurts badly. The left side of his guayabera was in shreds. He could see dried blood and the heavy swelling of his arm. This arm was totally immobile and felt like a giant weight.

The crash had spewed his duffel bag, clothes, books, and other stuff that he was bringing back home throughout the cabin of the Jeep.

At least, I can move a little, he tried to calm himself down.

Alejandro peered into the back of the vehicle and looked around. His duffel bag was soaked. He carefully reached behind the front seats until he found the bag that contained his leftover food.

He then found the liter water bottle. Alejandro grabbed it and opened it. He greedily swallowed the precious liquid. Hunger had deserted him. In fact, he was nauseous. His stomach felt gaseous and bloated. He seized the food bag. With his right hand, he opened the glove compartment and took out the flashlight. He tried it. It didn't work. He flung it into the backseat. Alejandro knew that he did not have any flares or candles.

I'll just take the food and water. I need to go back to the road if I have any hope of being rescued.

Cautiously, he inched over the glass strewn passenger seat and tried to open the door. It wouldn't budge. His right arm felt so weak. Clumsily, he stretched out and rolled down what was left of the passenger side window. With great effort and enduring shooting pains, he pushed himself off from the driver's seat and grasped the door at the window opening and pulled himself through the aperture with his right arm straining and burning from the effort. He started to slide over the window only to be scraped by shards of protruding glass.

He screamed out in agony. F__k! Moisture came to his eyes. Finally, he succeeded in sliding his wet and crumbled body out of the Jeep, falling the last half-meter. His left knee had caught on some ragged metal stripping causing him to hit the ground on his chin.

Cursing the heavens, he swore more and more profusely as he tried to pick himself up. He couldn't move. His guayabera and tan chinos were soaked with the reddish clay. His food bag lay just to the right of him along with the water bottle. He wiped his right hand on the partially dry area on the back of his pants.

He gasped. *Be cool! Let me relax a minute!* He tried to calm down. *Have to rest!*

He struggled, shifting his body back and forth, until his back was leaning on the vehicle, while at the same time reaching inside one of his pockets. His cigarette pack was only a little wet. After foraging around, he found a dry one. He still had his BIC lighter. He lit the cigarette and inhaled deeply. His watch said 6:22. At least it was still running.

After a long rest, he carefully tried to stand upright. His

left arm was immobilized. Alejandro picked up the food bag with his right hand and flung it over his shoulder. He then picked up the water bottle and staggered upwards toward the road. His head still throbbed with pain. His eyes hurt. He felt a deep pressure under his left eye. He took a deep breath and smelled the scent of wild lavender. Alejandro head turned to the side where he noticed that the Jeep had savagely slashed the wild red hibiscus on the side of the road. Broken branches created a walking path toward what remained of the road. He traveled about fifty meters to where the Jeep had begun to skid off the washout of the road. He glanced over his right shoulder as he reached the thinly paved route. The Jeep could barely be seen from the roadside due to the thick foliage. His only hope was to walk to the nearest pueblo.

How long had I driven from the crossroads last night before the mishap? He tried to calculate this in his aching head. *Let's see, I was going fairly fast and making good time. The intersection probably was at least fifteen kilometers back.* There had been no villages or haciendas around there as far as he could remember.

Should I continue forward in the same direction that I was going? He tried to think. *I have a little food and a half-filled bottle of water. Anyway, no one will be coming from behind because of the washout.*

He looked at his feet. He had been wearing white Adidas running shoes with three black stripes that were now caked with reddish orange mud. Alejandro now knew that he had been totally unprepared for such a road trip. He had underestimated what he needed. His mother had always bought him his clothing. Maybe fashionable, but not practical.

I could try to go back to the intersection and flag someone down. On the other hand, a car or bus approaching from in front of me would run into the same predicament. I would be able to warn them. I'll take a chance and go onward.

Stiffly, he hobbled for the first fifteen minutes. His left shoulder was still aching. The palm trees and banana plants let off steam as he passed. The air was perfumed by star jasmine and the birds were still singing their enchanted songs.

Life is good. I'm lucky to be alive. How true were my mother's insistences that each day one must smell the roses. Such is life. I'll be okay. His head felt giddy as it swayed from side to side as he advanced.

Beads of sweat emerged from his forehead. A black fly kept buzzing by his head. He tried to swat it, but was not successful. It was a humid day for the middle of May.

The road was no longer paved. Instead, it was more like a wide clay path sprinkled with large puddles of water. The insides of his sneakers were no longer dry, but squished in the reddish mud as he trudged along. Tire tracks were barely discernible. The rains seemed to have expunged them like an eraser removes chalk marks from a blackboard.

Alejandro noticed that the road had an upward incline. The hills that he was approaching had puffs of clouds surrounding them. There was no breeze. It probably would not rain for a while.

He placed one foot in front of the other. *Eventually, I'll get there. Wherever there is.* His mind started to drift. His eyes became unfocused. His lungs struggled to breathe the sultry air. *Suddenly, he felt nostalgic. I wonder what my family is doing?*

The sun was beating down on him. The only relief came from the shade of the trees. Every once in a while a black bird would fly by, cackling.

❧

Alejandro had grown up in the Colonia Las Lomas of Mexico City, the oldest of three children born to Señor Alberto Rubí and his wife, Dolores. The father was a consummate businessperson who was also active in politics. On several occasions, he was recruited to run for public office, but he always refused. He knew that he had more influence from the outside. On the other hand, Señor Rubí had a tendency to always back the underdog candidate in any contested election.

Dolores, his wife of over twenty-four years, came from one of Xalapa's oldest family, the Campos, who had made its fortune in coffee. She was deeply religious and believed everything was the will of God. She loved her children and was the buffer between them and their father. She was blessed with three, two boys and a girl. Alejandro was her oldest. Sadly, she had at least three miscarriages during her marriage.

Alejandro's fifteen-year old brother Ricardo was studying engineering in high school. Ricardo was the perfect student and his mother's favorite. Once a week she would bake him a guava pie as a reward for his successful studies.

The spoiled sibling was the seven-year old, Lupe, who was in second grade at Sacred Heart School. Lupita was preparing to receive her First Communion on the upcoming May 28th. She wanted a large party with all of her cousins and friends invited. And she especially wanted a three-tiered tres leches cake with a creamy frosting. She wanted her cake to be bigger than that of her classmate Gloria Guzman's at her recent birthday.

Oh, God! If she is so fussy now, how will she be when she has her quinceañera, thought Alejandro. But who could resist her dark brown curls and dark brown eyes when she called

Alejandro by his special nickname, "the Flame", with which she had christened him. Since her infancy, she loved to pull his reddish brown beard. He would always admonish her that his beard was a flame that would burn her. Her response was a cute giggle.

ཡ

Alejandro looked at his wristwatch again. It was almost nine o'clock in the morning. He still felt nauseous and his kidneys hurt. His lips were chapped. He could feel the cracked skin as he licked them.

There was a green, grassy mound over to the right. There was no breeze and he could feel the heat of the day starting to rise. He walked wearily over and sat down. He took a swig of water. Dizzily he looked into his almost empty food bag. He was still not hungry, but was exhausted. Sweat was beading up all over his body. He leaned back on the grassy knoll and rested his head on the lumpy food bag.

The sun was rising barely above the hilltops. A white egret gracefully flew across the blue sky. He closed his eyes. *I'll just rest for a few minutes.*

He felt something crawl across his hand. Alejandro stirred drowsily from his deep sleep. Far away there was the sporadic tap, tap, tap of raindrops falling on the jungle forest. It grew louder and more intense. A few raindrops fell onto his face. He was now fully awake. With caution he tried to raise himself up. Pain flared through his left shoulder. The skies were dark grey and opened up their tears on him. In a few minutes he was thoroughly drenched. It felt good as he showered in the rain. He opened his mouth and tried to catch some liquid sustenance. He opened the top of the water bottle in hopes of trying to replenish some of the depleted contents.

It's getting late and I haven't eaten all day. I should eat a little something. He crawled under the shelter of a grove of palm trees. There he opened his food bag. He tried to chew the day old bread that was now stale. He put the remaining part of the loaf out into the pouring rain. It softened somewhat with the moisture. Better. The bananas were good although they had been squished and were overripe. He had nothing sweet to eat. Not even gum. He picked up his water bottle and drank almost the entire container. *I didn't realize that I was so thirsty.*

Once more Alejandro glanced at his watch. It was just past four o'clock. He had slept nearly six hours since this morning. The rain had ceased and a rainbow appeared in front of him in the direction of his pursuit. How auspicious! He gathered up his belongings and resumed his trek.

He marched onward. He saw bugs of various sizes and colors flying around him. He rested. He heard birds singing. He walked some more. He rested some more. Alejandro felt a little better but he was still fatigued. The sun started to set. Noises in the jungle became amplified.

Alejandro lit up his second cigarette of the day. He knew that he had only about six or seven left. The cigarette was a little wet. He inhaled deeply. A smoke ring exited his mouth. A tiny lizard scurried across his path.

I can't believe I haven't seen anyone today. As he marched forward, he tried to examine his surroundings. *I really don't want to sleep in the jungle tonight. Should I have stayed with the Jeep?*

As it started to get dark, he looked for a place to overnight close to the road, but not close enough to get run over if a vehicle should come along. He tied his food bag and water bag to a tall bamboo. It was warm enough to sleep al fresco.

He laid himself down into a fetal position, resting on his right shoulder.

I'll never be able to sleep. His mind began to wander. *I wonder what Chuy is doing right now. He's probably down at the Rosarito Bar drinking beer with the local patrons, but not getting anywhere with the girls.*

Alejandro and his best friend Chuy had spent the last three years together at the Facultad de Derecho in San José. As a reward for passing their final examinations, their parents had sent them to Colombia for two weeks. They had a thousand adventures trekking from Cartagena to Bogotá. They had broken dozens of young girls' hearts. They had seen a hundred churches, museums, and archaeological ruins. They had just returned a week earlier.

The embellishments increased tenfold every time an event was mentioned. In reality, they each lost five kilos from being sick half of the time.

A month before graduation Alejandro had secured a legal position in a prestigious sector of Mexico City. He wondered if he should live with his family for a short time until he saved up a little money to live on his own. He thought that he was ready to have his own apartment since he was now twenty-two years old. *It would be so cool!*

Conversely, Chuy was going to take off a year to find himself. Chuy's parents were wealthy and they wanted him to get involved in the ruling political party. Little did Chuy's parents know that he was a hybrid of Trotskyite and Libertarian.

What I wouldn't give for a cold beer right now. Why is my head swimming?

He opened his eyes. He could hear crickets chirping all about. His mind was active. *I'm sure that there are no wild animals around here. Let me climb up this little tree. I can try to wedge myself between the trunk and some branches.*

Ow! My arm is killing me. He exhaled deeply, cursing his aches and pains, as he reached the first limb.

Alejandro started to close his eyes and soon his awareness faded away.

He fell into a restless stupor. There was a buzzing that zoomed by his ear. He subconsciously tried to swat at it. The sound finally went away.

Alejandro felt uncomfortable during this slumber. The hard wood knots were pushing along his spine. He tried to turn his body, but with little success.

The buzzing returned, but this time it was louder. Then he felt something prick him.

CHAPTER 3

BIG RED

Alejandro felt moisture on his forehead. It felt too warm to be raindrops.

I must be having a bad dream, Alejandro moaned groggily to himself.

Now he sensed what seemed to be a coarse thumb pressing lightly over his right eye. There was the smell of burning sage. An abrasive hand started to rub his forehead.

Slowly Alejandro began to awake. His mouth opened wide and he yawned. His eyes saw what appeared to be dozens of dark shadows surrounding him. It was difficult to make out the figures in the nocturnal light. He tried to recall if there had been a waxing moon during his drive. As he peered through the dimness, he thought that he could discern what seemed to be fluorescent yellow stripes around their eyes, but he wasn't sure. The shapes seemed to take on the appearance of some type of indigenous people.

Gradually, two hands were massaging Alejandro's forehead from behind. They were heavy and callused.

Who are these people? What is happening to me? Alejandro shrieked and tried to raise himself up. He was petrified. He wet himself. The native closest to him retreated for a moment, but came back and placed some banana leaves across Alejandro's chest.

They're f__king cannibals!

Alejandro lapsed into unconsciousness.

૭

As Alejandro awoke, he found himself on a bed of green elephant ear leaves in the middle of a round palm hut. His body was completely covered with a mealy powder that smelled somewhere between clover and orange blossoms. On his left shoulder there was a pulpy purple paste with thumb size pieces of aloe vera mixed in.

It must be morning, he thought, though there was not much light. *Where am I?* Alejandro heard voices outside. They were talking in some sort of guttural indigenous language. *It sounds like Nahuatl?*

He rambled a delirious rant to himself. *Who are these people? I just hope they are not cannibals. I need to get out of here! I'm not tied up. Just let me rest a little more. I just need to stay calm. What time is it? Do they speak Spanish? Can they help me?*

As he lifted his arm to look at his wristwatch, he was hit with such a wave of pain that he fell into unconsciousness.

૭

The smell of burning sage permeated the interior of the hut. A wizened face with black eyes circled with yellow rings was offering a small gourd to Alejandro. A wreath of purple feathers adorned his head that was crowned with a funny ponytail. He had elongated ear lobes with gold loop earrings hanging down. Who was this person? A witch doctor? Alejandro tried to raise himself up from the leaves. His left arm throbbed.

The dark wrinkled hand of the old man pushed the orangish gourd of liquid closer to him. Alejandro hesitated. *Could he trust this old man? He seems to want to help me.* Slowly, Alejandro took the drink, all the time staring at the native. He kept leaning gingerly on his right elbow. He looked at his benefactor and nodded. Alejandro was dehydrated. His lips were chapped. He put the gourd to his lips and sipped carefully, still unsure whether it would help or harm him.

The liquid was hot and tasted like the chamomile tea he remembered his housekeeper Inocente had given to him as child when he was ill. His "host" fixated on him inquisitively, but did not utter a single word.

"Thank you," uttered Alejandro in a barely discernible voice.

The response from the native who seemed to be some sort of a medicine man was incomprehensible. It was not Spanish.

"Where am I?"

There was no reply.

Great. These people don't even speak Spanish.

There was another figure wearing a big red feather crown standing behind the medicine man and he handed Alejandro another gourd. This one held a pinkish liquid.

Alejandro's eyes squinted as he looked about. The purple-feathered native kept circling around him waving burning sage branches in the air. Maybe he was even singing some incantations, Alejandro wondered.

Alejandro slowly put the first gourd down and took up the other. This one tasted very starchy. He drank it anyway. He felt something prickly moving in his mouth. He swallowed it before he could spit it out.

Little veins of pain radiated through the top of his head. *Let me think!* He searched his memory for Sister Paulina's fifth grade social studies lessons on indigenous peoples.

These people are more than likely bug eaters! Ick! Well, as long as they don't eat me.

Feeling slightly, but not totally, relieved that they were

not going to devour him, Alejandro laid his head back down. His body convulsed as he hiccupped. He felt his stomach bloating up. Alejandro saw his two hosts pick up the gourds and leave the hut.

He tried to suppress the thoughts of what vile insect or other creepy, crawling bug he had just ingested.

Very slowly, Alejandro began looking about the green-leafed hut. His eyes strained in the semi-darkness. What could he learn? There were no real clues as to who these people really were. This hut was made from palm fronds and was void of any décor. There was only access through a narrow door that was covered with more palm fronds.

He began to get drowsy. He shut his eyes. Alejandro's left shoulder ached. His head was woozy. Soreness ran throughout his body, from the bumps and bruises. And he definitely reeked. Despite the pain, he began to feel waves of comforting warmth start to wash over him, first from his mid-section, then radiating out to his limbs, finally, soothing his throbbing head.

This is better . . . I'm so tired . . . My mouth is dry . . . Please give me water . . . I want water . . . He fell into a deep sleep.

ॐ

For a day and a night, he fell in and out of semi-consciousness. At first light, he was awakened by three dark-skinned native elders who had surrounded him. His head was still sensitive. His vision was blurry and his eyes watery. He squinted. The faces of the natives were punctuated with thinly dyed concentric yellow rings around their eyes. They were speaking among themselves, looking attentively at Alejandro. He could not comprehend anything that they said.

He remained groggy. His eyes had trouble focusing.

One of the elders, who wore a red-feathered crown,

was holding an object in his hand. It was Alejandro's St. Christopher's medal. This is the one that his godmother, Justine, had given him for his First Communion. This native also had a strange ponytail and wore gold earrings.

The purple-feathered elder, who had also nursed him, offered Alejandro another gourd of a pasty liquid. The native in the middle, who appeared to be the eldest and wore a multicolored crown of feathers, spoke a few words to Alejandro. He pointed with an air of authority to Alejandro's left shoulder with his crooked finger.

Although Alejandro could not understand the words of this chieftain elder, he replied woozily, "My shoulder still hurts. My head is okay. Hard head, huh," he made a knocking gesture to his head. "Like a rock." This was his first smile in many days.

The chieftain elder nodded. Alejandro sat up to grab the gourd. It was only then that Alejandro realized that he was completely naked. His whole body was covered with a whitish powder.

His hosts themselves wore only loincloths.

The red-feathered elder, who was holding Alejandro's medallion, touched the young man's forehead with his forefinger and thumb. There was some chanting by the other two. Although Alejandro was apprehensive, he did not react. The hand went over to the cut over his left eye.

"Ouch!" Alejandro cried out.

This elder appeared to be some type of shaman. He continued to probe around Alejandro's head, repeating some type of murmurings in a soft voice. He touched Alejandro's left shoulder. A sharp pain went through Alejandro's body. The young man groaned.

The shaman reached around and applied a dark oatmeal-

like poultice gently on Alejandro's head and left shoulder.
Eventually, the three elders left. He wanted to get up. But
as he tried to rise, he felt weak and dizzy.

He tried to chase off the sleep that was rapidly defeating
his will to rise up and follow his hosts outside to discover
clues about his location, but his lids felt heavier and heavier
as the potion's magic pain relief took effect. Relieved and
relaxed by the concoction, Alejandro abandoned his desire to
get up, and instead he fell back into a slumber.

Alejandro awoke several hours later to the sounds of
women making high-pitched noises. There seemed to be a
tremendous amount of activity outside. *What was going on?*

The inside of the hut was bright from the noonday sun,
but was cool from the thick, palm fronds that made up the
roof and the banana leaves upon which he laid. The heat
lingered at the edges of the hut, and he could smell dried
straw coming from the outside. This reminded him that his
throat was parched.

He felt better, but his back still ached. He felt something
tickle one of his little toes. He looked down. It was a little
black beetle with a red-spotted shell and long legs crawling
up his leg. Maybe it was eating all the powder caked on his
body. He kicked it off casually. It was just a stupid bug.

Alejandro rolled on to his right side. He leaned up on his
elbow. *Take it slowly. You're not going anywhere.*

The wailing from outside had stopped.

Finally, his eyes were able to focus. Alejandro wanted to
stand up, but he didn't want to pass out again. He rolled
back over until he was on all fours, or really on threes, as
his left shoulder dipped due to the pain. He was unable to
support himself. He tried to crawl like a wounded animal

toward the opening of the hut. He moved forward with more like an upper body hop. He dared not put any weight on his left shoulder. He advanced slowly, squishing the large green banana leaf flooring, feeling the ground give way like soft but thin sponges as he did so.

He needed water. The leaf flooring ended and suddenly he was crawling on hard dirt. *Just a little further,* he told himself. He reached out and pulled aside the door covering. It was so bright outside. His eyes were overwhelmed. His eyes blinked rapidly, tears flowing from the searing pain caused by the brightness of the blazing sun.

Finally, he could make out several dark-skinned natives moving about in a village of huts. The majority of the tribe seemed congregated around three or four fire pits. The men and women were segregated into two groups and they were almost all naked except for their dark loincloths. The men were small in stature and wore their hair in a strange ponytail manner. Some were eating.

The women wore red and orangish-yellow wraparound skirts. Their breasts were fully exposed. Some were conversing with gesticulations, but Alejandro could not discern if they were speaking words or just uttering sounds. The few nearby children were unclothed.

No one seemed to be looking toward his hut.

Alejandro tried to imagine who these inhabitants might be. He did not see any horses, or burros, or any other pack animals. There were no visible dogs or chickens or pigs. Aside from the women doing some type of keening, he had not heard many sounds in the village. *How did this commune survive?*

Alejandro saw the native with the red-feathered crown among the other villagers. This shaman was talking to some young boys. He seemed to be talking to them with a patient calmness. Maybe they were his sons.

What should I do? I could get up and walk toward him. I don't have any clothes on, but who cares? And besides, I am still covered with this stupid, itchy white powder. He laughed in a giddy tone.

They don't seem at all dangerous. They've tried to heal my shoulder and my head. They've given me shelter. Alejandro continued to evaluate his predicament, but his head felt cloudy. *They've even fed me a little. Not much. But I'm thirsty right now. I shouldn't push my luck. "Be patient," my father used to tell me, but I never really paid attention. I was always screwing around. He was strict with me. I guess he had a right to be. I should have listened more and studied harder.*

Little by little he retreated into the hut. He lay back down on the leaves. He closed his eyes. The next moment he was back asleep.

A few more hours passed. As he lay in the dreamy fog emerging from a deep sleep, Alejandro heard the raindrops bouncing on the palm fronds overhead. Softy at first, then harder as the tropical storm made its daily visit to the forest. Drip. Drip. Faster and faster. Pitter-patter. Soon a deluge sounded outside the door. It was pouring rain. It was getting toward dusk, but the room was darkened more dramatically by the storm.

The hut entrance opened and in walked the chieftain with the multicolored plume headband who now wore an ocelot skin over his right shoulder. He was soaked. He smelled like a wet dog. The shaman with the red feather crown and four other tribesmen who were also wet from rain followed him in. One carried a torch.

The six natives stared at him. Their eyes looked bright.

They sat themselves around him. One of the natives, who had the face of a thousand wrinkles, produced a pipe and gave it to the "chief".

The pipe seemed to be made of a caoba wood and had a deep, red cherry-like finish, as if burnished by generations of hands caressing it as a valued part of their culture . . . or something like that. It had tiny figures carved around the barrel of the pipe, but in the pale flickering light, Alejandro could not discern what they represented.

The chief inserted the narrower end of the pipe into his left nostril and took a deep breath while he simultaneously covered his other nostril with his right thumb. This lasted for a few seconds and then he skillfully exhaled a thin, steady, and solid stream of smoke. The damp odors were replaced by a vapor that smelled like something between woody pinole and sweet mangoes. The anthracite grey smoke became heavy and dispersed slowly throughout the hut.

One by one the sextet of natives engaged in this ritual. The room was now saturated with the smoky cloud. Alejandro wanted to choke, but began to feel elated. He had no fear. His mind was totally disengaged from this phenomenon. He actually laughed aloud.

Finally, the elder with the red feather crown placed the pipe into Alejandro's nose. *Maybe this is some sort of religious ritual,* Alejandro surmised. *What is "Big Red" doing to me?*

Big Red uttered some guttural sounds to Alejandro. Alejandro tried to inhale, but started choking. Needles of pain shot through his head and left shoulder. He forced himself to try again. He inhaled. Then again. And then again.

This is like drinking with my compadres at the Black Eagle Cantina. These natives are cool, he thought. He was getting animated.

I feel like a child again, mimicking a dog. What is spinning? Oh, there's my friend, the little black bug that was tickling my toes. Man, I'm high! Bow-wow, little bug. A million colors spiraling! Everything is unreal.
One of the natives started to beat rhythmically on a small drum. Rat-a-tat-tat. Rat-a-tat-tat. Rat-a-tat-tat. *The beat seemed to emulate my own heart,* Alejandro sensed. Now his ears tickled. His body felt loose. He noticed that the throbbing of the pain in his head and shoulder seemed to diminish, giving way to the steadiness of the native's drumbeat. Waves of sound vibrated around his ears and throbbed throughout his body. He could feel a warm positive energy taking over his entire being. He seemed to be conscious, but not entirely lucid. As his mind willed his body to move, he felt himself floating upward, as if leaving his corporal pain on the ground. A sense of peace, calm and security enveloped him in a light, affectionate embrace. He was mystified.

The torch was burning out. The interior of the hut became darker and darker.

Alejandro once again closed his eyes, carried back to sleep on the waves of the slow, pulsating drumbeat.

CHAPTER 4

THE BED

On this day the air blew cool and moist. He smelled the sweet scent of lavender. Alejandro's body was totally at ease, although there was a trace of a headache. For the last few days he had recuperated in the hut with occasional visits from the elders. He felt light-headed most of the time, especially after the pipe smoking rituals. The medicine man had been bringing him gourds filled with the starchy sustenance while Big Red chanted. Alejandro was given herbal teas that smelled like a combination of anise and shoe polish. They reminded him of some of the medicines that his nanny Inocente had forced him to swallow when he was sick as a child. His left arm was discolored but seemed to be healing, and he had more mobility with it.

Man, I feel good today, he thought. His eyes were closed and his mind was in a semi-meditative state. *I am so relaxed. I just want to vegetate. Hanging out at the Cartagena beaches checking out the girls.*

A breeze glided through the room. Suddenly, Alejandro sensed someone or something near to him. He felt a mounting fear. He willed himself to slowly open his eyes. There was something eerie happening as he became more aware of his situation. He no longer felt the banana leaves under him. He felt soft cloth. It was like . . . like . . . like . . . a sheet! He was in a bed! He quickly opened his eyes.

In front of him was a frocked nun in a rocking chair

crocheting white lace onto the end of a piece of cloth. She was rocking ever so slightly, almost still, but moving enough for him to detect as he came out of his soporific state.

He felt confused, surprised, and fearful that he was still hallucinating from the native tea, smoke, or a combination of both. Or, even worse, that he had died and was in purgatory, condemned to atone for torturing the nuns at his Catholic elementary school.

"Who are you?" he croaked out weakly. His voice cracked from the dryness in his throat.

"I am Sister Beatriz," the smallish mestiza nun rose from her seat and placed her palm flush on his forehead, "How are you feeling?"

She held her hand there for a few moments. "You are very much improved. Your fever is gone and you are awake and talking." She gave him a smile. "All good signs."

He gazed at her in wonder. There was quite a contrast between this nun and his native, red feather bedecked benefactor from the village. She looked very different than the nuns he had in grade school. This one wore a black cornette headpiece that was folded upwards. It reminded him of a manta ray. The white wimple covered part of her chin and chest. Her tunic was black, but her scapula and sash were golden yellow.

"Yes. I guess I'm okay," he had raised himself a little in the tiny bed. "I hurt my head and arm in a crash a few nights ago."

"Yes, we know." She stepped back a little and looked intently at his forehead through her thick owl-eyed glasses. She reminded Alejandro of his third grade teacher at La Escuela de la Ascención. Both of them seemed to be in their thirties and had darkish skin.

Gracefully, she glided over to the bedside table. Sister Beatriz poured out a glass of water from an orange terra cotta pitcher. She turned back and carefully put the glass to Alejandro's lips, tilting it slightly. He met the glass by lifting his head slowly forward.

That was good, he thought, savoring every drop.

"More?" She had noticed that indeed he was very thirsty.

"Please, Sister," Alejandro looked around the small room that was simply furnished. She appeared to be friendly enough. "Where am I? Is this a hospital?"

"My son, for the moment, you must rest and save up your strength. Just rest. We can talk later." She dismissed his question and went to refill the glass. She turned to him, "Are you hungry?"

Alejandro tried to recall the last time he had eaten. He could not remember. "Yes," he replied meekly, as he felt his stomach protest against the water that was filling the void that had been growing since the accident.

"Is there anything that you cannot eat? We eat very modestly here, and we don't eat meat." She gave him another glass of water. "I probably can get you some breakfast if there is still any left over from this morning."

"Anything will be fine." He suddenly felt the urge to urinate. He hadn't voluntarily voided himself since the day after the accident.

Embarrassed, he found that he had no clothes on. He knew that he could not simply climb out of the bed and appear naked in front of the nun. "Sister, where is the toilet?" His face flushed as he tried to request this.

"There is a chamber pot in the corner," Sister Beatriz pointed with a slight grin as she lowered her eyes. "Modesty is indeed a virtue." Her smile widened. She made a half turn and left the room.

Alejandro pushed the cotton sheets away and slowly swung his body around until his feet touched the red tiled floor. His feet were unsteady. They felt cramped. His limbs burned. Carefully, he inched his way to the chamber pot. He lifted the ceramic lid. Deliberately, he began to urinate, feeling a burning sensation as he did so. After a few minutes he finished and rinsed his hands and face with the pitcher of water and small basin that lay on a small four-legged wooden bedside table.

He felt better now than he had when he arrived at the native village, although his body was still tired and his mind shaky. He crawled back into bed. He took a few deep breaths to relax.

Alejandro's eyes slowly scanned the room. It was whitewashed and had almost no furniture except for the nightstand, a table with a water pitcher, and the nun's rocking chair. There was a black wooden crucifix hanging on a near wall. Through the large indented window portal a nice breeze blew the simple manta curtain.

His head fell back onto the coarse cotton cushion and his eyes closed. He thought, "How did I get here? How lucky am I to be in this hospital."

All of a sudden he was hit with a nostalgic sense of familial obligation that confused him. He felt that he should be calling his parents to let them know that he was all right.

Sister Beatriz seemed nice enough. Yes, she did remind him of Sister Carlota at his elementary school with her thick glasses. He recalled that the students used to call her "La Tecolote" because she resembled a comic strip owl. This brought a smile to his face. Alejandro knew that she was a very strict arithmetic teacher. *But why did they have to learn how to add, subtract, multiply, and divide inane numbers?* His desk mate at that time, Hugo, had said that he would pay someone to count for him when he grew up. Alejandro had heard a few years ago that Hugo was working as an accountant in Guadalajara. *That's the way life goes!*

ॐ

Sister Beatriz knocked on the door and came in with a wooden tray of food. She placed the rectangular carrier on the table next to the bed. She reached behind Alejandro's head and pushed the pillow upright against the wooden headboard. "Sit up," she ordered.

Alejandro instinctively obeyed. "Ay!" he grunted. His body creaked.

Expeditiously, Sister Beatriz lifted the tray from the table and placed it on Alejandro's lap. She went back to the rocking chair and resumed her crocheting. It looked like an article of clothing. Perhaps some sort of mantilla.

Alejandro quaffed the glass of orange juice with the slice of lime. It was so sweet and refreshing. Sister Beatriz gently reminded him to take it slowly.

He salivated as he began to attack the food. The corn tortillas were steaming hot as he greedily scooped up the black beans, pico de gallo, and jicama. There was a cup of red herbal tea that tasted like hibiscus. He ate faster then he should have. Unfortunately, he became sated before ingesting a third of the plate. His eyes had been bigger than his stomach that now had ballooned. But he kept eating anyway. He successfully disguised a few belches during his meal.

Finally, Alejandro put his orange cotton napkin back onto the tray. Remembering his manners, he said, "Thank you, Sister. That was very good."

"The Good Lord always provides when there is a need."

She put the food tray back onto the little bedside table. "Maybe next time you should say grace before you start eating," she gave him "the nun's stare".

"Yes, Sister." He faced heated up and turned red. He had known better.

Sister Beatriz went back to the rocking chair. She put her hands together, raised her eyes upward, and seemed to utter a sotto voce prayer.

Alejandro's stomach felt acidy. "Sister, how did I get here?" He looked at her with such an innocent expression like a puppy staring at his master. He was trying to use his boyish charm to find out this information.

"Rest, my son. We'll have plenty of time to talk," she returned the angelic look.

"But when can I call my parents?"

She stared at him with her face contorted, but did not answer. Her eyes blinked. He thought that she was about to say something. But instead, she rose from the chair, signaling the end of their conversation. She picked up the food tray and left the room.

Within the next few moments, Alejandro became homesick thinking of the vacations that he and his family took every December in Acapulco. The beautiful azure skies with puffs of white clouds. The cool ocean breezes that offset the penetrating sunlight. The majestic foamy caps on the aqua seas. They loved playing in the water and building sand castles.

His sister, Lupe, would be pestering his parents for mangoes. Lupe was his special sibling, ever since she came home from the hospital in her mother's arm, swaddled in frothy ivory lace.

"Dro! Dro! Dro!" she used to call him when she was a

small toddler. In fact, she still sometimes called him this, even though she was now older.

His brother, Ricardo, was a pest who always wanted to tag after the older Alejandro, trying to copy his every move as little brothers often do.

The two brothers would tease each other as to who had the lighter or darker skin. They would end the verbal polemics by jumping into the breaking waves. The water was cold. They came out only when they were summoned a dozen times by their parents.

Señora Dolores Rubí, his mother, would be looking at them with her plaintive brown eyes. "Santa Maria! Please come out of the water when I call. Hurry up and get cleaned up. We are having dinner with the Perez family tonight."

"Yes, mamá!" they would respond in unison as they ran to their cabaña. Ricardo pulled Lupe's hair as he passed by. Lupe would then let out a blood-curdling scream that she had perfected since she was two.

The waves coming in. Pounding the surf. Pounding the surf. Pounding the surf.

"Alejandro!"

As he was turning to look back at his mother's smiling face, he heard someone urgently call his name from behind, "Alejandro!"

His memory faded to black . . .

CHAPTER 5

THE PENGUINS

There was a quiet whisper. Sluggishly, Alejandro opened his eyes. In front of him, three nuns were standing. Two others had joined Sister Beatriz. They were all dressed in a similar manner.

His dream had been so wonderful. So tranquil. He could have slept forever.

Sister Beatriz approached him and put her palm on his forehead. "How are you feeling, my son?"

"Fine, Sister. Thank you." He was now on his best behavior because a waddle of penguins surrounded him. The students had nicknamed the nuns when he was in grade school because of their black and white garb.

"Here, my son, I brought you some more juice." She lifted his head up carefully with her left hand and held the juice to his mouth.

"Slowly, my son," she reminded him.

He took the glass with both of his hands. He swallowed the orange juice, savoring every gulp.

When he finished, she took the glass and put it on the nightstand.

"My son, these are Sister Agatha and Sister Clara."

"A pleasure to meet you. I am Alejandro Rubí"

Not reciprocating, Sister Clara immediately began an inquiry. "There are some questions that we want to ask you."

"Sure. Anything." *The typical bossy nun,* he thought.

Sister Clara came closer to the bed. Sister Agatha remained silently in the background.

"Alejandro," she said in a soft tone. "Do you mind being called Alejandro?"

"No, Sister." He lowered his eyes. He felt like he was back in his old grammar school. The students had to obey the nuns without question. They knew that their parents would punish them for any transgressions that the sisters would bring to their attention.

"When did the accident occur?" inquired Sister Clara.

"I think it was about four or five days ago." He tried the best that he could to describe the stormy night and the subsequent events. He was hazy on most of the details.

"Were you alone?"

"Yes, Sister."

Why isn't she asking me about my injuries? He thought. *How strange!*

"Where was the accident?"

He was surprised that a doctor had not yet been in to see him. At least, to ask him how he felt. *What a strange hospital!* He pondered.

"Why were you going to Mexico City?"

"To see my family. I have a new job that I am just starting. I just graduated from law school in San José," he was responding in an excited tone. "Excuse me, Sister, when can I call my family? They're probably worried to death about me."

It was at this time that Sister Beatriz broke in. "Señor Rubí, I'm afraid that will not be possible. There are no telephones here . . ."

Alejandro blurted out, "What kind of a hospital is this?" His body was noticeably shaking. Now he was half-angry, half-worried.

Sister Beatriz put her hand on his shoulder.

At the same time, Sister Clara somberly continued, "This is not a hospital. This is the Abbey of Our Lady of the Flowers."

As she spoke, Alejandro could not believe his ears. His brows furled upward. He was shocked. *Where in the hell am I?*

"You were left at our front gate early this morning by the Momos. That is how you came into our care. We have no contact with the outside world except for the natives."

"But, Sister, I need to get home. I have to call my family," he pleaded.

"We understand. But the best thing that you can do right now is to rest. You've had a traumatic experience. This is the only way for you to recover." Her eyes softened his agitation.

A sigh escaped from him. Alejandro knew that Sister Clara was right. But at the same time he couldn't spend a long time here. He knew that his family would be worried. And how about his best friend, Chuy? And he had to start his new job and make the right impression. A thousand thoughts raced through his mind. The middle finger of his right hand started to tap on his body nervously.

"But, how does one leave from here?"

"We've never been further than three kilometers from here since we joined the Order," replied Sister Beatriz.

"Well, how do you get food? Or mail? Or . . ." Alejandro was surprised regarding the isolation of the abbey.

"Excuse me, Alejandro," Sister Clara interrupted him, "While we have not taken a formal vow of silence, we still are not permitted to speak anymore than necessary. We may be overstepping our limits presently. I suggest that you rest now. Perhaps we can talk more tomorrow."

Alejandro was dumbstruck. He wanted to continue the

dialogue. There were dozens of questions that filled his mind when Sister Clara informed him that he was not in a hospital. He wanted answers. He wanted them now.

Sparks flew inside his skull. His had shortness of breath. He began hyperventilating. His head was pounding and he felt dizzy. *"Oh, man! I'm not well yet,"* his eyes starting to open and close slowly. *"I feel like crap!"*

He tried to look at the nuns. They looked like amorphous figures. *My mouth feels so dry. I need water.*

"What is this place? Where is this abbey?" He started to yell in a frenzy.

"Please excuse us, Señor Rubí. I have just heard the bell. We've got to go to our afternoon prayers. Sister Beatriz will bring you your dinner after vespers. Do you need anything else right now?"

Sister Agatha and Sister Beatriz had already started to exit the room.

"No, . . . no, Sister," he responded agitated.

The last nun then began to follow her colleagues.

"Your clothes are being washed today. So much mud and all. You poor thing," Sister Clara tried to console him. "You need your rest. Tomorrow a nice bath will be prepared for you," she said empathetically. "Until then, I'm afraid that you'll have to use the pitcher and basin. We live an austere life here, Señor Rubí."

Sister Clara turned around and followed the other two nuns out of the room. The large wooden door closed behind them.

The bed creaked as he slid back under the bed covers. His head rested on the pillow as he stared up at the wooden ceiling. His mind was spinning. He felt unsettled. Alejandro started to have delusions.

୬

He woke up in the middle of the afternoon wet from sweating. Alejandro now lay awake wondering about his circumstances. Here he was in a frigging convent! Fate had played a nasty trick on him. When he rejoined his friends back in Mexico City, he would be the butt of a thousand jokes. *Hanging out with nuns? Is this the only type of women that would have you? Were there any virgins there besides you? Did they reaffirm their vows of chastity when they saw you? Ha, ha, ha.* It would be terrible.

How could I endure the razzing? I need to start thinking about how I can embellish this disaster. Surely this could surpass the exploits of Don Giovanni.

Instead of these owl-eyed nuns, I'll conjure myself on an island of mermaid-like damsels who even Odysseus could not resist. Alejandro closed his eyes and began to doze off again. He would be the honored guest of a Palladian mansion fit for a Greek god with its Dorian columns and mosaic floors. The seductive sirens would feed him grapes and massage his feet with perfumed oils. The land of milk and honey.

Alejandro jumped suddenly. He had been startled from his prurient fantasies by the sudden knock at the door. A moment later Sister Beatriz entered with a tray of food. He tried to calmly recover from the surprise and smiled at her sheepishly.

"Are you okay, my son?" she inquired as she bent forward.

"Oh, yes, Sister. I'm just a little hungry," he replied. He pulled the bed cover up over his bare chest as she placed the tray on the stand next to his bed.

"We have some news for you. A bath has been set up for you down the hall. You can bathe tomorrow. It took four of us to carry the tub up the stairs," she chuckled. "It hasn't been used in years." She retired to the rocking chair by the window and started crocheting.

The dinner tray contained small terra cotta bowls that had steam rising from them with tortillas on top of a tan cotton napkin. The hot tortilla was the first item that he grabbed. He didn't mind the discomfort. The vegetables had been cooked in olive oil. His mouth watered. They tasted delicious. The yucca swam in the juice of the black beans. He sopped up the liquid with another tortilla. He mouth chewed slowly and he relished every bite.

He watched Sister Beatriz as he ate his meal. She rocked as she crocheted. She seemed preoccupied. Perhaps she was praying.

Alejandro was feeling better. His left shoulder only had a slight tingle, but still had swelling. There was no more excruciating pain. His head felt clear. His father always reminded him that he had a hard head. Maybe tomorrow he could get up and walk around.

At least Sister Beatriz seemed nice. She was much kinder than Sister Carlota from the third grade had been to him. *What possesses a young woman to become a nun?* He thought. *Love of God? Fear of Life? Not knowing what to do in this world?*

His mind started to wander. *In a few weeks I'll be starting my legal profession. I'll be good. Darn good.*

From the window the pitter-patter of rain sounded. The breeze whirled outside ever so slightly. Alejandro could feel a slight temperature change although it was still mild. He felt a slight chill. Sister Beatriz walked over to the window and stared out. She secured the window.

She came back toward Alejandro and picked up his empty tray. "I need to close the windows in this building. There will be another storm tonight. God bless you, my son.

I'll see you in the morning."

"Thank you, Sister." Darkness started to penetrate the room. "Good night." Alejandro noticed that there were no candles in the room.

"Good night, my son," she seemed to be amused as she left the room.

The rain started to come down heavier. The storm made him recall his traumatic experience several days prior.

Suddenly, he felt sullen. His mind started to race. There was a foreboding in the air. He began to breathe deeper. His heart started to pound. Alejandro's dull aches became more acute.

What does this tempest bode for me?

CHAPTER 6

CLEAN SHEETS

Tap. Tap. Tap. There was knocking at his door. It woke Alejandro up. It was Sister Beatriz with the breakfast tray. Today he was provided with orange juice, hot hibiscus tea, and toasted bolillos with honey. There were even two bananas.

"Good morning, my son. How did you sleep?" she inquired as she fidgeted with the tray.

"Fine. Thank you, Sister. This orange juice tastes really good." He was trying to be polite and act amiably with the nun.

At home I would be dipping my pan dulce into my café con leche. Inocente would bring me a soft-boiled egg already cracked and peppered, he reminisced. He felt that although Inocente was the family maid, she was like a second mother to him.

He peeled a spotted yellow banana. Alejandro hated bruised bananas, but he had to be discreet here. He gnawed off the end. It was not as mushy as he would have expected. He took a bigger second bite. He squished it between his teeth. His third bite was smaller. He savored it as it slowly slid down his throat. *It isn't that bad,* he thought.

Carefully he ate around a darkened portion of the banana, casually breaking it off and placing it nonchalantly on his plate. He dipped the remainder of the banana into the light amber honey. His tongue could taste the orange blossom and mint of the syrupy liquid. His nose smelled the aroma of orange blossoms.

"Hmm. That's good!" he grinned. He licked off the sweet, sticky liquid that had dripped onto his fingers. *Yum!*

While he was entertaining himself with his breakfast, Sister Beatriz was rocking herself in the rocking chair. He folded over the banana peels as he munched on his morning meal.

Unexpectedly, Alejandro heard another knock at the door. Sister Clara entered carrying two giant white cotton towels.

"Good morning, Alejandro. Here are the towels for your bath. After your breakfast, you may use one of the towels to wrap around yourself. The other to dry yourself off," she instructed officiously. "Go out this door and turn left and proceed to the very end of the hall to the double doors. Enter there and you should be fine."

"Thank you, Sister, " he said deferentially. He was so ready to bathe. He knew that he must be soiled from head to toe, not to mention reeking of foul body odors.

"Please be careful, Alejandro. Dry yourself well. The floors are very slippery."

"Yes, Sister."

"Let me see." Sister Clara put her elbow into her palm and rubbed her plump chin. "Is that all I need to tell you?" she said rhetorically.

"Sister, what about my clothes? You said that I might get them back today," he hesitantly inquired.

"Oh, yes. Your clothes should be here by the time you've finished with your bath."

Sister Clara's eyes shifted over to Sister Beatriz and gave her a quick glance.

Instantaneously, Sister Beatriz rose from the rocking chair and took the tray from Alejandro's lap. The two nuns left.

He didn't want to tarry in bed. He knew that was emitting a stench and wanted to bathe as soon as possible.

Lifting his right foot out of the bed first, he righted himself and sat on the edge of the bed. He reached for one of the white cotton towels. He stood up and tried to wrap the towel around himself. This reminded him of the toga parties they had at the law school on those festive Saturday nights.

Taking the second towel in hand he started to walk across the floor. He hadn't noticed the slight chill of the surface under his feet before. He pushed down on the tarnished door handle and pulled the door inward. He looked outside. His eyes awoke to the brighter light. He looked left down the hallway. He turned his head to the right and saw a window that seemed to look outward. In front of him was a well-polished staircase railing.

Alejandro leaned over the railing. He saw that the stairs descended to a lower level. He felt dizzy for a second. He pulled his body back. He felt a twinge of pain. Across from the central stairwell there were three other wooden doors.

He was curious to know if the nuns slept there in cloister type rooms. *What kind of nuns were they? They sure talk a lot. Obviously, they hadn't taken a vow of silence,* he thought. *They certainly don't resemble the Carmelites.*

Cautiously, he turned to this left, walked down the hallway, and passed another door before he arrived at the double doors. Strange. Nobody was around. It was so quiet. Too quiet, it seemed.

Alejandro opened the double doors and in the middle of what appeared to be a storage room was situated a small white bathtub. Well, sort of. It was more of a basin in which to wash clothes. Much of the enamel coating had eroded away. It looked like a pinto pony. There were patches of water on the floor that made it slippery.

But this is better than nothing, he thought. There was a small footstool that had a big bar of soap on it.

It's probably lye soap that will eat away my skin!

He placed the one towel on the bench and picked up the bar of soap. It smelled quite fragrant, like sandalwood. He let the towel that had draped him fall to the floor.

With one hand on the edge of the tub, he raised his right foot over the side.

F__k! The water is frigging cold! Don't these nuns know how to take baths? Probably not. That would be carrying the vow of poverty too far, he surmised.

He had submerged his other foot into the water and assumed a crouched position. He started to shiver. Slowly he slid more and more of his body into the small tub. Goose bumps blanketed his entire body.

Alejandro dipped the soap into the water and lathered his hands. He rubbed the white snowy suds through his reddish-brown beard and his face. Then he continued the soaping to his ears. It tickled and he had to smile. He continued the process onto the rest of his body.

With his hands cupped, he rinsed himself. The water turned a clayish ocher color from mealy pastes, mud, and blood. He lathered his hands again and started to wash his hair.

He felt a slight knot on the left side of his head. It still hurt a little. A dead black beetle fell into the water from his scalp.

F__k! I wonder how long that's been with me?

The goose pimples started to recede. His body was now adjusting to the temperature of the water. Alejandro sat in the tub just soaking. He was trying to relax.

This sure beats the humid nights.

He lathered the soap again and gently glided it over his body. It seemed to add sheen to his light skin. He closed his eyes and tried with little success to submerge more of his body. He dunked his head. His fingers tried to rinse and untangle his hair. His head resurfaced. Time to get out. He reached over the side of the tub and grabbed a towel. He rose slowly so that he wouldn't splash too much water onto the floor. First, he dried his face, and then, he towel-dried his hair. The ambient temperature seemed mild, but cool. Carefully, he wiped away the film of soap and scum from his body.

On the edge of the tub he raised his right foot and dried between his toes. Then he straddled the tub and put his left foot on the edge facing in the opposite direction. After he toweled off these toes, he tried to mop up the water on the floor. He wrung out the wet towel over the tub.

Alejandro then left the wet towel lying over the tub. The other towel was still on the footstool. He grabbed it and pulled it around him.

He looked around.

What should I do with the soap?

He carefully reached into the tub and retrieved the slippery soap and placed the wet bar back on the stool. His eyes made one last inspection. Everything looked okay.

Slowly Alejandro tiptoed across the floor still dripping water, even though he had been careful, as he left the storage room. There was still no sign of activity in the passageway. He treaded lightly past the whitewashed stucco walls back to his room. He noticed that there were no paintings or tapestries or murals on the walls. Not even crosses. Very austere.

Nonchalantly he flung open the door to his cell. He was

in his Elba. He was greeted by a burst of a lavender fragrance. Before he could comprehend the source of this aromatic bouquet, he saw her. She was changing the sheets on his bed. She looked at him silently and smiled.

Her bright smile melted his heart like a lit candle. The ivory teeth gleamed like a thousand stars in the night. Her garnet lips flamed his desire. The face that launched a thousand ships culminated in her violet eyes. Alejandro had found his Helen of Troy. She was a young girl. Not really a grown woman. Her cinnamon-colored body was tiny and thin. Her braided black hair swept over her cinnamon neck down to her waist. The tresses ended with little white ribbons.

Alejandro was breathing with difficulty. His heart was palpitating throughout his corporeal frame.

"Good morning," he said meekly.

"Good morning, señor," she replied in a very simple manner, her eyes diverted from him. "I'll be finished in a moment." She continued making the bed.

It was only at this moment that Alejandro realized that he was only wearing a towel. "Oh, excuse me," he blurted apologetically.

"No problem, señor. Your clothes and things are over on the rocking chair. After I leave, you can leave your towel. I'll pick it up later." She gave a little curtsy.

The girl gathered up the soiled bedding and slid past Alejandro. She never looked directly at him. She left the room expeditiously.

Alejandro stared at the door as she left. He had been mesmerized. Cupid's arrow had found its mark.

He ran his fingers through his hair. It was the best that he could do without a comb. His shirt and underwear were neatly folded and laid on top of his freshly laundered pants.

It also looked like the guayabera had been sewn where it had been torn. Alejandro put the shirt up to his nose and sniffed. It smelled so fresh and clean. It had a lavender scent. His maid, Inocente, would have been envious. He carefully put on the shirt and buttoned the bottom three buttons.

Moments later he had finished getting dressed. However, there were no shoes or socks. *I wonder what happened to them?* His handkerchief was tied up like a pouch with a little hemp string.

Undoing the tie on the handkerchief was difficult. Finally, his face lit up with cheer. In the middle of the handkerchief lay a trove of a few coins, a bottle opener, his lighter, a crushed pack of cigarettes or what remained of them, and something resembling a package of chewing gum. There was no wallet. He could have lost that in a million places. There was no watch. Time was standing still for him anyway. There were no keys to the Jeep. They were probably still in the vehicle.

Alejandro laid himself back on top of the bed. *What should I do next? I feel restless.*

He stared up at the wooden beamed ceiling. His eyes locked.

Who was that girl?

CHAPTER 7

THE LUNCH

As he was lying in bed, Alejandro's thoughts kept drifting to the beautiful, cinnamon-skinned girl with the radiant violet eyes.

It is so cool to meet such a girl! Chuy, eat your frigging heart out! I need to find out her name. What does she do around here besides make beds? He wondered.

Alejandro rolled over onto his stomach and dug his face into the pillow. He loved the smell of lavender. He tried to remember the girls that he had dated in San José. None could compare with this sexy little goddess.

Then all of a sudden, his body tensed up. *Oh, holy crap! She's probably a nun! Or studying to be one. Why am I such a jerk? What would she being doing here if she wasn't a nun or novice? Oh, Jeez, I need to go to confession. I probably committed a frigging mortal sin! Probably at least a dozen! How could I have fallen from heaven to hell in a flash? The devil lured me into a trap, and I was caught without a fight. I'm such a frigging idiot! I must be the worst sinner in the whole world, thinking such thoughts about a nun.*

Alejandro was now in a foul mood. He wanted to kick the wall or punch the door. He was afraid that he would be struck down dead for such lustful thoughts in a nunnery.

He put the pillow over his head. He wanted to disappear.

Knock . . . knock. Sister Beatriz entered. He turned over and sat up. He did his best to hide his shame.

"Well, how was your bath, my son?" she said to him with a cheerful smile as she repositioned the pillow back under his head.

"Fine. Thank you, Sister, " he responded rather meekly. He did not look her straight in the eyes. Instead he focused on her mouth. It was a trick that he had learned when he was young and was getting scolded by one of his parents. He could avoid the pain of the piercing and punishing eyes in this manner.

"Now you have clean sheets and clean clothes. You must feel like a real human being again."

"Yes, I do. Thank you." *Why was she so damn cheery?*

"Perhaps you would like to join us for lunch. It must be very challenging to you to be confined to this room," she said inquisitively.

"Yes, Sister, that would be nice." *Anything would be better than this little room.* He was getting restless.

"Good. I'll to fetch you in a little while. You'll meet some of the other sisters of our Order."

"Thank you, Sister."

Sister Beatriz started to turn around to walk out, when Alejandro blurted, "Sister, I don't have any shoes."

She cackled. "Don't worry, my son. We'll find you some sandals or something." She then left the room.

A while later there was a rap at the door. Sister Beatriz entered the room. In her hands she held what looked like sandals from a previous century.

Alejandro swung his legs over onto the floor. He still felt a little woozy, but the bath had been helpful. She handed him the leather sandals. At least they were clean, although they had been well worn. *Maybe they belonged to one of the staff,* he thought.

"Thank you, Sister."

"You're welcome," she smiled. "As soon as you put them on, we can go downstairs."

His hands fumbled with the straps as he tried to hurry. Finally, he had them fastened. His toes hung over the front of them. *They are a little too small,* he thought, *but I'm not complaining.*

Alejandro stood up. "I'm ready, Sister."

The two walked toward the door. He tried to get to the door first in order to open it for Sister Beatriz, but she beat him to the exit. It seemed that she was not accustomed to having the door opened for her. She opened it herself and he followed her out.

She turned left onto the hallway. He had difficulty keeping pace with her. He lagged behind a few steps.

"Easy, my son," she cajoled him. "Take your time. We aren't in a hurry."

His head nodded.

They walked down the hallway and turned right to the stairwell. Sister Beatriz glided down the stairs. Alejandro gingerly took each step one at a time. His feet tried to make sure that he had secure footing. Halfway down the stairs, Sister Beatriz stopped and turned around looking upwards to Alejandro.

"Are you okay?" she said in a concerned tone.

"Yes, Sister. I'm fine," he quickly responded. He had no desire to go back to the room. It was like a deserted island. He would tough it out.

They continued down the stairs. He saw huge wooden entryway doors in front of them that led out of the residence. Each of the orangish-brown oak doors had multicolored ovals of impaneled stained glass. *How come they have such ornate doors?* He thought. *This is a nunnery.*

However, at the bottom of the stairs the two made a left turn and continued about twenty steps to the entrance of the dining room. There they entered. Alejandro's head circled the room and noted the details. The dining room did not seem very large. Here, there were no paintings or adornments on the walls.

In the middle of the room was a long rectangular table. Sitting around the table were four nuns, although it could have accommodated eight persons. Sister Agatha was at the head of the table.

Sister Beatriz pointed to the empty seat to the right of Sister Agatha. Alejandro proceeded to that chair, pulled it out, and sat down. Sister Beatriz sat on the other side of him.

Alejandro lowered his head and for a moment stared at the empty wooden bowl situated in front of him. Each bowl around the table had a large wooden spoon accompanying it.

It was so solemn, so quiet. Alejandro slowly raised his eyes to the two nuns who sat across from him whom he had not yet met. The pair seemed so young.

These two nuns seemed to be concentrating their attention to the middle of the table. Unlike the other nuns, this pair wore white veils rather than the black cornette headpieces.

Suddenly, the smaller and thinner of the pair blurted, "I'm Sister Sophia. It is very nice to meet you. I pray that you are feeling better."

Sister Clara shot her a reprimanding glance. "Excuse me, Señor Rubí, for our lack of manners. We seldom have guests here and the sisters have been filled with anticipation in meeting you."

Alejandro nodded like he understood what she was trying to communicate.

"You remember Sister Agatha," continued Sister Clara. "And this is Sister Consuelo." Sister Agatha and Sister Consuelo politely bowed. "And of course, Sister Sophia." "It is a pleasure to meet you all. I'm actually glad just being here."

I'm back at The Ascension Grammar School again. This will be another good story to share with Chuy. Eating lunch with a bunch of nuns. Chuy wouldn't believe it.

From a door opposite him entered a short, heavyset mestiza woman with long black braids wrapped into a bun and wearing a yellow kitchen apron over a cream-colored manta indigenous dress. She was carrying a ceramic tureen of what seemed to be a broth. She placed the soup bowl next to Sister Agatha and ladled out three large spoonfuls.

"Thank you, Marica," said Sister Agatha.

Marica, the cook, then continued to serve Alejandro and the other four nuns.

"Normally, we adhere to periods of silence throughout the day, my son, but today we may relax this discipline," stated Sister Clara.

The nuns nodded their heads in unison with tacit approval. Marica had left the dining room and had returned with two wooden boards of bread. Steam rose from the large loaves.

"Sister Sophia, please lead us in prayer."

"Bless us, O Lord . . ." Alejandro silently lipped the words in the saying of grace. He realized that he had not said grace when Sister Beatriz was catering his meals to him upstairs. His face reddened a little, but in reality, he hadn't said grace before meals for years. This situation reminded him of being back in grammar school, although in those days there was a lot of kicking under the table during the meals.

"Amen."

"Amen," echoed the remainder.

The bread was taken in turn by each.

Alejandro savored the first spoonful of the foamy broth. It was delicious. It had a hearty taste. It actually tasted like a potato-leek soup. It could have used a little pepper or salsa, he thought, but there were no condiments on the table.

Sister Sophia broke out into a little giggle. "Excuse me, Señor Rubí, but you have some soup in your beard."

Sister Clara rolled her eyes and sighed. Her expression said that Sister Sophia needed a lot more training. *The innocence of youth,* she thought.

"Thank you, Sister," Alejandro said somewhat embarrassed. "Sister, how many nuns are here in the Abbey?"

He was trying to change the direction of the conversation.

Sister Agatha seemed dumbfounded by the question. She had a look of consternation. She gave a quick nod to Sister Clara.

After a few moments, Sister Clara replied, "Currently, we are eight. You have met several of us. Mother Superior is with Sisters Teresa and Anna. They are in the other residence. You will have an opportunity to meet them soon."

Eight nuns? Other building? I thought that this was a full-fledged abbey. This is a recluse.

"So, Sister, this is a small Order?"

"Yes, we belong to the Order of Our Lady of the Flowers that was founded over five hundred years ago. Unfortunately, throughout the years, our numbers have dwindled dramatically. We are all who remain," she responded in a somber tone.

"I don't mean to be impolite, but what do you do here?" Alejandro inquired curiously.

"Our Order is dedicated to world peace and harmony. We spend our time in prayer. We dedicate thoughts, words, and deeds to this end. We even grow our own food and produce honey."

To Alejandro, this sounded like the religious propaganda that he had been taught as he was growing up. *How could one be for such lofty ideals as world peace, if one did not interact with the real world and with real people?*

While at law school, Alejandro had become more cynical about platitudes and rhetoric. *What really is important? Ideals? Family and friends?* He remembered fondly the intellectual writings of Unamuno.

He dipped his bread to soak up the last of the broth. Alejandro wanted more, but he would not ask for more.

"My son, would you like more soup," invited Sister Beatriz.

"No, thank you, Sister," he replied with restraint.

Marica came back into the dining room, carrying what looked like a small bowl.

"We have a treat for you, my son," smiled Sister Beatriz.

Marica placed the bowl in front of him. It smelled wonderful. It was coffee! Coffee! Coffee!

Alejandro looked around the table. No one else was having any. There was no cream or sugar, but he wouldn't complain.

He sipped the hot liquid. It was on the bitter side, but it was better than nothing. He stared into the black-brown liquid. It reminded him of the days in law school when he and Chuy would go to the Café Paraíso each afternoon. There they would discuss the finer points of legal precedents and distinctions. Ultimately, the conversation would degenerate into base talk about wine, women, and song. The hyperboles increased a hundredfold each day.

Suddenly, there were ringing sounds. Sister Agatha was rotating a small bell in her hand.

"Sisters, it is time for our afternoon prayers," Sister Clara said. Turning to Alejandro, "Señor, you may stay until you are finished. Marica will assist you. I pray that you had enough to eat."

"Oh, yes, Sister. Thank you very much. This was very nice," he politely tried to express his gratitude. Moving his head in a sort of a semicircle, he said, "It was nice meeting you all." He bowed forward slightly. He was grateful for the break in the monotony.

The nuns pushed in their chairs in a precise manner as they prepared to leave. Their facial expressions were now solemn. No one spoke.

Alejandro relished the remainder of his coffee. He rose from the chair. He too was methodical about pushing in his chair.

Marica started to clear his dishes.

"Thank you for the wonderful meal, señora, " he smiled at her. Marica reminded him of Inocente, the maid of the Rubí family. She had those dark, sensitive brown eyes.

Alejandro turned around to leave.

"You're welcome, Señor Rubí."

Alejandro left the dining room. Sister Clara remained alone in the hallway. Was she waiting for him?

He walked toward the base of the staircase. He took a few paces toward the front doors.

"It would be nice to take a little walk after that wonderful meal. I feel my strength coming back." The double oak doors seemed to invite him outside.

"Alejandro, it is probably best that you retire to your

room. We wouldn't want you to have a relapse. I need to consult with Sister Beatriz on what you are able to do now."

Obediently, he nodded affirmatively to Sister Clara. He put his right hand onto the railing and started to walk up the stairs.

Sister Clara disappeared into a nearby doorway. When she opened the door, he could hear the low drone of the other nuns praying.

That is probably their chapel, he thought. It wouldn't do me any harm to pay a little visit there.

Finally, after a slow ascent, he reached the top of the staircase. He turned left and went back into his room. After relieving himself in the chamber pot, he removed his pants, and crawled into bed.

His eyes closed as he tried to recreate the luncheon scene in his mind. Oh, how grateful he was to have finally gotten out of his confining room.

This place probably has a million secrets. At least, that is what I will tell Chuy. Well, I can't exaggerate too much for after all, this is a convent. A sacred sanctuary.

His eyelids remained closed as the rains started to fall. The drops could be heard beating against the building.

The room got darker and darker.

Alejandro's head started to feel hot. There were electric currents charging through his brain. He started to dream about the Sunday walks in the plaza with his parents when he was the only child. They would buy him an ice cream. He loved to run around the gazebo.

This custom ceased when his siblings came into the picture. His father and mother spent more and more time with the younger ones. He resorted to doing mischievous pranks in order to get his parents' attention.

"Alejandro!"

CHAPTER 8

SMOKE

The outdoor birds were singing loudly and sweetly. The mourning doves were cooing. His body felt the fresh coolness of the dawn coming through the open window. The early morning sunshine had filtered into the room. Alejandro had attempted to look out of the window, but the view was partially obscured by a large orange-red madrona tree.

There was an authoritarian knock at the door. Sister Beatriz walked in with a breakfast tray.

"Good morning, my son," she smiled.

"Good morning, Sister," he replied half-asleep. "I guess I slept through dinner last night."

"You mustn't try to do too much, too soon. You need your strength."

"Yes, Sister, " he replied respectfully. *But I'm not doing anything,* he thought to himself.

"I'll return in a while. Enjoy."

Alejandro gulped down his orange juice. His throat had been so dry and he had been very thirsty. He took a big bite of a mango. His mouth captured its soft flesh. The tortillas were still hot and steaming. He dipped them in the little bowl of honey. How he loved this sweetness! This sure could compare to Inocente's kitchen.

He was still wearing his shirt from yesterday. His mother would have scolded him for sleeping in his clothes, "Your clothes are not pajamas!" Were all mothers taught to say this? It was probably one of the Ten Commandments of Motherhood.

He put the tray on the little table and went to the corner to use the chamber pot. At the basin he washed his face and combed his hair by running his fingers through it.

There was a slight tap at the door. The girl from the prior day entered the room carrying a clean towel.

"Good morning, señor," she greeted him without looking at him.

"Good morning to you." His heart skipped a beat.

"I am just going to straighten up the room and get you a clean towel. Is right now convenient? I can come back later if you like."

"Oh, no! Please stay! I have already finished my breakfast." He didn't know what to do. Alejandro was nervous. She was so lovely. He felt his heart pounding. The blood pumped hotly through his veins. His face became flushed. He moved away from the bed.

The girl exchanged towels and was making the bed as Alejandro stood by the window trying to decide what to do. He spied his old handkerchief near the washbasin. He went over and opened it. He picked out the crumpled packet of cigarettes. He turned the pack over. Loose tobacco fell to the floor. There were only a few cigarettes left. Two were broken, to describe them in the best sense. He found a whole one that was bent.

He found his lighter and flicked it. It didn't work. He flicked it again without any better results. Finally, on the eighth or ninth attempt, a flame appeared. He nervously lit the cigarette and inhaled deeply.

Oh, man! I haven't had a smoke in days. As he exhaled, he started to choke. He looked up at her. His eyes were tearing.

The young girl was glaring at him. She had stopped making the bed.

"What are you doing, Señor Rubí?" she exclaimed in a severe tone.

He was about to answer, still unable to catch his breath, when Sister Beatriz walked in.

"What's going on here?" she barked. "Melissa, please leave the room!"

"Sister, I haven't finished making the bed."

"Never mind, girl, just take the tray."

"Yes, Sister," she replied with her head down.

Alejandro was aghast. He felt nauseous and was unable to speak.

Melissa quickly exited the room as she had been directed.

"My son, please extinguish that thing. There is no smoking here at the convent," she said sternly.

Alejandro opened the chamber pot and dropped the cigarette in. "I'm sorry, Sister. I didn't know."

Sister Beatriz started to calm down. "Yes, my son. This convent was built almost four hundred years ago. It is made of very old timber and fragile stucco. We try to minimize the fire hazards around here. Actually, part of the convent burned down several years ago. It was such a tragedy. Thank God, the remainder miraculously survived."

"I'm sorry, Sister," He repeated. Alejandro felt like he was back at his grammar school in the colonia, being scolded by the nuns for fighting.

"Don't worry, my son," she put her hand on his shoulder. She seemed to have regained her composure after what seemed like an overreaction. "Mother Superior is quite allergic to smoke. We have to be very careful around here."

"Yes, Sister."

"I know it must be difficult for a young man like you to have to comply with all these rules. You'll soon get used to things around here."

"Sister, when will I be able to contact my parents? They are probably worried to death about me."

"The Momos come here sometime between every ten days or up to a month to bring our supplies. No on knows exactly when. It depends. They were the ones who brought you here. It'll be a little while before they'll be back here again." She turned away from him and started to leave.

So those were the natives who found me, he realized.

"Sister, is there any reason why I must stay in my room?"

She turned back. "You really should rest. You need your strength."

Alejandro felt that she was treating him like a child. He decided to push a little. "A little sunshine and a little exercise might do me good," he proffered.

"Well, a little exertion shouldn't hurt. Just be careful. It is not only for your own sake, but for ours as well. The young sisters yesterday were talking about you. They should have been praying to God. Temptation is everywhere. Even in innocent forms."

She turned around and silently left the room.

Alejandro was left speechless. He didn't know what to think. *I hope that Sister Beatriz was not upset because that girl was alone in the room with me.* He could empathize with her dilemma. Over the years he had been very protective of his seven-year old sister, Lupe. He didn't want to be the cause of this girl being excommunicated from the nunnery.

I've probably already committed a dozen mortal sins just thinking about her.

Suddenly, his mind paused. *Why wasn't she at the luncheon*

yesterday? He wondered. Sister Clara had not mentioned her as a nun. *Maybe she was just a novice?*

Still, I don't want to get her into trouble.

Alejandro ineptly tried to finish making the bed. He was out of practice. It ended up looking lumpy and sloppy.

I need a plan of action. A plan of action to do what? A plan of action not to go crazy. You are already crazy. He could hear Chuy laughing at him. The two of them would often get into polemic discussions reviewing their legal studies of the day. Each vigorously supporting one position or another. Arguments would abound, each getting progressively more outrageous, until they engaged in name-calling.

Professor Peña at the Law School instructed them in rhetoric and forensics. He would say that when the law is on your side, but the facts of the case are not, the best strategy is to argue the law. On the other hand, he would say that when the facts are on your side, but the law is not, the best strategy is to argue the facts.

Then one day Chuy naively asked the professor what should one do if neither the facts nor the law are favorable to one's case. The fly fell into the web and the spider chortled, "Well, then argue like hell!" The class burst into laughter and applauded the professor. Chuy recoiled in his seat from embarrassment.

Alejandro didn't know exactly what day it was. It must have been a week since the accident, but it seemed like a year. He wanted to find out when the Momos were coming back. *What kind of supplies did they bring the nuns?* He pondered. Maybe the girl could help him, if she was allowed to come back. *I need to drive out those lustful thoughts I have about her. What did Sister Beatriz call her? Melissa?*

CHAPTER 9

THE VIEW

When Sister Beatriz returned with his lunch tray in the afternoon, she found Alejandro in an upbeat mood.

"How are you, my son?" she inquired. She laid the tray on the little table. The rectangular wooden carrier seemed very plain and quite old.

"Fine," Alejandro replied joyfully. He leaned over and took the white cotton napkin. He placed it on his lap as he sat on the edge of the bed. He reached over and with a large spoon took a taste of the vegetable soup. It heated his mouth. It was delicious. It actually tasted spicy. He liked heat in his food. The more chilies, the better.

Fresh sweet peas, white corn, leeks, and anise seed were submerged in a red peppery, pulpy orange juice base. There also was a hint of lemon grass, ginger, and coriander.

The steam rose from the corn tortillas. He grabbed one and tore it in half and halved the half. He dipped the quarter tortilla in the soup, soaking up the appetizing juices.

The aroma from the soup made his nose get stuffed up. His eyes started to water.

"My son, I've talked to Mother Superior. She will permit you to walk about on the abbey grounds. She does admonish you to follow our rules and not to overexert yourself. She says that if something should happen to you, we are leagues away from help. Do you understand?"

"Yes, Sister," His pleas had been answered. "Thank you,

Sister!"

He took hold of the ripe banana and started to peel it. On the tray there was a small ceramic ramekin filled half way up with honey. He took a chunk of the banana and dipped it in the honey after pulling off some of the silky strings that still clung to the fruit. He savored it with gusto.

"When may I start walking, Sister?" he inquired eagerly.

Sister Beatriz looked at him pensively and after a pause replied, "Soon we'll be going to prayers. You will probably hear the bell ring. After we are done with our prayers, we have our daily responsibilities to do. That would be an appropriate time to go out for a stroll. Please remember that although we haven't taken a full vow of silence, we do observe a peace and quiet rule of conduct here. Therefore, there should not be any idle chatter with the sisters here. Do you understand?"

"Yes, Sister."

Sister Beatriz sat herself down in the rocking chair and began crocheting. Alejandro continued to eat his meal. He ended by drinking the glass of orange juice with its slice of lime. It was so sweet. It was the best that he had ever tasted.

"Are you finished, my son?"

"Yes, Sister. Thank you." He noted that she never admonished him about not saying grace before his meals.

She rose from the chair, picked up the depleted food tray and left the room. She had seemed a little quiet. It was like she was preoccupied. Maybe she was stressed because she had to watch over him. His father used to say that after three days both fish and relatives begin to smell bad. Of course, Señora Rubí chided her husband for saying such outrageous things to their children.

Alejandro and Ricardo used to laugh when their father said this. It was certainly true about his father's cousin,

Socorro. They called her Aunt Socorro, but they didn't know why. She tried to be nice to them, but they used to make fun of her because of her red dyed hair and heavily rouged cheeks. She would slip them coins, and then would try to hug and kiss them. Her perfume overwhelmed them with a cloying, snow cone sweetness. Her sixty-seven years had eroded her sense of smell and also her hearing.

Ricardo and he would whisper behind her back. She would look around, but she couldn't find them. At times they would pretend to speak to her by only moving their lips. She in turn would pretend to hear them by nodding her head as if she understood.

There was a knock at the door.

Alejandro waited for the door to open. Nothing happened. "Come in," he called out.

The door opened half way. The young girl peeked in, holding the edge of the door with both hands.

"Señor, Sister Beatriz says that you may go out for awhile."

He was now standing in front of her. "Are you coming with me?" he asked surprising even himself with his boldness.

"No, señor. I can't," she said modestly.

She walked past him to the bed. Alejandro recalled that she had not been able to finish making it that morning. She started rearranging the bed linens.

"I'm sorry if I got you in trouble this morning," he said apologetically.

"Oh, you didn't get me in trouble. Things have changed around here lately." Melissa seemed apprehensive to continue conversing. She kept her back to him.

"Are you some sort of nun?" he blurted out. He couldn't believe that he asked the question so shamelessly. No manners. No respect. Sister Beatriz had warned him about disrupting the serenity of the nunnery. But in Melissa's presence he could not control himself. His heart put his mind in a frantic state.

"I'm sorry . . ." he started to say.

"No, señor. I'm just a servant here at the abbey," she turned around and faced him.

"I'm sorry if I offended you by asking."

She looked up at him for a moment. Her eyes penetrated his soul. Her lavender fragrance enraptured his senses. As he inhaled her scent, the perfume traveled down the back of his mouth and touched his tongue. He could sense her essence. The taste was of a sweetness that slid down his throat like the finest Madeira wine from the San Ángel Inn Restaurant in the Colonia Álvaro Obregón in Mexico City.

"No, señor. I just do the cleaning here for the nuns. I make the beds. I wash their clothes. And other chores," her voice seemed so naïve. "And now for you, too."

"I'm sorry for being a burden, but thank you for helping me."

"You're welcome." Her head bowed downward.

"Tell me your name again," Alejandro pressed.

"Melissa."

The door closed. The girl had quickly disappeared right after she had finished making the bed. The sudden departure by Melissa took Alejandro somewhat by surprise, since she had not finished making the bed. He slipped on his newly acquired sandals with some difficulty. His toes stuck out because the sandals were a little short. He departed from the room.

He peered down both sides of the hallway. Melissa was nowhere in sight. But he could still smell her essence as he inhaled deeply.

What kind of power does this angelic creature have over me?

Yesterday I went to the left to the storage room. Let me now go to the right. He started walking slowly on the wooden slatted floor toward the window. It took him about eight steps to reach the curtained window.

It was so bright outside as Alejandro pulled back the white manta curtain. It was so beautiful. He was in paradise.

This second story vantage point overlooked a magnificent, ornamental parterre garden that could rival the Fontainebleau. Each section of green yew bushes contrasted with another. There were sections of red roses, white daisies, yellow daffodils, and pink tulips. *It was glorious. I'm in the Garden of Eden! The family maid, Inocente, would have been chattering a kilometer a minute. "How beautiful this is! How beautiful that is!"*

In the middle of the garden courtyard was a little round fountain. There was a path that led from this structure to a set of marbled steps that wound up to another two story building about a hundred meters away. The tan colored structure was slightly uphill from his observation point. It had six windows on one side with beautiful purple bougainvilleas climbing over its walls.

The front of the structure had a simple entryway with a Roman archway portal. *What is that building?* He wondered. *Who lives there? Maybe some of the nuns live there.*

Craning his neck more to the right, he looked downhill to the groves of trees. They looked like fruit trees. Mangoes, figs, avocados. Maybe a few olive trees. He thought he could catch a glimpse of some beehives.

He had a whole world to explore. He recalled when his father used to take them on strolls through Chapultepec Park for their Sunday family outings. The azure blue sky pulled his sight to the left. The uphill climb some distance away saw steps ascending a steep grade. He could barely discern what looked like a parapet. There also seemed to be rows of trees.

As his eyes explored, he looked for movement. He thought that he saw Sister Sophia coming down the hill with fresh flowers in her arms.

He took a deep breath. The air was so fragrant. He stayed observing for what seemed a few seconds. In reality it was almost an hour.

During this period he saw no one entering or leaving the other building. He did see another nun walking gingerly down the path from the upper parterre. She was also carrying a basket. He could not ascertain if it contained fruit or flowers.

His eyes started to feel heavy. He was tired, yet exhilarated. He decided to go back to his room. Tomorrow he would explore the gardens. He fell into a deep slumber.

CHAPTER 10

EL SOMBRERÓN

The next morning Alejandro woke up in an upbeat mode. He had dreamt about Melissa. *What would it be like to hold her hand? To stroke her hair? To taste her lips? To touch her?*

His rapture was interrupted when Sister Beatriz entered with the wooden food tray. For several days she had been bringing him food. Alejandro didn't know if he was in a hospital or prison cell. He wanted to go downstairs to eat rather than spending so much time in his room.

"Good morning, my son."

"Good morning, Sister."

"How did you sleep?"

"Fine, Sister."

"Did you venture through the gardens yesterday?"

"No, Sister. I thought that I would do that today. If that's all right?"

"Oh, yes, my son. It is."

Sister Beatriz took her customary place in the rocking chair. Alejandro drank his orange juice hurriedly. He savored the fresh mango. Each bite was juicy. He was making quite a mess with the sticky nectar running down his forearm.

Inocente would have scowled at him and said, "Slow down, son. You weren't raised on a farm. Don't be such a piglet." She would have smiled because he would have wiggled his nose in response and they both would have giggled.

Alejandro was sopping up his tortillas dipped in honey,

when his ears perked up. He heard a commotion outside of his window. He looked at Sister Beatriz. At first it seemed that she hadn't heard anything, but then all of a sudden, she sprang from her chair. She rushed toward the door and the left the room.

"What is happening?" Alejandro leaped from his bed and went to the door. He saw Sister Beatriz scurrying down the stairs. He had forgotten to put on his sandals. It wasn't important. He decided to follow her.

Sister Beatriz hurried through the ground floor corridor and opened the double oak doors. *She sure moved fast for a nun,* he thought.

Alejandro followed through the doors. The sunlight blinded him. He squinted. His eyes blinked. It had been a week since he had been outdoors.

There was nothing but blurred images ahead of him. He ran into a yew bush.

"Ouch!" he cried.

Alejandro hobbled slowly up a gravel pathway. He winced with pain as the sharp pebbles bit his tender feet. He started to hear screaming and crying. He saw four figures in front of him. They seemed huddled around something on the ground. It looked like a log. No, another figure. As his eyes adjusted, he noticed that Sister Beatriz was with Sister Clara, the novice Consuelo, and a hunched-over indigenous woman. They were hovering over another nun. What had happened?

As he approached the cluster, he suddenly noticed the bloody clothing. It was Sister Sophia lying on the ground! Her eyes stared upwards into infinity. Pools of blood were beside her. Her left arm was missing. Alejandro's stomach was constricting with an acid reflux. A feeling of nausea overcame him.

Sister Agatha approached the group from the other side. She was carrying blankets. She handed them to Sister Clara. A native woman with short black hair and bangs who wore an orange apron left running toward the second building.

Sister Agatha looked at the nuns without uttering a word. The nuns reacted instinctively and immediately wrapped the body in the blankets.

Sister Agatha turned and walked back toward the other building.

The two other nuns and the novice struggled as they carried the body into the kitchen of the first building. Alejandro tried to help although he felt lightheaded and queasy. They put the body on the wooden table in the kitchen. Marica sobbed profusely when she saw the remains of Sister Sophia.

"Marica, please help us clean her up," requested Sister Clara, placing a hand firmly on the cook's shoulder with a knowing look that seemed to convey much more.

"Yes, Sister," she responded as she started to remove the victim's wimple.

Alejandro noticed deep puncture wounds on Sister Sophia's neck and throughout her garb.

He felt a touch on his shoulder. He looked around. There was Sister Beatriz teary-eyed.

"Go back to your room. I'll be up in a little while."

"Yes, Sister."

He obediently went back to his room. He was surprised to see Melissa finishing making his bed. She was weeping. Her violet eyes were swollen with tears. She didn't say anything to Alejandro. She simply left the room.

Alejandro was thoroughly depressed. *I'm not sure I've ever seen a dead person before.*

Certainly, not one that looked so maimed. What kind of accident was it? He thought. *She seemed so sweet.* He tried to throw up, but succeeded only in experiencing dry heaves. His innards seemed to have calmed down.

What had happened? He was getting agitated and started to pace around the room. He ignored the pain throbbing from the soles of his feet. His mind was whirling. He was tiring himself out. He was getting dizzy.

He dropped himself onto the bed and his head fell back onto the pillow. He looked up at the ceiling and then closed his eyes. *What was the worst thing that he could recollect?* He recalled the time he got caught smoking at his grammar school. The school principal lashed his hand with a small leather whip. And then when he got home, his father flogged him again. He was grounded for two weeks.

The door slowly opened. Sister Beatriz entered. She had brought Alejandro a cup of chamomile tea. She sat in her rocking chair.

"Are you okay, my son?"

"Better, Sister" he opened his eyes and rubbed them.

"Sister Sophia is dead. We are now making final preparations for her funeral. There will be a wake this evening in the chapel. You are welcome to attend, if you would like."

"Thank you, Sister. What happened to her?" Alejandro asked her in a somber tone.

"Well, my son," she said slowly and drew a long breath, "our Order has been here for many, many years. We have survived fires. We have survived diseases. And hopefully, we can survive the greatest danger of them all . . . man."

"Sister, I don't understand," his face contorted in bewilderment.

"For many decades we have had good relations with the

Momo natives. However, in recent years, our supplies from them have been routinely ambushed and plundered. There is an evil creature outside of these walls that has killed our friends and stolen our food. We have not seen or heard from him for over a year. Now he is attempting to enter our holy sanctuary." She started to weep. "This time he has gone too far!"

"Who is this devil?"

"El Sombrerón," she answered in a quavering voice. "The Momos have named him 'El Sombrerón' because of his devious disguise."

"Who is he?" Alejandro's criminal law studies were coming back to him. "Does he act alone?" He needed to get the facts. He had to get the answers. Maybe he could discover how the savage murder occurred.

"El Sombrerón is a cursed disciple of Satan. He kills for pleasure and sport. He also steals the supplies being brought to us by the Momos. Sister Sophia was such a precious, little thing. So innocent!" She started to break down again, but regained her composure. "Some say that he is descended from the fierce tribe of the Caribes. Others think that feral animals raised him. I say that he is the devil incarnate!"

Sister Beatriz gave him a sketchy description of the assassin. The killer was short and dressed all in black. He also wore a big hat that hid his face. Alejandro felt that there were some salient facts that were intentionally being omitted by her. He didn't know why he thought this, but he just sensed it.

Alejandro remembered how his Tio Tino would sometimes tell horror stories to him, his siblings, and his cousins when they visited him in San Pedro. Their uncle would wait until it was very, very dark or the weather was stormy. He would scare the youngsters when he spoke in his deep and dramatic voice about the chupacabras, the satanic goat suckers, who drank the blood of their victims. These creatures looked like spike-backed devils and would prey upon misbehaving children. The children would cry and have terrible nightmares after his tales. Alejandro's mother was never happy with her brother for teasing the children.

"Sister, are you going to send for the authorities?"

"No, my son. It would take such a long time before they could arrive. They are so far away. By the time we could make contact with them, the body would be decomposed and the stench would be unbearable."

"But how is this El Sombrerón ever going to be brought to justice?"

"There is Divine Providence, my son. And besides, we must follow God's will, no matter where it may lead."

"Sister, that won't stop the killing," he retorted rather aggressively. "You're all in danger!"

No one was safe with a murderer lurking around. All the nuns would be in constant peril. *What could he do to protect them? And Melissa?* He didn't want this delicate flower plucked from his life.

CHAPTER 11

THE WAKE

The evening was grim with nebulous skies. The quarter moon was on the horizon peeking behind the grayish clouds. Only a handful of little stars were visible.

The vespers bell tolled.

Alejandro had tried to clean himself up the best that he could under the circumstances. The remainder of the afternoon had been quiet for him. Alejandro never did leave his room to explore the outdoors.

Sister Beatriz appeared in the room after she had knocked on the door.

"You may accompany me to the wake, Alejandro."

"Yes, Sister."

The two left the room and walked down the stairs together. They entered the chapel on the main floor of the building. In addition to the four nuns that he already knew, there were three more sisters kneeling in the front row. There were also two native women behind the nuns.

Alejandro genuflected and went into the back pew. He crossed himself as he looked at the simple table-like altar. Sister Beatriz looked over to the three unknown nuns. The trio all turned around and nodded their heads as they viewed Alejandro. He did not make eye contact with them.

He kept his eyes looking forward. Behind the altar, there was a colored wooden statue of the Virgin Mary. In front of the altar, there was a long wooden casket on two sawhorses.

The box looked like it was made of pine. There was no ornamentation. Alejandro was not surprised at the plainness of the coffin since the abbey itself was just as simple. He could smell the lilacs that were in pots behind the casket. The small candelabras on the sides of the chapel were lit and emitted little puffs of black smoke.

This scene brought back sad memories to him. He had always disliked funerals. Alejandro remembered that when he was five years old, his godfather had died. It had seemed like hundreds of people dressed in black were congregated around the carved Philippine mahogany casket at the funeral. There were thousands of flowers. Alejandro had met his first cousins, second cousins, and even third cousins. He couldn't remember one tenth of their names. His mother was sobbing. She and his godfather had grown up in the same neighborhood.

Alejandro's father kept pacing in and out of the cathedral after smoking with his compadres. His father and his godfather had been best friends growing up together. Señor Rubí had bestowed on his friend the greatest gesture of affection by making him Alejandro's godparent.

Señora Rubí had hugged Alejandro as her eyes welled up with tears. "Oh, my little one. Why did he have to die? Oh, Holy Mary!" she had wailed. Alejandro could still grimly remember that scene. His hands were now sweaty. He dreaded having to go through another depressing event.

However, that funeral was surely a strong contrast to the one taking place in the quiet chapel. This one was so serene. He sensed an absence of feeling and emotion.

One of the three nuns in the front rose and approached the coffin. She turned around and faced the tiny audience.

"Dear friends, we are gathered here this evening to pay

our final respects to Sister Sophia. We know that her soul is in heaven. We will miss her friendly smile. Let us pray." She seemed to be aiming her comments toward the abbey staff and Alejandro, rather than to the nuns in front of her.

Alejandro saw that this nun looked old, but yet was very articulate. She was thin and wore thick hexagonal glasses. The lenses looked dark, almost as if they were smoked. She seemed to speak with a slight accent. Alejandro had never seen her before. Maybe she was the Mother Superior.

The assemblage prayed silently after her austere words.

Alejandro kept turning his head around. He noticed that Melissa was not present. He wondered why she was not part of this congregation.

"Tomorrow we will bury the body of Sister Sophia in her favorite place in the garden, next to the laurel bushes." The elderly nun returned to her seat and knelt down to resume her praying.

One of the two remaining unknown sisters rose slowly. Her bulky form waddled carefully over to the coffin and directed herself toward the gallery in slow motion. She seemed to be older than the former speaker. She hesitated. Her face was puffy and had a million wrinkles. She also seemed to be the most heavyset of the nuns. She wore dense round-rimmed glasses. *Maybe this one was Mother Superior,* Alejandro conjectured.

"My children," she began in a cracking voice, "for many years we have lived together in peace. Providence has blessed us with its bounty. God has sent us many blessings. We have much to be thankful for. But now we have been assaulted by evil from the outside world!

Man can no longer interfere with God's will . . ."

Alejandro became startled. He hoped that she was not

referring to him. It wasn't his fault that he was at the convent.

She staggered back to her original seat, with her hands in front of her, almost as if she were blind.

Several nuns rose and left the chapel.

Sister Beatriz whispered to Alejandro, "My son, you are free to leave."

"Thank you, Sister. By the way, I don't want to be rude, but who were the nuns up in front?"

"The one who spoke first was Sister Teresa. She assists Mother Superior," she replied. "The second one was Mother Superior."

"Sister, if I can be of any assistance with the burial, please let me know."

"Thank you for your offer. But we have a duty to make sure that you recuperate fully. However, I will discuss the matter with Sister Teresa."

"Yes, Sister. Good night." Alejandro rose from the pew and left the chapel. It was dark as he walked up the stairs to his room.

What a strange day! He wondered if Sister Sophia had family. This led him to think about his own family. They must be quite concerned about him. They probably had assumed that he was dead. He needed to contact them as soon as possible.

In his bed Alejandro tried to sleep, but he was haunted by strange thoughts of death and evil spirits lurking about. It was like he was having a nightmare while being awake.

The winds outside of his window began howling. The night became blacker. There was an onslaught of rain. The storm came and lightning crashed in the skies.

CHAPTER 12

THE BURIAL

The sunlight seeped through the window and the rays awoke Alejandro with a tickle. He had a nightmare about El Sombrerón during the night.

Now the air was fresh and sweet smelling after the night rain.

Getting up, Alejandro walked over to wash his face. *I wish I had more clothes. I wouldn't even mind another bath. Maybe I'll ask Sister Beatriz.*

Alejandro lay on top of his bed until there was the routine knock on the door by Sister Beatriz. He had almost fallen back to sleep.

He felt a bit in a crabby mood. He didn't know why. Perhaps he was stressed.

Alejandro remembered studying for his final examinations at law school one night. He had finals in contract law, commercial law, and legal ethics, all on the next day. It was almost midnight when Chuy barged into his room.

"Come on, güey!" his friend beckoned. "Let's go!"

"Where to, man?" responded the surprised Alejandro in a semi-comatose state.

"To get a beer!"

"Are you crazy, man?" He shook his head no.

"Come on. You need one. You're uptight."

"I have to study. I have three finals tomorrow."

"So? How much do you think you're going to learn in a

hour?"

"I want to make sure I get passing grades."

"Listen, Ale. Tomorrow you're going to be totally exhausted and frustrated. You're going to be a frigging wreck. You need to relax."

"So a beer is going to relax me and help me pass my tests?"

"Sure, why not? It can't hurt, you uptight jerk."

"I shouldn't." Alejandro knew that he was already tired and could hardly concentrate. He wouldn't last much longer. "Okay. Maybe one. Only one." Perhaps a short break wouldn't hurt.

"Only one, I promise."

Chuy and Alejandro escaped to the local cantina and saw several classmates there.

Alejandro and his friends closed the bar at 4 in the morning. He went back to his room and got two hours of sleep.

He barely remembered taking the first two tests. His mind and body were on automatic pilot.

During the third examination, the pages of the test seemed blank. It was as if it took centuries for him to start writing. When the proctor called time, Alejandro was feverishly scribbling down everything that his brain cells had stored.

"Señor Rubí. Señor Rubí. Are you all right?"

"I'm almost done. Just a second!"

"Señor Rubí. Are you okay?"

Alejandro opened his eyes. Sister Beatriz was standing over him. She put the back of her hand against his forehead. She held it there for a moment.

"I don't think you have a fever."

Alejandro raised himself up. Sister Beatriz had placed the breakfast tray on the bedside table. Alejandro instinctively went for the orange juice.

"My son, the burial is in an hour. Mother Superior has invited you to attend if you feel well. You don't have to force yourself. You are not under any obligation."

"Yes, Sister." He slowly drank his juice with lime slice. He had been thirsty and the liquid was satisfying. He was thinking about the burial. He felt bewildered. While he was told that it was not compulsory to attend, the fact that Mother Superior invited him seemed to make it very important. He told himself that the prudent thing would be to go.

Sister Beatriz retired to the chair near the window and resumed her crocheting while Alejandro continued to eat his breakfast.

He devoured the fresh fruit and bread, barely savoring any morsel. Suddenly, he paused.

"Sister, forgive me. I don't want to be rude, but do you think that I could have another bath. And some clean clothes. I think that I don't smell so well. And I do want to attend the burial." He could not refrain from grinning sheepishly.

Sister Beatriz paused for a moment and then replied, "Why, of course, my son. We'll see what we can do. But unfortunately, there isn't enough time for your bath before the service."

Alejandro perceived a slight change in the attitude of Sister Beatriz. It was like now she was a mother figure, rather than a nun. His forehead furrowed. He wondered about the transformation.

"It was so hectic yesterday," her voice had taken on a somber tone. "We forgot about you. Are you done with your food?"

"Yes, Sister. Thank you."

She came over and picked up his tray and exited the room.

He felt better. He ran his fingers through his beard trying to dislodge any remnants of food.

About an hour later Sister Beatriz returned. Alejandro was already dressed and waiting anxiously.

"Do you still want to go to the burial service, my son?"

"Yes, Sister."

"How do you feel?"

"Fine, Sister."

"Okay. Then follow me."

Sister Beatriz escorted him out of the building. They walked through the entryway patio to the garden grounds. Alejandro's eyes hurt from the beaming light. He could see beads of water on the leaves of the flowers and bushes from the previous night's storm. Everything smelled so fresh in contrast to the mustiness of the abbey.

She walked next to him on a gravel path for about a hundred and fifty meters up a slight grade. They approached a set of stairs and walked up to a different tier on the grounds. They had passed hundreds of colorful plants and vegetation. There was the sound of bees humming. It was like the Garden of Eden. This was so antithetical to the pallor of death that was hanging over the abbey.

As they approached a clearing, they observed the nuns who were praying quietly over the burial hole. Alejandro suddenly realized that what he had thought was the sound of bees humming was really the nuns praying. Sister Teresa was facing the congregation. Melissa, Marica, and the unknown older woman were in attendance. All three wore black lace veils over their heads and shoulders. This reminded Alejandro of when some of the ladies that had attended his godfather's funeral had been wearing black mantillas.

Melissa glanced at Alejandro. He caught her gaze. Their eyes met. She immediately dropped her countenance and kept on praying.

"My children, bid farewell to the corpus of our Sister Sophia. May she pray for us now that she is with our Heavenly Father," directed Sister Teresa.

Four of the nuns grabbed the rope handles of the casket in unison and started to lower it into the earth. On the one hand, it seemed odd that the sisters were pallbearers, but conversely, there were no men around except him. Alejandro advanced to try to assist them, but Sister Beatriz softly intercepted him with her arm. She gave him a cautionary look. He ceased his attempt.

The nuns lowered the coffin with ease and began interring it with dirt. This was done in such an efficient manner that it looked like it had been choreographed. Maybe other nuns had died recently, he surmised. He would have to find out.

Mother Superior ambled up to the grave. Sister Teresa handed her a pink rose in a ceramic pot. Sister Teresa had dug a little hole on top of the grave using an old spade. She then took the rose from Mother Superior and gingerly planted the rose. Melissa gave her a towel to clean her hands.

There was a short period of silent meditation before the gathering dispersed.

Alejandro kept staring at the rose. He turned to Sister Beatriz.

"I would like to see where it happened, Sister."

"What, my son?" Sister Beatriz's face looked like she was in shock.

"Where the tragedy occurred."

Alejandro did not know why he was so inquisitive. Maybe because he was bored and needed some stimulation.

She put her hand to her chin and stared at him for a moment. "I don't see why not. I could use the walk myself," she replied.

Sister Beatriz starting walking further up the hill. Alejandro followed. He turned around to look at the total estate and could see the two large edifices separated by beautiful gardens and orchards further down the hill. An adobe wall surrounded the abbey grounds. It was a lovely sight.

"Sister, isn't today Sunday?" Alejandro tried to make light conversation on the walk.

"Yes, my son," she looked at him curiously. "Why do you ask?'

"Well, there's no Sunday mass," he hesitated.

"You are correct, my son," she patiently answered. "We haven't had a priest around here for a long time."

"Well, what about Holy Communion and confession?'

"We do the best we can under the circumstances," she gave him a strange smile and pushed on ahead.

Silently, they strolled for a few minutes more and then veered to the left. They continued up to a black wrought iron window that had been built into the abbey wall. The grating had seemingly fallen off and was dangling from the opening. Alejandro felt alarmed that the hole in the wall had not yet been repaired.

Then Alejandro saw the damaged wicker basket on the ground a few meters away. He noticed wilted flowers scattered all around. At the base of the wall, there was evidence of dry blood splattered. He also observed bits of black cloth in the bushes.

"Please don't touch anything. Rafaela is going to clean this mess up."

He started to feel nauseated. Alejandro knew that he could not succumb to his queasiness. He took a deep breath and exhaled slowly.

"This is where El Sombrerón entered and attacked poor Sister Sophia. She was picking flowers as part of her daily routine," she pointed to the grill. "See here. He came through this breach in the wall."

"Shouldn't we put the grating back up, Sister?" he nervously added.

"The fastenings are old and probably wouldn't hold. Rafaela is bringing up some protective hedging."

Alejandro scrutinized the open breach and tried to visualize a solution. He stared at the black wrought iron. It didn't look rusted, but some of the bars looked like they had been eaten away. The cuts look jagged, he thought.

He continued to analyze the situation. It would probably be too difficult to use wooden planks. They would shrink and expand with the rains. New iron grating was probably nowhere to be found.

There was a rustling behind them. It was an old hunched-over woman laden with a hemp cloth sack filled with leafy branches. This was the native woman who had been with Melissa and Marica at the burial. She also carried several sharp sticks. She laid down everything near the opening.

"Señor Rubí, this is Rafaela. She is our gardener and bee keeper."

"A pleasure, señorita." Alejandro assumed that all the women within the walls of the abbey were unmarried.

"The pleasure is mine, señor."

Rafaela's face had the character of having been subjected to thousands of days of sun. It was dark with a galaxy of freckles.

Taking a sharp stick, she started to poke little holes in the dirt in front of the opening in the wall. Alejandro was perplexed on why Rafaela had no real gardening tools.

"My son, are you ready to go back?"

"Sister, if you don't mind, I would like to help Rafaela."

Sister Beatriz eyed him for a moment. "Yes, you may. But do not overdo it, my son."

"Yes, Sister."

Sister Beatriz turned and headed back to the convent.

Maybe I can find out some things about what goes on around here. What kind of things might Rafaela tell me? Alejandro frowned. *Things are so strange.*

CHAPTER 13

WATER

Alejandro singled out one of the whetted sticks and attempted to emulate Rafaela. Although she was twice his age, she dug three holes for every one of his. She had a dark complexion and Alejandro assumed that she had a Momo heritage. Her black hair had blocked bangs. She was slender and had a slight hunched-over back. She wore a white manta indigenous dress protected by an orange gardening apron. She also had on cloth gloves to protect her hands.

Systematically Rafaela laid down her stick and poked the branches into the holes. The rain from the prior night had made the ground easy to work with. Alejandro was awkward in his attempts and ended up with mud all over himself. After trying to dig about a dozen holes, he felt shaky. He had to stop digging.

The next step for Rafaela was to position the sharpened stakes in the opening near the wall. This took on the form of a palisade that appeared that it might protect the abbey.

She paused for a moment and told Alejandro to wait where he was. Then Rafaela left him. He heeded her request.

He kept wondering about El Sombrerón. He had surmised that the killer had entered through the breach in the wall. Why did he attack the nunnery? Would he return? They had to be prepared.

During the summers of his youth, his parents would take the family to his uncle's in the country. His uncle owned a plantation in the outskirts of Xalapa, Veracruz.

Alejandro, along with his siblings and his cousins, had to pick fruit and vegetables along side the laborers. It was hard work, but his father declared that it built character. The children all complained, but made a game of it. Sometimes Alejandro would place a worm in his cousin's basket. She would scream. Everyone would get scolded. The next day the same thing would happen. He, Ricardo, and Lupe would laugh.

However, under no circumstances would any fruits and vegetables be discarded, thrown, squashed, or wasted. The fruits of the Rubí clan's labors went to the farm workers. The families of the workers were also allowed to glean the fields after the major harvest. There was respect for the earth. There was respect for the harvest. There was respect for the workers. Alejandro's uncle cared for his men and would not deny them their subsistence.

Señor Rubí would then treat his children to the amusement park in Chapultepec when they returned home to Mexico City.

Finally, Rafaela returned with two pails of water, one at each end of a pole that she carried across the back of her humped shoulders. Alejandro tried to assist her in taking the buckets off the pole.

Carefully, Rafaela poured out a little water on each planted bough. She then patted each one down with her tiny foot. The water pooled around the lowest branches.

Rafaela eventually emptied the two pails, but had covered only about a third of the newly planted area. She affixed the buckets back onto the pole.

"I'll be back," she informed Alejandro.

"I'll go with you. Let me take that." Alejandro lifted the

pole off Rafaela's shoulders. It was heavy. Although Rafaela was small, she was a strong woman. She probably had spent her entire life in a garden or working in the fields.

They walked back down the path. Before they came upon the burial place of Sister Sophia, they turned left onto the red clay path. The vegetation on each side was dense. As they continued, he began to hear the sound of gurgling water. They moved up an incline and approached a large pond that was being fed by spouts from the fountain wall.

The water looked clear.

Alejandro leaned over and lowered the front pail into the pond. It splashed. The water was cold. Suddenly his body lurched forward with the extra weight and he almost lost his balance. Rafaela grabbed him and saved him from falling into the pond. She shook her head.

He was embarrassed.

"Turn around," she ordered softly. He did so.

"Squat down." He obeyed again. She pushed the bucket on the back of the pole downward. The water filled it within seconds.

"Good," she signaled.

He righted himself. The weight was heavy, but not quite overbearing. *I can't believe that she could carry such a load. She must be strong as an ox.* He felt guilty about having lived a life of privilege.

She started out walking in front of him to return to the wall and to the new plantlings. Rafaela hiked quickly. He could not keep up with her. He scraped his elbow on the bushes along the path. The scratch caused his arm to twinge.

Alejandro forced himself to focus on Rafaela's heels as he labored behind her. He didn't look right or left. Finally, they arrived at the breach in the wall. He was covered with sweat and was panting. The caked mud collected on his body made him feel dried out and itchy.

Rafaela resumed the watering of the plantlings. Alejandro was too tired to assist her. His muscles were burning from the weight of the water. Finally, she finished. There was only a small area that remained to be done.

Despite his overwhelming fatigue and pain, Alejandro picked up the pole again. His face grimaced. The two traipsed back down to the pond at the high end of the gardens.

This time Alejandro was more cautious in filling up the water buckets. The pails were now like two boulders dragging down his shoulders. His right elbow ached from the gash. Rafaela started back. Alejandro did not try to keep up with her. He was more circumspect on the return, avoiding the attacking branches off the path while attempting not to spill the water. He could barely keep his balance. At last they arrived back at the small plot of branches.

Once again Rafaela emptied the buckets on the remaining section of the newly planted earth. Alejandro was so exhausted that he didn't even attempt to help Rafaela. His arms and legs felt like lead. She finally finished.

"Thank you for helping me, señor."

"I really didn't do anything."

"Well, until we see each other again." She lifted the pole and the pails. She started to leave but turned back to him. "You seem like a nice young man. Please be careful. Danger is all around us."

She resumed her retreat, leaving Alejandro still sprawled on the ground. *No one was safe while El Sombrerón lurked about,* he pondered.

After about ten minutes, he picked himself up. He was covered from head to toe with mud and sweat.

Alejandro dragged himself down the path. He felt weak and lightheaded. The sun was on its descent. He hadn't eaten since breakfast.

When Alejandro approached the red clay arterial path, he turned onto it. *I'm thirsty. I'm hot. I'm frigging dirty. I need some water. Water. I'll get some water.*

Alejandro finally reached the pond. He dropped to his knees at the edge of the water. The bordered stone lip of the basin had several chips in it and missing tile pieces. He leaned over and stuck his head in. It was so refreshing. He came up and spit out the water. He pushed his hair back with his hands.

He splashed water onto the front of his body, trying to cool off. This was an oasis. The fountain was designed to replenish itself through the ingress of water coming from the hill above and spouting from anthropomorphic-looking gargoyles. The water circulated in the pond, then exited through an egress, and finally funneled itself into very narrow levada irrigation canals. He dunked his head in and out again. He could see a mosaic design at the bottom of the pond. It looked like an ancient coat of arms.

It was then that he finally noticed her. Melissa was on the other side of the pond. She was washing clothes.

CHAPTER 14

DIRTY LAUNDRY

Melissa had spotted him immediately upon his arrival at the pond. She had silently observed him as he had dipped his head into the water. She had thought he was behaving rather strangely. This was not how they bathed at the abbey. Alejandro did not have anything to dry himself off with. He was soaking wet. Nevertheless, he started walking toward Melissa.

He felt drawn to her. Her natural beauty. The splendor of the surroundings. The warmth of the sun and the faint humming of bees. They made him dizzy. He was in heaven.

She tried to resume her washing without looking at him. She took the bar of soap and rubbed it into the garment with her hand. Back and forth. Back and forth. The water in front of her became discolored as if it was a milky ink from a squid.

"Good morning."

"Good morning, señor."

"What are you doing?" He knew what she was doing, but was uncertain about how to converse with her.

"Washing clothes," she said simply.

His eyes took a walk over her. Melissa's wet cinnamon skin shimmered in the afternoon sun. Her violet eyes sparkled like little jewels as she stole a quick glance of him.

"I hope that I'm not bothering you," he asked disingenuously.

"Oh, no," she said a little too quickly. She had pretended

not to notice his stare that moved all over her body. She was feeling a warm glow within herself. "This is one of my daily chores."

Maybe the trout was nibbling?

"Are you sure? I can leave." He threw out the lure again.

"Yes, I'm sure. I have to wash all these clothes this afternoon because of Sister Sophia's burial. Normally, I wash clothes in the morning . . ." She had slowed down the laundering and now was fully facing Alejandro. "And afterwards, I clean up your room."

Alejandro now felt awkward. He was momentarily embarrassed that she was really his servant girl. Then he caught himself and tried to change the subject, "I didn't get to know Sister Sophia. What was she like?"

She turned her back to him. He didn't know how to react when Melissa's body spun away from him. She seemed to have withdrawn like a tortoise retreating into its shell. She remained motionless for a few moments. He sensed that she was in pain.

Melissa somberly gazed back over her shoulder toward Alejandro. There were tears in her eyes. "Sister Sophia was very sweet. Very sweet." Her voice cracked.

Alejandro felt terrible about trying to hit on her. *How could I be such an insensitive jerk? She is grieving. I'm so selfish. I wasn't thinking about her feelings or her grieving. I was trying to charm her, rather than comfort her. What a fool, I am!*

She had completely stopped washing clothes now. The waters of the pond became calmer. Her reflection off the waters became clearer and clearer, but her face had become cloudy. She wiped her eyes with a swipe of her forearm. Melissa took a deep breath. She was trying to regain her composure.

"Melissa," he said softly. "May I call you Melissa?"

"Yes, señor."

"You may call me Alejandro. My father is señor."

"Yes, señor."

He laughed aloud breaking the tension. She was so polite. So innocent. She was like a beautiful gardenia that would spoil if touched by human hands.

"Where are you from? Are you from here? Where is your family?" He started to pepper her with questions.

"I don't know," she answered.

"What do you mean?" he probed. "I don't understand."

He knew that his Law Professor Peña would have reprimanded him for asking compound questions. How could she answer three questions at the same time? He needed to improve his lawyer like skills and sharpness.

I can't waste my time here forgetting everything that I have learned. I need to get back to Mexico City as soon as possible.

"The good sisters told me that I was found on a sunny hillside not far from here by a priest that used to live here at the abbey. Father Rivoli. I was less than a year old when they brought me here. This place used to have an orphanage."

"Who were your parents?"

"I don't know. They told me that my mother had died and that my father had abandoned me."

"Wasn't there a note or something?"

"No."

A leaf of a water lily gently floated by, leaving a champagne-like trail of bubbles.

"So the nuns raised you."

"Yes. But really it was Marica. I have been hanging onto her apron strings since I could walk." She beamed as she reminisced about her childhood at the nunnery.

"Were there other children in the orphanage?"

"Yes, but that place burned down many years ago," The expression on her face turned to sadness. "There is no more orphanage."

"What did you do while you were growing up?" Alejandro was unsure why she had become sullen.

"The sisters schooled me in religion and some academics."

"Did they want you to become a nun?"

"At first, I believe they did. But later on, I heard that they did not think so. You have to understand that the abbey was more than a novitiate school for prospective nuns. Up until recent years, it was an orphanage for young girls. That was why I was here.

"Anyway, the choice was mine. Entering the sisterhood has to be voluntary."

"Melissa, have you ever been outside of the abbey since you were brought here?"

"No."

"I can't believe it!" he blurted out unexpectedly. He felt sorry for the poor thing.

"Why not?" she responded self-assured. "I'm perfectly content here."

"Don't you want to explore the world? Go to other countries? See how other people live?"

"No. Why should I? I'm fine here" she was now defensive. "The sisters take good care of me. It's not important."

The tone of the discussion has suddenly become heated. She seemed a bit offended. Was he questioning her life? Was he judging her by his standards?

"Señor, I think I need to go back now." She had slipped off the hook. The trout was no longer biting.

"Melissa, don't go," Alejandro knew he had alienated her.

"Please don't go. Tell me more about yourself."

"There isn't much to tell, " she was aloof.

"Where is Father Ravioli?"

"Father Rivoli!" she corrected.

"Sorry, Father Rivoli?" *What an idiot, I am!*

"They said that he left the abbey when I was four or five." She stood up. "The Father was always very nice to me. Everyday he would give me pieces of papaya. I don't remember seeing another priest here since then."

"Who comes to visit the abbey?"

"Just the Momos."

"And why do the natives come?"

"To trade. We give the Momos fruits and vegetables and they bring us supplies from the villages way far away."

"What kind of supplies?"

"Soap. Needles," she then gave the slightest grin. "Even eye glasses for the sisters."

"And for all these years, you have been able to take care of yourselves?"

"Yes. God has been good to us."

"What will you do when you get older?" He was trying to recapture her attention. He wondered if the nuns were indoctrinating her or if she really believed what she was saying.

"I don't understand what you mean."

"When you get old enough to get married."

"I don't know. I've never thought about it."

Alejandro clicked the back of his teeth with his tongue. His head turned slightly and he looked pensively upward. *Were the nuns actually educating her or protecting her? She seemed to be treated more like a servant, maybe even a slave. Was she in the same predicament that he was in?*

"Have the nuns taught you about men and women?"

"I've read the Bible, if that's what you mean."

Alejandro paused for a moment. He was in a quandary. He knew that he was pressuring her, but he was also curious.

"Have you met any men before?"

"Yes. The Momos."

"Who are these Momos?"

"All I know is that they are natives who live in villages somewhere outside our gates."

"How often do the Momos come here?" He saw an opportunity to discover crucial information that could be useful in leaving this place.

"I think they come within a few days of the new moon."

"Are there any other natives or people that come around here?"

She nodded no.

I see. Have the nuns told you about men?" He prodded again.

"Yes. Men and women are children of God. Men help the species procreate. They are an essential part of the breeding process. Males furnish the seed for the mother's egg."

You ask a dumb question. You get a clinical answer. He noticed that she was finished with her washing. The water was now sudsy in front of Melissa. He looked up at the three nozzle head fountain spouts that fed fresh water into the pond. They were in the shapes of insects.

"Women are the queens for the propagation of the species. Men are the agents to assist in that process."

"Oh," he reacted uncomfortably. It sounded like a textbook answer. *Where did she learn this feminist propaganda?*

Melissa picked up the wash. She started to walk away. She stopped and looked back at Alejandro. Her eyes locked onto his. It seemed that she was wondering if he was going to accompany her. Her look told him what to do.

His heart palpitated. He jumped to his feet quickly.

"I have to hang these clothes up," she told him.

"Sure."

They walked back toward the convent. Neither one spoke. They came to the other fountain that was halfway between the two buildings. She stopped.

"Until the next time, señor."

"See you soon, Melissa."

They each went their separate ways.

CHAPTER 15

DELIRIUM

Alejandro had fallen into his bed. He was so exhausted from trying to help Rafaela. His entire body ached from transporting the buckets of water. His head throbbed with a slight headache. He soon drifted into a fitful slumber. His body tossed and turned throughout his sleep. Perspiration beaded on his body. His throat felt parched.

Hours passed and then suddenly he woke up. There was a certain stillness in the air. It was unnatural. He was unaccustomed to the dead silence. No birds. No wind. No rain.

Alejandro relieved himself in the chamber pot in the corner of the room. He drank some water from the water pitcher. Then he walked over to the window. The crescent moon was shining. There were no clouds in the dark skies. The last time that he recalled seeing the moon was before the accident. *What in the hell is wrong with me? I hope I didn't get heatstroke today.*

Growing up, he and his brother, Ricardo, would paint their faces black when there was a full moon. They would wait until Lupita came into the family living room. The two boys would pretend to be chupacabras and scare her half to death. She would scream and go running to her mother. The pair would then go hide themselves in the closet until things settled down.

His mind began to race. His head felt feverish. Alarming

images bombarded his brain.

Maybe El Sombrerón was some sort of chupacabra, the legendary monster that would attack goats and then suck their blood. No, that only happens at the cinema, he pondered. Why would El Sombrerón attack the nuns? In his legal studies, he recalled the professor postulating that most criminals were really cowards. These bullies tended to victimize children and helpless ones. Many of them had been victimized, raped, or abused as children themselves. Maybe El Sombrerón was this type of tormentor.

Alejandro fought to stay focused. What were the facts? The Momos themselves probably had weapons, and could protect their families and villages. But the nuns were defenseless. Nothing to protect them from El Sombrerón except for the walls that surrounded their abbey. They led a very vulnerable existence in almost total isolation except for their contact with the Momos.

I need time to consider the totality of the situation. How can the wall be fortified? It would be difficult to put sharp stakes on the wall. It would take dozens of trees and as many days.

Traps probably wouldn't work either. They would have to be camouflaged or covered up. And chances are that one of the nuns would inadvertently injure herself.

Maybe we should just fill in the opening in the wall with adobe mixed with straw. That would be a simplest alternative. The grated window had served no practical purpose anyway and had made the abbey vulnerable. I should discuss this with Sister Beatriz. Everyone is so vulnerable around here, especially me. I was a real weakling in front of Rafaela today. Or was it yesterday?

He felt drained. He imagined himself in front of a mirror talking to his alter ego. It was a blurred image.

And I need to see that Melissa is protected.

What? She barely tolerates you. She only talks to you to be polite.

But I like her.

How can you like her? You barely know her. You sound like Don Quixote acting as the champion for his true love, Dulcinea.

But she is kind.

Right, you like her because she is kind. You like her because she is as pretty as a flower, don't you?

Why, yes.

Let's be honest. Would you be willing to stay here at the convent with her for the rest of your life without ever being able to leave?

Well, no. I need to return to my family.

See, you sound like a lawyer or even a politician. A very cerebral thinker, but no real commitment to truth or virtue or even love.

That's untrue. I love my family.

Then why don't you just leave?

I can't.

Why not? Just tell the nuns that you are leaving.

What about the Momos?

What about them?

Shouldn't I wait for them? They are supposed to deliver some supplies soon. They could show me the way back.

Why, are you afraid?

Of course not. Afraid of what?

Afraid of getting lost? Afraid of starving to death? Afraid of El Sombrerón?

No, I'm not!

Alejandro's delirium now ebbed and flowed. He convulsed and sweat soaked through his clothing. He moaned. His skin reddened.

He opened his eyes for an instant.

I need some . . .

He then lapsed back into his frenzied state.

CHAPTER 16

CLEAN BEDDING

When he awoke, Sister Beatriz was hunched over him. She was applying a cool, wet cloth on his forehead.

"I think that you overexerted yourself yesterday, my son," she said softly. "Rafaela told me that you really worked hard with the planting."

"Not really, Sister."

"Well, we thank you for your assistance. You are truly heaven sent."

She reached over to the tray and grabbed a glass. She placed her right hand behind his head and raised it.

"Here, drink this."

Alejandro quickly downed the orange juice. He almost felt like he was getting addicted to this wonderfully tasting elixir.

"Thank you, Sister."

"How are you feeling?"

"Quite tired. I'm a little achy. My back hurts. It's like all my energy has been drained from me."

"Maybe you should stay in bed and rest today," she gently suggested.

That was the last thing that he wanted to do. He wanted to go to the pond and see if he could find Melissa.

"Yes, Sister," he replied. He knew that he should obey. Nuns always had to be obeyed.

"Maybe if you feel better this afternoon, you can have a

bath. How does that sound?"

"Fine," he pretended to be enthusiastic. It was better than nothing.

Alejandro ate his breakfast as Sister Beatriz continued with her crocheting. She was doing another garment. He wondered if the nuns traded their crocheted items with the Momos.

His thoughts drifted to the security of the abbey. *Could the Momos protect them? Should I talk to her about my dreams last night? About the wall? About leaving this place?*

Probably not now. They need my protection. Or am I really fooling myself. I couldn't even defend myself against a lame flea.

"Are you finished, my son?"

"Yes, Sister. Thank you."

I wonder if Melissa will come today? He closed his eyes. His cheeks were sensitive and felt hot. He probably got too much sun the day before. He had not even eaten dinner on Sunday evening. Yes, he would take it easy today.

Alejandro became very drowsy and then dozed off. His slumber only lasted about twenty minutes. When he awoke, Sister Beatriz had gone.

Why do I get so tired after every meal? I need to be more alert. More active. I wonder if there are any books around here that I could read? I could try to write some letters, but to whom? There were no postal services. This is getting to be so boring. I need to find something to do. I need to get out of this room and explore this place. I don't like feeling like an invalid or prisoner . . . but, on the other hand, I'm in no position to question the nuns. What can I do?

Alejandro lay in bed for a while staring at the ceiling. Then came a soft knock at the door.

"Come in," he called out.

It was Melissa. Her almond shaped eyes gazed at him. His face reddened. She was so beautiful, he thought.

"I'm here to clean the room."

"Okay. Just a moment." He tried to slip on his pants modestly while she glanced toward the window.

Alejandro rose from his bed and walked past her toward the chair.

Melissa started to change the bedding.

"Sister Beatriz tells us that you are not feeling well."

"I'm okay. I'm not used to the sun anymore," he shaded the truth.

Melissa didn't continue the dialogue. For Alejandro, it was a challenge to engage her in a conversation.

"When do you do the laundry at the pond?"

"Usually in the late morning."

"Every day?"

"Yes. Except Sundays, of course."

"Are you going to do wash today?"

"Yes, of course," she glimpsed at him for a second in a bewildered sort of way.

Back home in La Colonia Las Lomas, Inocente would do their laundry twice a week. Sometimes she had her niece help her. Two years ago his father had bought Inocente a heavy-duty washer and a large dryer. With Alejandro being away at law school, the washing task was more manageable.

Alejandro remembered when he had tried to wash his own clothes while he was in school. He had poured bleach in with the laundry soap. His jeans were ruined and several colored shirts bled their colors. Chuy had laughed at him.

But Alejandro had the last laugh. Chuy's clothes had a pinkish tone when his best friend attempted to do his own wash.

Finally, Alejandro and Chuy solved the problem by hiring the law school's janitor's wife to do their laundry.

He felt a little embarrassed that his mind had drifted away for a moment. He tried to change the subject. "Would you like to take a walk with me?"

"I have work to do," she had finished changing the bed. "Where would you want to go?"

"The abbey grounds. I haven't explored them yet. I'm sure with you as a guide, I could discover many things."

"I don't know. I'll have to ask for permission." She started to depart.

"Melissa, are there any books around here?"

"Only a few, I believe. Most of them were destroyed by a fire many years ago."

"What do you read?"

"The Bible, of course," she quickly responded.

Alejandro wondered if she was very religious. He should behave better around her. He knew better than to take advantage of her youth.

"Would you like mine?"

"I'm sorry," he apologized. "Your what?"

"Would you like my Bible?"

"Why, sure. Thank you." He stared into her violet eyes. She returned the look in a reassuring manner.

They remained in this posture for almost a minute without saying anything further. She then made a half turn and walked out of the room. He thought that her hips had swayed suggestively as she left. Or was it his imagination? Or his desire?

Oh my God!

Alejandro fell back onto the bed. He smiled up at the wood beamed ceiling.

She's so beautiful!

ை

Sister Beatriz returned in the afternoon. She gave him permission to take the bath that he desperately needed.

CHAPTER 17

STRAWBERRIES

Alejandro slept well that night. His body was clean. This morning he felt rejuvenated.

At breakfast time, he asked Sister Beatriz if he could go out. She gave him permission to do so.

He ate his meal with gusto. He especially liked the honey on his bread. However, all the sugar made him jittery. His hands clapped nervously. He wanted to take off.

"Just be careful, my son. Don't overexert yourself."

"Yes, Sister."

He left the building and rushed up the same path that Sister Beatriz and he had walked two days before. He passed the fountain that had multicolored tiles impaneled about it. He walked up the grade to the grave of Sister Sophia. The pink rose was blooming brightly. He stood there for a few minutes. His mind was racing. What a crime it was that she was murdered. She was a nun. She was innocent. Why did El Sombrerón attack her? He wondered.

His head craned back and forth, almost in a half circle. He saw that no one else was around. He decided to check the breach in the wall.

Alejandro hurried up the sandy path kicking up gravel as he did so. He found his way quite easily. When he approached the wall, he did not immediately recognize the site. He had been looking for little plantlings less than a foot high. Instead he found a thick hedge of blackberry vines.

Am I in the wrong place? What accounted for the phenomenal growth? This can't be the right place! But it has to be! He told himself.

He continued moving along the sand-colored adobe wall. It was an uphill trek.

Carefully, he negotiated his way through the waist high star jasmine. Alejandro breathed in *deeply. He was overcome by the perfume of the vegetation. How could such a potentially dangerous place seem like heaven?* He dwelled more on his questions about El Sombrerón. His eyes squinted from the brightness of the day.

He approached some flowering cherry trees and decided that he had walked too far. He made an about-face.

Alejandro had a more difficult time walking downhill, but now he took his time. He was getting tired. He came upon the blackberry brambles again. He went on past them and soon came into the flower gardens. Fuchsias, azaleas, camellias, daffodils, tulips, and dozens of types of multicolored flowers blanketed the area. There were bees everywhere. His olfactory senses were filled with the hypnotic scents.

Alejandro decided to detour from the way he had originally come. His body was wet with sweat and his mouth was dry. He was thirsty now.

I'll go back to the pond. The water will be cool and refreshing. Maybe Melissa will be there.

He strolled on and finally reached the pond. Unfortunately, Melissa was nowhere to be found. Maybe she had already finished her chores.

He laid his body face down on the edge of the pond. With his right hand, he reached into the cool water and drank. A few flower petals and leaves floated on the surface, but the water itself was sweet and pure. From observing the pond's fountain spouts and the upward slope of the hill behind them, Alejandro surmised that the waters came from an underground spring up the rise. This could be one of his future explorations.

In the cool Decembers back home, his father would take the family to the mountains, about seventy-five kilometers from Mexico City. The family would spend a week or so in rustic lodgings. The accommodations would include hot showers, a kitchenette, and small electrical appliances. This was his father's idea of camping. The trip would include fishing. Ricardo and he would have to clean the fish that they caught. This led to a lot of mischief. More than once did Lupe find a fish eye in one of her shoes. But being sent to bed after dinner without dessert was worth it to the brothers.

However, what Alejandro enjoyed most on these excursions was soaking in the hot springs. The indigenous people had enjoyed this ceremony for hundreds of years. It was so relaxing. It was spiritual. It was cathartic. His body tingled. He felt energized. His head was clear and relaxed. His body and soul were healed.

Every year his father pronounced that he wanted to start each New Year with a clean heart and soul. Alejandro wanted to follow his father's example.

At the moment, he was resting on one elbow and tracing circles in the water with one finger as he daydreamed.

"Hello," said a soft voice behind Alejandro.

He turned around. It was Melissa.

"Oh, it's you. You startled me."

"I'm sorry."

"Have you finished your chores?"

"Yes. Sister Beatriz helped me."

"Why is that?"

"She knows that you require more work," she said with her face painted with exasperation.

"Like what?" he exclaimed defensively.

"Your laundry for one thing."

"Sorry about that. I didn't realize I was such a burden."

Melissa refused to retract her insinuation, but instead asked, "How are you feeling today?"

"Much better, thank you," he inhaled. "I took a walk to the hole in the wall today. Do plants grow unusually faster here?"

"What do you mean? I don't understand what you saying," she frowned. "These grounds are blessed with good harvesting. Flowers and plants always grow well here."

Alejandro turned his back away from her and started making circles in the water again. Alejandro liked the challenge that she was presenting, but had reservations about her youth and innocence. *Chuy would be egging me on and telling me to go for it. But it was too dangerous! But Chuy would remark, "Oye, pinche, that's what makes it so exciting!"*

"Are you hungry?" inquired Melissa.

"A little."

"Come with me." Melissa started to extend her arm toward him, but withdrew it quickly as he got up by himself.

They walked to the right of the pond and caught a path that zigzagged up the slope to a place of several small dirt mounds covered with little green plants laden with red berries.

Melissa climbed on top of one of the mounds and beckoned Alejandro to join her. She sat down although the ground seemed a little moist. He sat next to her.

Very deliberately she looked about, selected a bush, and picked three ripe strawberries close at hand. They were large and magenta. She reached over and placed them in Alejandro's hand.

He tasted the first. "This is delicious. Thank you!" He devoured the other two.

She picked about a dozen or so more. She ate a few also, but gave the majority to Alejandro.

"Everything Rafaela touches grows fabulously," she said nonchalantly.

"So it seems," he smiled with reddened lips. He liked the fact that she was actually talking to him today, rather than simply answering his questions listlessly.

Somehow Melissa seemed more at ease today. She was talkative and friendly, and almost playful. Alejandro wondered why there was a sudden change.

Maybe I had come on too strong. She really hadn't met any men before. The nuns have probably indoctrinated her to believe that all men are evil.

"You know, Alejandro, I read about the Garden of Eden in the Bible and it's just like here." Her face beamed and she turned her head and eyes to the sky.

It was the first time that she had addressed him in a familiar tone. He could spend time in paradise with her.

Be careful! Remember what happened to Adam and Eve! But this is not Eden!

"Would you like more?" she said innocently.

"No. No thank you." Her words melted his heart. He wanted more of her. He could almost taste her.

Alejandro wanted to talk to her forever. He told her about his family and his law studies. She listened attentively. When she didn't understand something, she would politely interrupt him. He would patiently explain it to her; sometimes having to rephrase his answers more than once.

"Why did you go to law school in San José?" she had asked.

He gave her at least three different answers. Besides wanting to live independent of his family, he really didn't have a good response.

Chuy would probably characterize this interchange as an adventure of Tarzan of the Apes. Melissa would be Jane. Chuy, of course, would tease him about Alejandro being more like the chimpanzee than like Tarzan. *Don't bore her with your boring personal life, cabrón. Talk to her about the stars, the sun, and the moon.*

It was highly evident that Melissa had been sheltered and protected at the abbey. *How could such a precious flower survive in the outside world?*

Finally, she told him that they should return. They started to walk back and stopped at the pond. They both took a quick drink. On the way down to the lower fountain, they encountered Sister Clara.

"Good afternoon, my children."

"Good afternoon, Sister," they chimed.

"Melissa, my dear, I need your assistance. Would you please come with me?"

"Yes, Sister."

Melissa turned to Alejandro. Her violet eyes seemed to say good-bye.

Alejandro wandered back to his room. He took a deep breath and exhaled.

What a nice day in paradise!

CHAPTER 18

MENTAL

That night he had dreamt about Melissa.

In the morning Alejandro was cheerful when Sister Beatriz arrived with his breakfast.

"You are recovering, my son."

"Yes, I am, Sister," he replied as he heaped the viscous honey onto his bread.

"I'm glad that the fresh air helped you to recuperate yesterday."

"Yes it did, Sister."

"I think that the worst is over for you now. Mother Superior says that you have her permission to explore the grounds. She doesn't want you to be treated like an invalid or a prisoner. Just know that this place is very extensive and that you should not stray too far." Her face gave him a maternal smile that lifted her little pale-colored cheeks.

"Oh, no, Sister, I don't feel that way at all. It's just that I need to get back to my family and my home as soon as possible." *Had they read his mind?*

"Things could be worse, my son. Providence acts in strange ways. You remember the story of Moses?"

"I think so. He was involved in the seven plagues against the Egyptians."

"That's correct, my son. He saved the Hebrews because God told him that it was his destiny."

"Oh, I kind of remember now. There was the parting of

the Red Sea and the Ten Commandments." Alejandro had read little of the Bible, even in school. However, when he was young, he had seen some movies with Charlton Heston or Yul Brunner. He and his friends would go to the cinema on Saturdays and watch the Hollywood films with Spanish subtitles. He loved those chariot races and sword fights.

The quinoa porridge was especially delicious this morning. He still had a young man's appetite. His tongue savored the sweetness and texture.

Sister Beatriz left the room shortly thereafter.

About an hour later, there was a tapping at the door. It was Melissa.

"Good morning, señor."

"Good morning." He wondered why she had reverted to addressing him in a formal manner. He hoped that she hadn't gotten into trouble with Sister Clara.

She offered him some clean clothes. They were a simple white muslin blouse like shirt and corresponding pants.

"Thank you. Where did you find these?" he inquired without thinking.

"I made them myself," she replied with hesitation. "Are they okay?"

"Yes, they're great!" he tried to recover for his thoughtlessness. "They are really great!"

"You think so?"

"Yes. Yes, I do."

"I can fix them if they don't fit. I have never made such clothes before," she said, blushing as she held them up.

Melissa reached out and gave him the shirt and pants. He brushed her hand as she did so. It was warm and delicate. His hand stroked the soft sleeve of the shirt.

She went over to make the bed.

"Melissa, are you washing clothes today?" He already knew that she washed clothes almost every day.

"Yes," she answered with a puzzled look on her face.

"Would you like to go for a walk with me?"

"When?"

"After you're done washing." At least, she didn't say "no" right away.

"I have chores to do."

"Can't they wait?" he asked impetuously.

"No. I have to help Marica."

He felt rejected. Alejandro was maybe a little sensitive. He knew that he had been a little too aggressive.

There was a long silence. She continued to straighten out the bed and tidy up the room.

"Melissa, do you want to grow up to become a nun?"

"I don't know. I haven't thought about it much." She paused. She ruminated for a moment or two. "I don't know any other life."

"Marica and Rafaela are not nuns," he suggested.

"But they are different. They weren't orphans like me when they came to work here." Her face was very still.

"Don't you ever want to visit foreign places like Madrid or Rome or Paris?"

"No. Why should I? I have everything here."

"Do you have freedom?"

"Freedom is in your mind," she replied dryly. "I can do whatever I want."

Her cognitive processes overwhelmed Alejandro. She is really naive or she is really profound. She had interesting ideas. He was attracted to her. He didn't know why. It was like the spider and the fly. His mind was confused. Did he dare pursue her?

"Tomorrow, we can," she said in a casual tone.

"I'm sorry. What about tomorrow?"

"Tomorrow we can take a walk. I will ask Marica if I can do my other chores earlier in the day."

"Great!"

"Let's meet at the pond before midday."

"Great!"

He lifted his head and grinned as she left the room. His heart was pounding. His physical desires were calling out. Yes, her little body looked enticing. If Chuy could only see him now, his friend would be so jealous.

CHAPTER 19

THE POEM

The next day came. His blanket had fallen to the floor. He had slept restlessly during the night. *Was he doing the right thing with Melissa? Was she just being coy? What if the nuns found out?*

At breakfast, Sister Beatriz noticed that Alejandro was not very talkative. He seemed to be preoccupied. He ate only about half of his breakfast.

As she departed, she said, "Patience, my son. Patience."

"Yes, Sister."

Did Sister Beatriz know what he was up to?

Alejandro finished getting dressed. He decided to go to the pond early and wait for Melissa. He wouldn't care if she took her time.

He ambled along slowly, humming to himself along the way. He saw Rafaela tending to her flowers across the way and waved a good morning to her. She gestured back in approbation.

Alejandro was acting like a schoolboy on his first date. He had forgotten about the possible threats of danger to the nunnery.

Chuy really needled Alejandro when he had taken a first year female law student out to dinner. Chuy had warned him, "Be careful, my friend. She is not only beautiful and from a good family, but she is also intelligent." He teased Alejandro. "Too smart for you."

Unfortunately, his good friend had proved himself to be correct. Half way through the dinner, Alejandro and his guest got into a debate over the property rights of criminals. That was the first and last time they dated.

Alejandro's father had also often reminded him that golden eagles didn't breed with bald eagles.

Alejandro bent over and looked at his reflection in the pond. His hair was messy. His beard was scraggly. He looked like a bum. It's no wonder that Melissa was not interested in him, he thought.

He closed his brown eyes. He felt their heaviness. He sighed. But she did agree to go on a walk with him today. He could hear the water gurgling from the fountain spouts. There was no breeze. There was the buzzing sound from the humming of bees. The faint scent of flowers in the air tickled his nose.

Alejandro opened his eyes to cloudless, blue skies. He heard a slight rustling behind him. He looked around. He spotted Melissa as she made her way up the path.

"Good morning."

"Good morning," she rejoined. She did not greet him by name.

How should I deal with her? I'm probably thinking too much. I need to go with the flow. I'll just keep quiet and let her talk.

"It's a lovely day," he proffered.

"Yes, it is," she agreed.

"Did you finish your chores?"

"Yes, most of them."

He stood there, just staring at her. Her cinnamon skin stirred him. Her violet eyes melted him. Her pretty mouth penetrated his soul. He remained quiet.

She finally asked, "Would you like to go for a walk now?"

"Sure," he awkwardly replied. His desire to explore the grounds of the abbey had subsided for the moment. He was under her spell.

"Let's take the center path over there," she pointed.

Alejandro had not previously noticed the opening in the hedge about thirty meters away. It was on the opposite side of the pond. They walked side by side to the beginning of the path.

The route was paved with large, irregular granite flagstones. The reds, greens, and grays had faded over the years. A ten-meter high clay-colored cliff bordered the left side of the path.

The way bowed here and there for about a hundred meters against the curvature of the slope. Star jasmine bordered the right side of the pathway. It seemed never to have been trimmed. The right side also had brick pillars about as high as his knees every five meters.

"Who paved this?" He had stopped for a minute. "Surely not the nuns?"

"The original builders of the abbey were native workers."

"Momos?"

"I don't think so. It was way before them."

"Where do these tiles come from?" The masonry looked like it was Grecian or Roman. It reminded Alejandro of some of the best architecture in Mexico City. "Are the tiles imported?"

"I don't know," she shrugged. "Maybe Rafaela knows."

He thought that it would not have made much sense to transport these heavy tiles from distant places. Maybe there were Mayan quarries within a transportable proximity to the abbey. His mind had switched into a problem-solving mode.

"Who comes up here?"

"No one. It has been abandoned for ages. At least, that's what I've been told."

Gradually, they approached a set of stairs that rose to an elevated mesa. Alejandro's curiosity was even more piqued. The abbey seemed to hold many secrets.

Here the tiles were blue and very ornate, but faded. It was a type of floral design. Several were cracked or broken. Most were covered with an opaque mud. There were another set of ascending stepping-stones, but there wasn't any hand railing.

"What are these?"

"Stairs."

He was not winning the war of words with her. His breathing was becoming labored. The sweat was beginning to dot his forehead.

"Where do they lead?"

"You'll see," she hinted with intrigue.

She hopped the first two steps and turned around to see if he was following her. He started upwards. She continued climbing more stairs. He pursued slowly and carefully. He was watching his step as he was trying to watch her.

After taking about a dozen or so steps, Alejandro turned around. He was panting. He could not see the convent buildings. They were hidden by an expanse of trees, brush, and the cliff.

Melissa seemed to glide up the flight. She was already at the top while he was only half way up. He was winded. As he labored at each step, he saw sand and weeds between the cracks in the tiles.

When he was away at school, his law school building had almost as many stairs. But there were cigarette butts, gum, and trash that evidenced an advanced civilization. Here it seemed as if everything had been abandoned for eons. Finally, he reached the top. He was breathing through his mouth. He was exhausted. Melissa was waiting for him. She was grinning. They rested for several minutes. When he had recuperated, they proceeded to an open landing. Although tall weeds overran the tiled court, Alejandro was amazed at what he observed. There was a long rectangular pool. It extended for about 100 meters. It was only half full and the tainted water was emerald green. About thirty meters away was a fountain that depicted mask and bee reliefs. The fountain was not working.

Pavilions and overgrown yew bushes flanked the area around the pool. A colonnade and a balustrade of grape vines, in turn, encapsulated this. Additionally, dozens of broken pots were sprinkled around the pool. It must have been majestic at one time.

Alejandro stood there gawking at all the splendor. Alejandro took a deep breath and blew out slowly. He was tired. His hand grabbed his chin and his eyes tried to capture the entire scene.

"I wonder what all of this is?" he asked rhetorically.

"This is a place I sometimes come to when I want to be alone." Melissa had volunteered an answer.

"I can't imagine you ever wanting to be alone."

"Oh, yes, Alejandro, there are times." Her voice took on a serious tone.

"Who built this?" His curiosity was overwhelming him.

"I don't really know. Someone said that the original owners of this place were a rich Spanish family. They were nobles or something like that. I heard that they donated this to the cloister. I don't know really."

"Who does know?"

"Maybe Rafaela. I only pick up bits and pieces of things. These things are not important to me."

Alejandro was bewildered. He wondered why anyone would want to live in such an isolated place. One theory might be that they were fugitives, he suspected. His eyes looked downward and he noticed a little mosaic work. It was sparsely portrayed on the ground. He could not make out any of the motifs.

"When was this place built?"

"I don't know. Maybe Rafaela would."

Poor Melissa did not know much. Alejandro's picture of her being young and naïve was affirmed. He decided that he wanted to explore further along the pathway. He reached out and touched the top of Melissa's left shoulder, gently guiding her turn. The two went along the right side of the pool. It was difficult for him to try to absorb everything he saw. There was so much.

As they edged around the pool, Alejandro saw that pavilions were protected by a row of pomegranate trees that were bordered by a granite banister. There were little red flowers on the trees. A few looked like they bore little red bulbs. Alejandro was fixated on this. He inhaled their scents again and again. Suddenly, he felt at peace. He was no longer thinking. He was no longer trying to find answers. He was one with nature and beauty.

They stopped and leaned against the stone railing. There was a calm silence between them for several minutes.

She was standing next to him. She was close. Alejandro turned his head and looked at Melissa. She was so beautiful. His body started to awaken. His heartbeat started to increase. She had taken his soul hostage.

He stared at her longingly.

"Melissa, have you ever been in love?"

She was taken aback. "What do you mean?"

"I mean have you ever fallen in love?"

"Well, of course. I love God."

"No, I mean with a human being."

"Well, no," she replied with hesitation. "I think I'm too young." She tried to deflect the question. He had caught her off guard.

Alejandro pressed her a little harder.

"Do you want to fall in love?"

"I don't know." She was embarrassed. "Why are you asking me such a question?" She struggled to regain control. Her face reddened and she turned away from him. She was not prepared for this.

"I just want to know about you." He said it softly so as to be disarming. He took a step closer to her.

"No, I have never been in love," she returned unabashedly. Her face was flushed as she responded lowering her eyes to a pile of dried, spotted leaves.

"Life is good,
It is like food that nourishes the soul.
But love is better,
For the soul is enriched.
Yet, life with love is the best,
As the soul is sweetly nurtured."

"What are you reciting?" she inquired of him perplexed.

"A poem . . . a love poem. A love poem to you." *There I said it.*

She peered at him. Her eyelids blinked. Her head jerked back. She was embarrassed. Her mouth was open, but no words were coming out. She looked like she was in shock. Her body had withdrawn into a protective cocoon. Her arms were folded over her chest.

He reached for her hand. She stepped to the side.

"Melissa," he said softly trying to get closer to her.

She turned her head. "I have to go now."

She hurried off. Alejandro was left humiliated.

I have been such a fool. I blew my chances with her. I hope she doesn't tell the nuns about me.

CHAPTER 20

THE PICNIC

Alejandro had another rough night sleeping. His thoughts were centered on Melissa. She had rejected him. He was preoccupied by this unrequited affection for her. He felt guilty. He knew that he shouldn't have tried to come on to her. She was too young. What was he going to do now?

First light came and Alejandro was wide-awake. *I just have to go home. I'm tired. I'm bored. I really don't have anything to do. Adios, Melissa.*

Quit your whining, baby. Be a man. She is not the first to dump you. She won't be the last.

He fidgeted in bed. *Get me out of here!*

The morning passed routinely. Sister Beatriz brought him breakfast. She was smiling and chatty with him. She seemed to be in good spirits. He still didn't understand what the nun's qualified vow of silence was at the abbey. Sister Beatriz could be a chatterbox at times. Maybe Melissa hadn't told them what had happened at the pool.

"I finally finished my crocheting. Now I can work on some clothing . . ."

At about 11 a.m. there was a tapping at the door. Melissa entered the room long after Sister Beatriz had departed.

"Good morning, " she said.

She was behaving as if she was in a more favorable disposition. She had a nice little smile today. Her eyes seemed to be twinkling. She had not spoken in an angry manner with him. No silent treatment.

"Good morning, Melissa," he said glumly.

She began straightening out the bed.

"I can meet you up at the pool after I do my chores, if you would like?" she asked him gently.

Alejandro was stunned. It was as if someone had hit him in the head with a hammer. He blinked his eyes in disbelief. His forehead furrowed.

"Why, sure," he said reflexively with a weak grin.

"Good, I'll meet you at the upper pool at midday."

She had finished making the bed.

"See you later," Melissa said and departed from the room. There seemed to be a spring in her step.

Alejandro jumped into his bed.

"Oh, man!" *I can't believe it! I'm in love!*

Alejandro cleaned himself up to the best of his ability. He hadn't felt so energized for weeks. Maybe months.

A little while later he left his room and strolled toward the upper pool. He thought that he should try to act more properly with Melissa that afternoon. Doubts had been creeping into his inquisitive mind. *Why the sudden turnaround?* She had been angry with him yesterday. And today she was little Miss Congeniality. He was perplexed.

Alejandro passed by the upper fountain and took the path to the stairs, and finally to the upper pool. The air smelled sweet with jasmine plants. There was a slight lofting breeze. He could hear the distant buzzing of the bees. He sat down at the edge of the pool. His stomached growled. He was hungry. He preoccupied himself by watching little insects skimming on the surface of the water.

After what seemed like an eternity, Melissa finally arrived. She was wearing a white dress and was carrying a wooden food basket. Her braids were capped with tiny white ribbons.

"Hello, Melissa."

"Hello."

"You've come."

"Why, yes. I told you that I would."

"Oh, that's right." Alejandro again fell into a mental daze and was having a difficult time conversing with Melissa in an intelligible way.

"Alejandro, are you hungry?" She motioned toward the basket.

She had never addressed him in such a familiar tone before!

"Yes. Like, sure!" He always had an appetite.

"Let's sit over here." They went over to a patch of grass between the pool patio and the pomegranate bushes. She took out a large cranberry colored tablecloth and the two laid it outstretched on the ground. He laid himself down on his right side. She kneeled down and started to unpack the basket. There was a loaf of bread, some mangoes, and a bottle of the amber-colored mead nectar.

"Let me help you."

"No, I can do it," she gave him a smile. *Was she being polite or devious?* He wondered.

She broke off a piece of bread and handed it to Alejandro. He took a bite. It was fresh.

Melissa gave him more bread and he ate it with gusto. She joined him in eating and they shared the nectar.

"This is fantastic. Thank you."" He took another gulp of the elixir and handed the bottle back to her. She took a swallow.

"Yum!" he smiled. He was enjoying.

"Yum? What is yum?" Melissa queried.

"Actually, it's yum-yum. Twice as good as yum!" he laughed. "It means delicious. I'm just teasing you."

"Yum-yum," she echoed.

"This is such a great place," he continued.

"Yes, I have lived here all of my life." She handed the bottle back to him.

She gave him a mango and took one for herself. It was scrumptious! It was sweet! It was juicy! She bit into her mango. He saw liquid dripping down her arm.

They drank more and more of the nectar.

He was feeling more and more euphoric.

Alejandro started to laugh. And then she began to giggle also. She had the most beautiful smile. Those white ivory teeth. She smelled of lavender. She intoxicated him.

Alejandro reached over toward her and with his right forefinger gently stroked her cheek. He looked into her violet eyes. He met no resistance.

His hand cupped the side of her face and her delicate chin. Her head tilted slightly and she exhaled. She was as relaxed as if she were a cat being petted. Her cheeks blushed. She seemed to be elated.

Alejandro and Melissa said nothing to one another. She closed her eyes and gave a heavenly sigh.

Alejandro took hold of both of her shoulders and gently pulled her next to him. He felt her warm body. She did not struggle. She opened her eyes. He put a piece of mango in her mouth. She savored it smiling.

He leaned over and brushed her right cheek softly with his beard. She cringed with a smile from being tickled. She put her hand on his shoulder. He took another piece of mango and put in halfway into her mouth. Before she could consume the whole thing, he bit the other end. Her face beamed. Their lips touched and then she chewed through the mango. She giggled joyfully.

Alejandro gently kissed her left eyelid and then her right. He continued kissing her about the face. Softly. Sensuously. She would pull back every once in awhile when his beard rubbed lightly against her. He licked her lips with his tongue. He lapped the sweet mango juices from her mouth.

Melissa sighed. Alejandro kissed her. His right hand caressed her. Their lips touched again and again. They embraced. She pressed herself against him.

Slowly, he pecked her neck. She dug her fingers into his back as she extended her neck with pleasure. A wave of passion and hot blood shot through his body.

Alejandro felt the small of her back and massaged it in a circular motion for a while. She was entranced with the newly found sensations.

Another wave of arousal swept through his limbs. He took her little finger and put in into his mouth. He sucked it. He bit it. She moaned.

A heightened awareness overcame him and he rolled his leg between hers. He was breathing heavily. She was gasping also. She dug her nails deeper into his back.

Carefully, he pulled down one side of the top of her dress. His mouth kissed her cinnamon colored shoulder and longingly explored the swell of her breast. His tongue left witness on her chest.

Melissa took a deep breath. Her stomach flattened. Her legs longed to stretch out.

The moments turned into minutes. The swelling was like the lighting of the candle of life. The tip tingled as the wick became afire. Alejandro softly fondled one of her small breasts and mouthed it again. His tongue found bumps on the coffee colored areola. He licked her. The nipple became hard. He bit her breast gently. She winced.

Alejandro's back arched. From the tips of his toes to the top of his neck hot blood ripped through him. He was reaching out for her. He paused for a second, and reached over for the bottle of nectar. He took a swallow and then gently secreted it onto her breasts. The elixir ran down the front of her chest toward her belly button. He licked it up. He drank it up. He lapped it up. Melissa wailed with pleasure. Her legs enveloped his.

The hardened stimulation pressed against her warmth. He lifted up her dress and stroked her thighs. His hand reached up and touched her. Melissa was moist. She coiled her legs tighter around him. He tried frantically to pull his pants down. She grabbed him. They kissed. They tasted each other. They were melting together under the midday sun. He entered her. He felt a little resistance. She let out a sharp scream, but then bit her lower lip. He throbbed. He ached. The movement of the ocean. Swelling. Cresting. Falling.

The foaming and frothing on the pristine beach was the climactic tsunami. The candle had melted and had waxed the cave of love. The erotic volcano had exploded and amorous magma had engulfed the virginal forests.

The two lovers kissed and embraced for more than an hour afterwards.

Overhead, there was a buzzing sound. A bee soared by and then flew in a figure eight pattern with intermittent waggles over Alejandro and Melissa. And then it flew away.

The paramours squeezed each other. Then slowly they got up and packed the basket. They made their way back gradually to the building looking into each other's eyes.

CHAPTER 21

MOTHER SUPERIOR

Alejandro came back into the building room exhilarated. His chest heaved from exhaustion. His body tingled from the day's experience. He was ravenous. He went into the kitchen, but no one was there. He grabbed a few bananas and an old bolillo from the kitchen table and went up to his room.

He threw himself onto the bed. He envisioned Melissa in her splendor. He could still smell her essence of lavender. He could taste her kisses. His mouth watered. He longed for her again. She had left him, saying that she would see him again the next day.

He could feel her body against him. He drifted off into the sweetest of sleeps.

ی

The next day dawned.

There was a loud knock at the door. Sister Beatriz entered with his breakfast. She was not smiling.

There were no salutations or pleasantries.

"Señor Rubí, Mother Superior wants to see you in her study after our mid-morning prayers."

"Yes, Sister."

While Sister Beatriz did not seem angry, yet she was not friendly. *Oh, my God! Did they find out about Melissa and me? How could they?* His stomach churned. So soon!

"Mother Superior lives in the other building. Her study is on the first floor. I'll come by a few moments before your meeting in order to accompany you over to her."

"Yes, Sister."

Sister Beatriz seemed severe toward him. Or at least she was trying to act stern.

Alejandro ate his breakfast voraciously. His mouth felt so dry and he had trouble chewing. He was quite thirsty. He wanted more orange juice, but did not want to ask for more. Sister Beatriz expeditiously picked up his tray and left.

He tried to clean up, but he didn't have any unsoiled clothing. He stroked his hair and beard with his fingers. He hoped that there were no loose food particles visible. His breathing was shallow and his hands felt sweaty.

A few moments before the assigned time, Sister Beatriz returned. They walked out of the first building in silence. The only noise was the gravel underneath their feet. They passed the fountain in the middle of a garden courtyard. He saw a few nuns working among the plants. He noticed the humming of bees. As he and the nun entered the second building, Alejandro guessed that the second building was the mirror image of the first. But here, the interior floors and walls were made of beautiful woods. There were tapestries and paintings on the wall. This setting, contrasted to his building, was ornate and elegant. Hmm, he thought for a moment. They advanced down a corridor and Sister Beatriz opened up one of the two doors that led into the study. Behind the lavish rosewood desk sat Mother Superior.

"Señor Rubí, may I present to you, Mother Superior Regina Coeli of Our Lady of the Flowers Order."

"Come in! Come in!" she beckoned, waving with a frail and wrinkled hand. He had remembered her from the wake and the funeral. She seemed ancient.

"I am honored, Sister." He stared at the aged nun, but she

did not make eye contact. Maybe she was blind. Her glasses were very thick.

"Sister Beatriz, you are excused."

"Yes, Reverend Mother." She departed without hesitation.

"Señor Rubí, how is your health?"

"I think that I am almost fully cured, Sister," he answered nervously. He really didn't know how to answer the question without putting himself in a tenuous position. He inconspicuously rubbed his wet palms on the back of his shirt.

"I have been apprised of such," she said in a patronizing tone. "Señor Rubí, we here at the abbey lead a challenging life under the best of conditions. We are not accustomed to having strangers in our midst."

"Yes, Sister." He was trying to pay close attention.

"Especially, a man." There was a little edge to her tone.

Alejandro tried to recall what she ranted about at Sister Sophia's eulogy. "Yes, Sister." He knew that the ax was about to fall.

"You are a guest. Melissa is a child. Our child. A child of the abbey. You must not take advantage of her."

His face reddened. "But, Sister," he tried to protest.

"Enough!" she angrily raised her voice. "I don't want to hear anything. I want you to promise me that you will not see Melissa again."

"Yes, Sister." What else could he say? He was dumbfounded. He had found love and it was suddenly stripped away. He just wanted to flee and forget this strange place.

What would Melissa say when he told her that he couldn't see her again? How would she feel? She probably would cry. I could almost cry myself!

But wait! How did they find out? Did Melissa tell them?

He surmised that they already had subjected her to an interrogation and a similar admonition. They probably also had her promise that she would not see him any more.

If I were back at school, Chuy and I would be at the local cantina drowning our sorrows with a few beers. This reminded him of the time that Chuy's long-term love interest (of six months) dumped him for a medical student. Chuy was crushed. He lost about five kilos from a lack of appetite. For a solid week, the two had gone to bars to dialogue about love and betrayal. Within two weeks Chuy had found someone new.

"Sister, when will I be able to leave?" he blurted. "My parents don't know where I am."

At first, Mother Superior did not respond.

Then she replied, "I don't know."

This is strange, he thought. *Shouldn't she know?*

"Señor Rubí, please join me for dinner tomorrow night."

"Yes, Sister."

"It will be in the dining room next door."

"Yes, Sister." *This is strange. One moment she is warning me and then she invites me for dinner. I don't understand.*

"Until tomorrow. And remember what I said."

"Yes, Sister."

He turned on his heel and left. *Wow! That was creepy! I can't wait to get back to Mexico City and see my family.*

CHAPTER 22

THE SONNET

Alejandro started to return to his room. It was still before midday. *Would Melissa be making my bed? Almost certainly not. They probably had relieved her of that duty,* he surmised.

Dozens and dozens of thoughts were cluttering his head. She probably would not be laundering his clothes anymore. Maybe Marica would have to do it. But eventually, Melissa would have to wash clothes at the pond for the others. Alejandro took off in that direction.

Melissa wasn't at the pond as he had hoped. He decided to wait. He splashed the water with his hand. *Melissa is probably in trouble because of me. I need to talk to her.*

He was feeling sad that she was destined to remain in the abbey forever.

What would my father advise? Señor Rubí would almost certainly agree that Melissa was a pretty girl, but would admonish him that she was not to be treated like a ball of yarn to be played with by a cat. She deserved to be respected in the same way he regarded his mother.

He stopped splashing and just stared into the pond. His eyes watered. His heart felt heavy.

And under similar circumstances, what would his mother do? His mother would feel empathy for Melissa. She would want to comfort the girl and tell her that everything would be all right. His mother would worry that in a few years, Alejandro's sister, Lupe, would bring both tears of sadness and joy to her.

Señora Rubí knew how it was to be half-girl, half-woman. As for Chuy, he would probably cite a new popular theory about love and relationships. He always parroted what the latest magazine opined about men and women. Moreover, he always knew which politician was having an affair with which movie star. However, his masterstroke was quoting the telenovelas as authoritative sources.

Alejandro waited and waited, but still there was no Melissa. He wet his head with water. The wetness refreshed him.

He treaded wearily as he returned to his room. He felt depressed and sad.

Upon entering his room, he found that his bed had not been made up.

Rats! This probably means that Melissa will not be allowed to enter my room again.

A tension in Alejandro's head began to build. He climbed on top of the bed and lay down. He felt a painful throbbing in his skull. His eyelids closed. He fell asleep.

A short while later, there was a knock at the door. A moment later, Sister Beatriz entered.

"How are you, my son?" She seemed softer now than her attitude toward him that morning.

"Okay, Sister."

"So it seems."

"Pardon, Sister?"

"I mean you seem to be recuperating rapidly. That means that you will no longer be treated as an invalid."

"Yes, Sister. I would be willing to work around the abbey doing a few chores." He did not want to be confined to his room. Maybe if he seemed to cooperate, he would be permitted to see Melissa.

"That won't be necessary. You are still a guest here."

She seemed to have seen through his transparent gambit to try to see the girl.

"From now on, I will no longer bring you your meals. For breakfast, you can eat in the kitchen with Marica. She will prepare it for you. The same goes for lunch. I will look in on you from time to time to see how you are doing." He guessed that meant she was going to continue to keep an eye on him.

"Yes, Sister."

Sister Beatriz started to leave, but hesitated for a moment. She murmured, "I know that it is difficult, but you must be patient. Everything happens for a reason."

She rushed out of the room. His head flinched. It seemed to Alejandro that she was going to break down and cry. He was bewildered. *What had happened? What in the hell was she saying?*

He looked upwards. He wrote his contemplations on the ceiling. *I don't really don't give a damn about any of this. I have to see Melissa! How can I do it?*

I'll write Melissa a note. I need to find some paper. Another love poem? His heart was enamored with every thought of her. *I'll find a way to see her! Who said I was bored?*

Alejandro started to drift into an ethereal world. He tried to remember a sonnet that he had learned in school.

"While my princess sleeps,
Stars in the skies are bright.
Softly the moonbeam seeps
Through the clear lunar night.
Oh, the cool, gentle breeze,
While my princess sleeps,
Blows lightly through the trees,

Echoes of the finch's peeps,
To her dreaming ear, to please.
Should the breathing arias
That for her I sing,
From the holy Ave Marias
To the joys that I bring.
Breathe on the gentle breeze,
And glance upon the awesome sight,
Through the swaying trees,
But be your murmurs light
As the hum of bees.
All the stars are glowing,
In the midnight sky,
Through the fields a blowing,
Lavender lusters lie.
Oh, a gentle sigh,
Bring no clouds to hide
Nor leaves to fly,
But stay near her side
To dream just like I."

CHAPTER 23

LOOKING FOR MANGOES

There had been a gentle rain earlier that morning. Alejandro had awoken to the sweet and cool morning air. He had spent the prior evening reciting his love poem to himself and had forgotten to eat something.

He had slept well that night, despite Mother Superior's admonitions. He had frequently run into trouble when he was a youngster in grammar school. He knew how to respond. Passive resistance. Simply say, "Yes, Sister," and then do whatever he wanted. It worked successfully most of the time. However, if that ploy didn't work, it meant being severely disciplined by his parents. "Alejandro!" his mother would yell.

Alejandro wet his face in the small basin on the little table. His fingers ran through his hair. He ambled slowly downstairs to the kitchen. He did not pass anyone on his way there. He found Marica washing some vegetables and fruits in the basin.

"Good morning."

"Good morning, my son," she returned softly. Her black eyes seemed so sad. The wrinkles on her full, parched face told that she had lived a very laborious and hard life.

"What would you like?"

"Anything. Please don't bother with anything special."

He sat at the large wooden table in the middle of the kitchen. Marica served him a glass of orange juice first. This was followed by herbal tea. He then had corn tortillas and half of a melon.

"How long have you worked here?"

"For decades."

"Wow! That's a long time. How did you come to be here?"

At first Marica was silent. She seemed a bit hesitant to engage in such a conversation with Alejandro. Finally, she succumbed.

"I was brought here as a young girl. My father left me here to work. I was about eight or ten years old. The nuns took care of me. I was a helper to Marisol, the previous cook. She died many years ago. I have been here ever since."

"This sounds like Melissa's situation."

That comment brought a silenced gaze from Marica. It was a forlorn look. She turned away from him despondently. She slowly put some dishes away.

"Marica, what is going on around here?"

She kept her back to him. She did not respond.

"I can't see Melissa! I can't go home! I can't do anything!"

She spun around. She had tears running down her ridged cheeks. This was similar to the recent response from Sister Beatriz.

"I would like to speak with Melissa one last time. She shouldn't be punished because of me."

"It is forbidden," she said in a stony tone.

"I love her. She shouldn't have to be trapped here." *I said it. I can't believe I said it! Chuy would be teasing me mercilessly. Why was Marica being so cold?*

Marica peered at him with consternation. Her eyes were fixed on his brown eyes. She was trying to see through his soul.

"I need some mangoes. Go to the orchard downhill from

this building and get me some, please." She had commanded him in a strange way.

"Yes, Marica."

"And be careful."

"Yes, Marica. Thanks for breakfast," he said meekly.

She picked up his dishes and turned away.

Alejandro left the kitchen and exited the building. He walked toward the patio fountain. He waved to Rafaela who was gathering fresh flowers uphill from him. He turned to the right, down a sandy path.

Have I made Marica angry with me? Why won't she help me?

Within the first few minutes, he passed almond trees, papaya trees, orange trees, and a host of other fruit trees. Bees were everywhere, busy pollinating. He even saw a few pomegranate trees. That was his favorite fruit, even though he had stained many a shirt trying to negotiate its consumption.

He trod downhill a little further. There were weeds between the rows of trees. There was a lot of fruit on the ground with cracked skins, simply rotting. It seemed to Alejandro that the nuns did not lack for food. Maybe they traded fruit and vegetables to the Momos for supplies?

The abbey buildings disappeared from his view. His shirt was wet with perspiration. The shade from the arboretum of trees cooled him down. It was pleasant.

The trees seemed almost indistinguishable to him. Here were the mango trees, he thought. No, they were guava. He walked on farther and picked some cherries. He sampled a few. They were dark maroon and very sweet. He spit out the stones.

Alejandro traversed the orchard and finally found the mango trees. The golden-red fruits were plump and soft.

How many should I pick? Probably as many as I can carry. I should have probably brought a basket or something.

Alejandro was tempted to bite into one of the mangoes and savor its juice, even though at the moment he wasn't hungry. His mouth reminisced about the afternoon delight he had with Melissa. He could almost taste her. Maybe he would take one back to his room for an afternoon snack.

He picked up a few and then some more. He had eight cradled in his shirt. He kept dropping one as soon as he put the last one in.

With his head bent over and the front of his shirt held up to his chin, he started his retreat back toward the buildings. It was a different path. He passed some lemon and lime trees.

To his right he spied a double-trunked avocado tree. Alejandro decided to detour. He had to urinate. He put down the mangos and watered the tree. As he was doing so, he noticed that nearby, there was a small rose-covered mound that led to the right. It had dozens of red roses with large thorns and thick vines. The scent of the roses was intoxicating. He picked up the mangoes again.

I'll bring Melissa some red roses. His mouth turned into a smile. As he approached the sweet scented blossoms, he saw an old, decrepit wooden shack. It looked abandoned. Alejandro wanted to investigate it but decided to walk around it first. He then became aware of some old wooden planks implanted on the side of the small bank of roses about twenty meters away from the little building. He approached the mound. The closer he came, the more he realized that the rose vines overran some type of door. A door that was an opening into the side of the small hill. Strange? *Maybe it was an old mausoleum or something?*

The wood was discolored and splintering. It looked like

termites had eaten parts of it. There were no knobs or handles.

Alejandro carefully put down his mangoes. His shirt was now all wet with mango juice and his hands were sticky.

He attempted to push aside some of the vines, but suffered a few pricks. There were specks of blood on his hands and arms. Using his feet, he managed to clear off a small area. He tried to kick in the door, but to no avail. Cautiously, he attempted to pull open the planks. At first, nothing gave. Then, there was a creaking. Finally, by taxing all of his strength, he managed to pry the door open.

It looked like a cavern. The opening sloped slightly upwards. He tried to look into the darkness.

He didn't have his lighter with him, and couldn't see more than about twenty feet in front of him. *Maybe it was some sort of subterranean tunnel. Maybe for burials? Maybe for protection? Surely there was no mining.*

It was too dark to explore. *Maybe I'll come back later on or tomorrow.*

CHAPTER 24

THE DINNER

With sweat rolling down his brow, Alejandro finally delivered the mangoes to the kitchen. Marica was busy preparing the afternoon meal. It had been a few hours since breakfast, but eating the fruit had staved off his appetite.

"Thank you, my son," she said in a courteous tone, "Are you hungry?"

"No, thank you."

He dropped several thorny stems of red roses onto the kitchen table. "Could you please make sure Melissa gets these?"

Marica was busy slicing fruit, but she managed an affirmative nod. So he left the kitchen.

He was passing the chapel when he noticed that it was open. He went in. There was no one around. He scanned the room.

Dutifully, he went over to the portrait of the Madonna with Child. He made a slight genuflection and crossed himself. He had often wondered why the Blessed Virgin was painted with such a pallid complexion offset with rosy cheeks. He had always imagined her with Semitic features, dark skin, and black hair.

Underneath the painting he spotted some candles. He snatched three of them and stuffed them into his pants.

Forgive me, Holy Mary, but I need these.

As he turned back toward the chapel door, Sister Beatriz

had just entered.

"My son, what are you doing here?"

"Paying my respects, Sister." *Had she seen him take the candles? She was sharp. All nuns could smell trouble kilometers away.*

"Remember, my son, your dinner with Mother Superior is this evening. I will stop by to escort you. Some clean clothes have been left for you. I suggest that you bathe beforehand." He could hear her sniff. He wondered if he stunk.

"Yes, Sister."

Without looking at her directly, he passed by her and left the chapel.

Upstairs he found his clean clothes on top of the bed. He gathered them and proceeded to the room at the end of the hall. The water in the tub was lukewarm. He wondered how many buckets had to be carried up the stairs to fill the little tub.

He immersed himself in the tub and dunked his head under the water. He lathered his whole body several times with a lavender-scented soap and afterwards, rinsed himself.

Alejandro fantasized about having Melissa in the tub with him. Like two sea otters sliding over each other in the glistening waters.

He got out and dried himself off. Alejandro was glad to put on the clean white cotton pants and shirt.

Now bathed, he went back to his room. He hadn't seen Melissa for two days. *Oh, I forgot to find some writing paper! Well, the poem was probably a dumb idea anyway. Melissa probably would have laughed at me. I hope she got the roses. Maybe I'll see her tomorrow.*

Later that evening, there was a knock at the door. Sister Beatriz entered. She was there to accompany him to dine with Mother Superior.

The pair strolled leisurely over to the second building and entered a small, but elegant room. He was apprehensive about the whole arrangement. *What would he say to Mother Superior?* The wall was strewn with secular tapestries that reflected a Moorish influence. The floor was carpeted with a Turkish type of Oriental rug. *They don't seem to have the vow of poverty here,* he noted mentally. *I thought this was a simple abbey. Where did all this luxury come from?*

A white linen cloth covered the vintage rectangular oak table. There were silver plate settings.

"Good evening, Señor Rubí," Mother Superior hailed him in a slow, drawn out voice.

"Good evening, Sister," he said with his eyes lowered in a deferential manner. The situation reminded him of having to dine with the adult friends of his parents. Very stuffy.

"How was your day?" creaked her voice.

"Fine, Sister."

Mother Superior turned her head for an instant toward Sister Beatriz who immediately excused herself and left the room.

Alejandro noticed that there were only two dinner place settings on the table.

"Please be seated." She pointed to one end of the table with a wrinkled old finger partially draped by her black costume. She sat at the other end that was about three meters away.

Alejandro sat down and placed the white linen napkin on his lap. He did not know what to say. So he decided to say very little.

At that moment, Sister Teresa entered the dining room through another door. Mother Superior fiddled with her thick eyeglasses.

Sister Teresa's appearance was noticed by Mother Superior. Without delay, Sister Teresa took his glass and poured Alejandro a healthy amount of the mead nectar. There was a quiet atmosphere in the room. It was solemn and somber.

After they had said grace, Mother Superior bid Alejandro to drink. He savored the golden liquid. It tasted like the mead elixir that he had shared with Melissa up on the hilltop. Maybe a little too sweet. But on the other hand, he and Chuy had drunk many versions of rotgut liquor during law school. He was willing to indulge. He needed to relax.

"We must be sure to build up your strength," she grimaced. Her yellow stained teeth hinged in the skeletal jaw.

Sister Teresa reentered the room with a tureen of soup. She poured Alejandro a bowlful.

He sipped the hot broth. It was a vegetable soup. It was delicious! He spooned it up with gusto. His mother would have reprimanded him for his poor table manners if she had been there.

Mother Superior continued to grimace at him. She did not seem to be consuming much, if anything. Now, he was too busy inhaling his food.

Next, Sister Teresa reappeared with a garden greens salad adorned with blueberries, almond slivers, and what seemed to be a concoction of herbs and spices. Each bite created a different and unique burst of flavor. Alejandro finished his second glass of nectar. Sister Teresa immediately replenished it.

Alejandro began to feel a little giddy. He was hoping for some red meat. Even chicken would do.

In came Sister Teresa with an aspic dish. Alejandro did

not know what it was. His parents had taken him to some very fine French restaurants in Mexico City. He knew that there were some strange and exotic dishes that people ate. Escargot, for example.

I don't know what this is. I'll try it to be polite.

The gelatinous mold shook as he tried to cut it with his knife and fork. His jaw tightened and he cringed. After several attempts, he conquered the task. The flavor was bland. Chuy would have suggested that it needed some salsa.

I'll need to drink a little more to wash it down.

Reluctantly, he continued to attack the aspic dish with very little enjoyment. Mother Superior hardly had spoken. Sister Teresa was meticulously attentive, replenishing his nectar glass at every opportunity.

Then, all of a sudden, Alejandro started to experience drowsiness. *I can't understand what Mother Superior is saying. Her words are slurred. Maybe I drank too much. I am not used to drinking anymore. What the f__k!*

His eyes were half shut. His vision now was blurred. He was in a hypnotic trance.

In the next instant, he felt euphoric. He began dreaming about beautiful things. Blue skies. Cool breezes. Pretty flowers.

He imagined that he had opened his eyes. Hugh owlish orbs were gaping in his face. He tried to move, but he couldn't. His body felt paralyzed. He felt gel being plastered onto his face. There was a sickening ambrosial scent that overcame him and made him feel nauseous.

No! No! Stop!

A long, raspy tongue began to lap the ooze from his face. It licked his cheeks. It licked his nose. It licked his mouth. It licked his arms. It licked his chest. It licked his stomach. It licked his legs. It licked his entire body.

The images were turning into a horrific nightmare. He was being assaulted by some sort of creature. The terrifying creature was physically molesting him. He could not move his arms to protect himself.

No! No! Stop!

The overpowering scents. The slimy secretions. Then Alejandro felt that his entire body was being sexually assaulted.

Stop! Stop! Stop!

CHAPTER 25

SUBTERRANEAN

Alejandro's head ached when he awoke the following morning. His mouth was dry. His body was sweaty and sticky. His kidneys were throbbing.

Man, I have a frigging hangover. That drink that Sister Teresa kept pouring me must have been some powerful brew. Oh, my head! I could use a cafecito or some tripe stew.

Slowly, in a semi-conscious state, he went over to the water pitcher and wet his hands. He rubbed them over his face and tried to clean himself. He had slept in his clothes. How did I get back to my room last night? Maybe the nuns carried me back? How embarrassing!

I still remember bits and pieces of my nightmare. It was terrible! It felt like some sort of evil monster was violating me.

After a while he staggered downstairs to the kitchen. Marica was not there. There was no one around. On top of the table was a bowl of fruit. It included a mango. Also, there were some bread rolls. He sat down and ate lightly, and ever so slowly.

Alejandro felt strange. He needed to get out of the building. He needed some fresh air. He wanted to do something. He grabbed some fruit and bread and left the kitchen.

Alejandro returned to his room. He noticed his little pouch on the little table. Hmm, he thought for a second, still trying to come out of his daze. He grabbed his lighter and the candles that he had hidden and took off. He left the building. So far he had not seen anyone this morning. Maybe everybody was at prayer.

He walked down to the orchard at a slow pace. He was feeling better with a little food in his stomach. He got disoriented a few times. Everything looked different. Eventually, he wandered back to the rundown shack and the rose-covered mound. The area still looked abandoned.

His looked around to see if anyone was watching as he made his way to the dilapidated door. With caution he pried it open. He took a few steps inward. There wasn't much light within. He stopped and flipped open his lighter and lit one of the candles. The opening seemed to be sloped slightly upward. This kept the rain out, he thought. It was an excellent shelter. *But why is it here? Where does it lead?* With the candle he could see between five and ten meters ahead.

However, it was difficult to ascertain how far the subterranean chamber or tunnel extended on from his position. He recalled that the underground catacombs along the Appian Way in Rome went for leagues. He was curious about this mysterious cave. He and his brother always looked for buried treasure when they were children. He decided that he had to explore this cavern. *Will I find anything?*

Let me count out paces. One, two, three, . . . The candle flickered as he slowly marched forward. At first the air was cool. Then it became warmer and smelled like rotting garbage. He reached out and touched the right side of the cavern. It was ragged and felt like shale.

The ground seemed smooth at first. *Eleven, twelve, thirteen, . . . Does the path start to go downward or is it level?* He could not tell. He was losing his sense of orientation and depth perception. He used his right hand to guide him along the side of the cavern. As he touched the wall, it seemed to feel harder or more brittle as he continued to explore the tunnel. At times, he would have to lower his head for fear of bumping it. The air became cooler again.

Now there was the miasmic odor of mildew. It almost made him feel nauseous. *Twenty-eight, twenty-nine, thirty,* . . . Alejandro almost tripped over a rock and barely held on to the candle. The passage seemed to veer to the left. The ground became coarser with little pebbles. It started to slightly slope downward. Now he was stepping onto gravel that made crunching sounds.

These pebbles remind me of when Chuy and I and our law school classmates would sometimes go to the beach on Fridays. We would drink beer or wine and tell outrageous stories. Girls were not allowed. The truth of the matter was that if anyone had a date or a girlfriend there was no need to go.

As night approached, Alejandro and Chuy would settle down in one of the caves along the sandy cove until high tide rolled in. The surf would pound against the barnacle-covered rocks. The mist would refresh them both from the harsh late afternoon heat.

Fifty-one, fifty-two, fifty-three, . . . His hand was taut against the wall. He tried to steady himself. He felt moisture on what now was solid rock. He started walking in little puddles. Every once in a while a warm drop would descend onto his face. He cringed. He hoped that it was water and not some type of bat guano. It was very dark. Outside of his steps, there were no other sounds. His eyes could not adjust to the murkiness.

Maybe I should go back. I don't know what might be further down this cave.

But Alejandro continued to push forward. Suddenly, he

felt something that resembled a granite slab. He paused. His right hand examined it. He moved the candle from left to right. It appeared to be an underground tomb. *Frig! Maybe these are catacombs where they bury their dead!*

Carefully, he lowered the candle. There seemed to be another sepulcher. And then there was another. There were etchings on the graves, but he could not decipher them. Alejandro was getting very nervous. He was sweating and breathing heavily. He brought the candle back to the left side of the tunnel. There were more tombs. He seemed to have discovered a subterranean burial ground.

Should I return and pretend that I never was here? I know that I have committed some kind of sacrilege. But Alejandro continued onward. Some force was pulling him further and further into the obscurity before him. He stumbled onto more tombs along the way. *Eighty-eight, eighty-nine, ninety,* . . . The tunnel opened into a large cavernous chamber, the size of a small church. He stopped and saw stalactites. *What is this place?*

His foot hit a rock and he almost fell. He dropped the candle.

"What the f__k!"

Fortunately, the candle was not extinguished. Alejandro retrieved the candle and as he did so, he detected the "rock" that he tripped on. It was a skull. It looked hideous. Small. No teeth. It was cracked and it looked ancient. *Who were these people? This place is too creepy!* Yet he did not retreat.

He walked from side to side in the chamber. He used his foot to sweep several more skulls lying on the ground. *Why weren't they entombed in the graves?*

Just to the left of him, Alejandro thought that he spotted another entrance into the chamber. He advanced slowly to the opening, keeping his back to the cavern wall. He entered the black abyss.

Alejandro started his pace count over again. *One, two, three,* . . . The air felt a little warmer. It had a pungent ammonia smell.

Twenty, twenty-one, twenty-two, . . . The tunnel took a sharp left turn. The wall was now craggy and uneven. The ground became smoother again. Alejandro was walking slowly so as not to trip.

Forty, forty-one, forty-two, . . . The odor became more putrid as he went further down the passage.

"No!" someone shrieked ahead of him, "No!"

Alejandro was startled and jumped back. He was frightened. *What in the hell was that?*

He broke into a cold sweat. Alejandro's heart palpitated. His candle was almost spent. His mouth became dry. He felt like he had to urinate. He heard another cry.

CHAPTER 26

FATHER RIVOLI

"Go away!" A voice in front of Alejandro shrieked. "I said go away!"

Alejandro was stunned. He was frozen in place. He couldn't comprehend what was happening.

"Hey, you, calm down!" Alejandro yelled back, cupping his free hand to his mouth. "I can't understand you!" He had regained part of his composure. He knew that attorneys were expected to take control of situations. It was the perception of control that mattered.

"Go away!" repeated the strange voice, weakening.

"Who are you?"

"Who are you?" the question was echoed back at Alejandro.

"What are you doing here?" Alejandro was trying to control his apprehension. "My name is Alejandro Rubí. I am a guest here at the abbey."

Alejandro took out the second candle and lit it with what little remained of the first. He could now barely discern that there was a cell several paces in front of him. He approached the bars. The smell stunned him. It was foul, like rotting flesh. He almost gagged.

His eyes could scarcely make out a skeletal figure with long white hair, inside the cage.

The nebulous form looked away as if the light was hurting its eyes.

"Don't hurt me," the shadowy figure pleaded. It cowered. Alejandro immediately recognized that this was an old man who spoke Spanish with a strange accent. The Spanish seemed stilted and archaic. *Who is this person? What is he doing in a cell?*

"Do you have any wine, kind sir?" the figure asked softly.

Although Alejandro initially felt revulsion toward this poor figure, compassion was now slowly seeping into his soul.

"Are you hungry? Here is some fruit." Alejandro remembered that he was still carrying some food leftover from his breakfast. "And bread."

For a few moments there was only silence from within the cell. But finally an emaciated hand poked through the bars. "Wine! I want wine!"

"I have no wine. Just food." Alejandro resigned himself with disgust. This would probably be the typical client that he would get when he started to practice law.

The old man snatched the offering. He gagged as he tried to gorge himself with the food. Alejandro was sickened by the bestial sounds he heard from within the cell.

Who is this poor creature? Why is he in a cell?

"Who are you?" inquired Alejandro out of a curiosity that had been intensified by the setting. His stomach was feeling nauseous while his mind was whirling.

"I am Father Rómulo Rivoli," the voice was no longer shouting.

Alejandro was surprised by the response. *Where had he heard that name before?*

"Where are you from?"

"I am from Valencia," Rivoli stated matter-of-factly.

Alejandro thought that explained one thing. This person had a Castilian accent. Those Spaniards talked with a strange lisp.

"When did you come here?"

"I came to Mexico in 1949," the priest paused and coughed. Alejandro thought that the old man was going to throw up. Rivoli finally regained his composure. "But I didn't come to the abbey until 1952."

"But why are your here? Here, in this cell?" Alejandro had not seen any evidence of any priests around the nunnery.

There was no response. Alejandro heard a quiet sobbing across from him.

"I'm a prisoner," the aged man said as he wept.

"Why are you a prisoner?" inquired Alejandro who was now in a concerned frame of mind.

"Because I lost my soul! I have sinned against nature!" he cried out. "I shall burn in hell for my sins!"

"Calm down," Alejandro hesitated. "You are a priest?"

"Unfortunately, yes. That is why my life has been so wicked."

Alejandro, in spite of his analytical mind, could not follow what Father Rivoli was trying to convey.

Professor Peña had admonished his law students many times to examine the facts of a case without emotion. They were not to prejudge any situation. One question would lead to another, and then to another, and so forth. The answers were never as complex as they initially seemed to be.

"I need wine!" the figure blurted out. "I am a prisoner."

"Father, please start at the beginning. This is very difficult for me to understand. Tell me how all this started."

The priest heaved a sigh. He burped.

Alejandro seemed to have reassured him. Father Rivoli began to relate to Alejandro that his parents were from Spain.

"Much has happened to me since my birth . . ." the priest

slurred his words as began recounting his life.

Rómulo Rivoli had been born in Valencia, Spain, in 1917. There, his father had worked as a minor architect for Don Alfonso Borja. Later Rivoli's family moved to Naples with the Borjas. Rómulo was subsequently raised in Naples. "I learned to read and write Italian. But since I had to study Latin, it was easy . . ."

Alejandro was having a difficult time understanding Father Rivoli who narrated his autobiography with mumbling and ranting. Alejandro's back was starting to ache and he had trouble concentrating on what the priest was saying.

"After the death of Don Alfonso Borja, my parents moved just outside of Rome with his patron's nephew, Rodrigo . . ."

Alejandro was tired of standing and finally sat down on the dirt. It was damp and muddy.

"My mother raised me isolated in our country home. She was a good woman, but to her way of thinking, there was no one around with whom to socialize. She was not satisfied with simple people in the towns. On the other hand, I loved the outdoors . . ."

Rómulo spent most of his youth nurturing the flora and the fauna of their estate. He could grow almost anything and he could tame all the animals as well. Those who knew him likened him to Saint Francis of Assisi.

However, with the outbreak of civil war, the aspirations of his parents returning to Spain were dashed. He couldn't remember all the details of the European conflict, but recalled that there was more than enough bloodshed surrounding him. For his protection, his father decided to send him to a Salesian seminary. Rómulo was an excellent student and finally was ordained in 1942. He continued his studies in chemistry and oenology with an emphasis in sacramental wines.

At the end of World War II, with the assistance of his father's uncle, Rómulo was given a position with Rodrigo's son, Cesare, the Archbishop of Valencia. Rómulo was sent to Cesare's sister's estate in Spain to tutor her children.

A year later Father Rivoli's parents died under peculiar circumstances. Then one day in 1949, his patroness approached him about escorting the Order of Discalced Augustinian nuns to Central America. He humbly accepted the request.

Provisions were loaded upon a ship. He and several former members of his patroness' staff formed an entourage for the nuns.

The journey at sea took five weeks. The oceans were rough and the weather was stormy.

"I was sicker than a dog. So was everybody on the ship . . ."

Father Rómulo started coughing again and stopped his recitation. Alejandro still could barely understand the majority of what the aged priest was incoherently recounting. Finally, the prisoner recovered and continued.

"I gave Extreme Unction to two passengers who later died aboard the ship, including the apothecarist, who had been treating the other passengers for mal de mer . . ."

The ship finally arrived at Veracruz and everyone disembarked, tired and sick. A party of Spaniards, Guatemalans, and Mexicans met the Order of the Augustinian Recollects there. They were to travel to Aguascalientes. For his part, Father Rivoli was sent to the San Tomás Winery in Ensenada, Mexico to work as a vinoculturist in order to assist in its wine production. The vineyards had failed to produce sufficient altar wines for the clergy. Additionally, he had brought on board the ship flowers, fruits, and bee hives from the old country to be introduced into the Mexican agriculture.

"The Mexicans taught me how to make excellent wine. . ."

"Excuse me, Father. My candle is almost out. I have to go now or I'll never be able to see my way out."

"Yes, yes, you are right. I understand. Be careful."

"Yes, Father."

"When will you return?" said the priest pathetically.

"Tomorrow. At about the same time."

"Yes. Good. Be careful, my boy, you are in grave danger."

Alejandro could not reply. He lit his third and last candle.

"Until we meet again." Alejandro wasn't sure that he would really come back. *This is so crazy!*

Alejandro retraced his steps. *One, two, three . . .* At about the count of thirty he reentered the chamber of the skulls and stalactites.

After groping to his right, he found the other exit to the passageway. About five minutes later, he saw the light at the end of the tunnel. It was so bright. He squinted his eyes as he continued toward the exit. At the opening he was blinded by the brilliance of the sunlight. His eyes were hurting, but the fresh air made up for it. He inhaled deeply.

Who is this mad man? I can't even believe he's a priest. What danger was this old man talking about?

CHAPTER 27

DIRTY CLOTHES

As Alejandro ambled back toward the building, he noticed that his clothes were soiled. He would have a hard time explaining how he had dirtied them. His hands were also filthy. They were caked with orangish-brown sticky crystals. *I should go straight to the pond to clean up. Maybe I'll see Melissa. Damn, I forgot to pick some roses. Probably too risky now.*

He walked past the fountain and continued up the path to the pond. Fortunately, he encountered no one on the way. There were just a few bees buzzing around.

At the pond, Alejandro tried to clean his pants and shirt, but with little success. He rubbed his face with his hands. His mouth detected a slightly sweetened taste. He speculated that the brown crystals resembled raw sugar. *How peculiar!* He thought.

He lingered at the pond for a while. His mind was inundated with the inane tale that the priest had told him. *Should I ask Sister Beatriz about this crazy man? Who is he? Why was he incarcerated? I just don't know. But I would probably be reprimanded for being someplace where I shouldn't be.*

Perplexed, Alejandro decided to stroll up to Melissa's secret garden. He reached the top of the stairs and went over to where she and he had shared their love and carnal knowledge.

There were beautiful flowers everywhere. Fuchsias,

begonias, petunias. His olfactory senses absorbed them all. He inhaled the wonderful scents: jasmine, honeysuckle, and columbine. He gently toyed with the petals of the lobelias, penstemons, and snapdragons.

Alejandro closed his eyes and drew in another deep breath. He exhaled. Then almost imperceptibly, he detected the undeniable smell of lavender. He spun around. It was Melissa who had snuck behind him.

They rushed into each other's arms. They hugged. They squeezed. They passionately kissed.

"Melissa, I've missed you," he lamented. "I thought that I had lost you forever."

"No, I won't let that happen." She had a scowled expression on her face.

"I'm sorry for whatever trouble I've gotten you into."

"Don't be."

"Mother Superior made me promise that I would never see or talk to you again."

"I know. Mother Superior is angry with me. But I'm not a little girl!"

She took his hand and put it in hers. She kissed him longingly.

"I won't give you up."

He lightly bit her lower lip. His mouth slightly sucked on her left cheek. His lips gently pecked her eyelids.

Her back arched in his grasp. He licked her ear lobes. He started to kiss her neck. She began to giggle and withdrew from him. She was ticklish!

She pushed him away and ran to an open area plaited with clover. He caught her. The two fell gently onto the soft, springy ground cover.

"Alejandro, I love you!"

"Melissa, I love you too!"

They eagerly embraced and kissed and kissed and kissed. He carefully pulled the top of her dress down and muzzled his beard against her chest. He tasted her. He wanted to devour her. Her body twisted.

Alejandro lay partially on top of her. Her body heaved and sighed with pleasure.

He felt a wet drop on his back. The clouds were rolling in. He felt another drop. At first he sheltered his beloved one, but within a few minutes a torrential downpour ensued. They were both were getting soaked. The rain was warm.

She smiled with her ivory white teeth. They laughed. They rolled around in the clover. They held each other close with unlimited fervor.

The heat of the volcano had reached out for her. The earth trembled. The volcano was erupting. In the middle of the downpour, they made love with ecstasy. It was burning. It was passionate. It was yielding to their natural impulses.

The rain finally subsided. They were both drenched. Alejandro's clothes were muddied and stained.

"Melissa, how would you like to come with me to Mexico City?"

"I don't know."

"What would you do if you stayed here?"

"I don't know."

"You can think about it." He had detected hesitancy in her voice. Alejandro didn't want to rush her, but he wanted to leave the abbey as soon as possible.

"Okay, I'll think about it," she replied coyly.

"From what I gather from Marica, I assume that the Momos should be coming soon. Maybe any day now."

Melissa did not respond.

He got up and reached down and pulled her up. They started to walk back. She hung onto his arm.

Alejandro rambled on about what he wanted to do when he returned to Mexico City and what kind of law he wanted to practice. She listened quietly, but then tugged on his shirtsleeve to get his attention.

"Alejandro, I really don't know what a lawyer is," she said meekly.

How could I be so dumb? Am I overpowering the poor thing? He turned to face her. He was about to say something, when she pointed to his shirt with a look of disgust.

"Alejandro, I should wash your clothes. They are filthy."

His first instinct was to say "no", but he had no other clothing.

"You should have a clean set of clothes in your room. I washed them yesterday." She had anticipated his needs.

"Thank you. I don't mean to add to your chores."

"It's no problem. It's something different. I'm glad to do it."

They continued their walk. Alejandro remembered how his clothes had gotten dirty in the subterranean catacombs. He surmised that if and when he returned to the subterranean passageway the next time, he probably would soil his clothes again. That would cause suspicion. That was the last thing that he wanted.

Should I tell Melissa about Father Rivoli? Probably not now. Not until I discover more about the incarcerated priest.

"Melissa, should I leave these clothes in my room?"

"No. I'm no longer permitted there. Leave them in the kitchen with Marica."

"Okay. Thanks."

The pair approached the pond.

"Wait here for awhile. I don't want them to see us together," Melissa instructed.

She kissed him and left him standing at the side of the pond.

A while later he returned to his room.

He changed out of his wet clothes into the dry ones that had been on top of the bed. Alejandro was shivering. He dried his hair with a small hand towel.

Into the bed he crawled. His thoughts about the incarcerated priest had disappeared. He now was obsessed with Melissa again. He was enamored with her. *How can I escape from this place with her?*

CHAPTER 28

DRUNKENNESS

Alejandro woke up in a spirited mood. The evening before, Sister Beatriz had visited him briefly. He had been under the bed covers. She had inquired how he was doing. He had replied that he was fine. He had tried to maintain a neutral appearance because he did not want to seem too happy or too sad for fear of arousing her curiosity.

Since he had been in bed, it seemed obvious to him that she would not spend much time with him.

She did not ask him about his wet clothes which were lying in a pile in the far corner of the room. He had wrung them out as much as he could over the chamber pot. In doing so, he had gotten the floor wet.

Sister Beatriz had left after a few minutes without ever sitting down.

This morning he cleaned up quickly. He hastened down to the kitchen. Marica greeted him. He was a bit on the chatty side. She was polite and friendly, but seem preoccupied. She was busy slicing up vegetables on the counter.

"Marica, would you like me to pick some mangoes today? Or some other fruit?"

"If you wish, Alejandro."

He had brought down his still-soaked clothes. She had taken them and put them in a straw basket. She then gave him some bananas, dates, and rolls for his breakfast along with some orange juice.

"I will need something to carry them in, please."

"There are some burlap sacks over there," Marica pointed to a wooden pantry that had clay pots on top of it.

"Thank you."

Marica continued her work in the kitchen. Then she started out the door.

"Excuse me, señor, I have to leave now."

He acknowledged her departure.

"Have a good day, " she said as she exited the room.

Alejandro waited a few minutes and then went to the pantry. He seized two burlap sacks. He inserted one inside the other. He didn't want to look for any wine. It would be too risky. He grabbed a couple of bananas and dates and bread from his breakfast plate.

He left the kitchen. As he approached the chapel, he peeked in. There was no one there. Furtively, he entered and grabbed a handful of candles and quickly stole out of the building. He saw Rafaela in the garden up the hill from him. He wasn't sure if she had seen him. He could barely hear the humming of the bees.

About ten minutes later, he was panting in front of the entrance of the subterranean passageway. He used one of the sacks to pull back the rose vines that partially impeded the opening. Then he took off his shirt and packed it into the burlap bag. He left that sack near the entrance of the tunnel. Carefully, he lit one of the candles.

Alejandro threw the other sack over his shoulder. He proceeded and repeated the cadence of the previous journey.

One, two, three, . . .

The tunnel became increasingly moist. Alejandro imagined that this wet part must be underneath a stream or runoff. Soon he passed the chamber of skulls. Then the air got drier and warmer. He had a little trouble breathing from the stuffiness and the foul smells. Finally he reached Father Rivoli.

Alejandro gave out a warning cry, "Father Rivoli, I'm back!"

"Oh, my friend, it is good to hear your sweet voice. I was in despair," the voice quivered. "I was afraid that you weren't going to return. Forgive my lack of faith."

"Well, I did come back. I brought you some food." Alejandro reached between the cold metal bars and handed the prisoner the contraband of fruit and bread. All Alejandro could discern in the dim candlelight was the small hairy creature. The stench that emitted from the incarcerated one was unbearable.

"Did you bring me wine?"

"Sorry, no. Just the food."

The priest grunted and then proceeded to devour the food ravenously.

"Thank you. God is merciful."

"So, Father, you were telling me how you came to be in this place."

"Next time, bring some wine."

"Okay. Okay," Alejandro thought it was best to pacify the priest.

"Well, where were we?"

"You were working for a vineyard in Mexico."

"Did I tell you that the Mexicans made good wine?"

"Yes, you did," Alejandro was fidgeting with impatience, but he knew that he couldn't push the priest.

"Well, I received an order from the Church to join the Sisters of Our Lady of the Flowers here in Guatemala . . ."

Sometime in 1952, he arrived at the abbey after a six-month journey on foot. Here he found himself in a large colonial estate in the midst of plains and valleys. Rivoli had learned that the Spanish family that had originally owned the villa since the early thirties was unsuccessful in growing grapes because of the hot, humid climate. They had switched to mainly fruit trees that subsequently flourished after several years. A cholera epidemic had invaded the neighboring territories and demolished over half of the villa's inhabitants and populations of the local indigenous villages. The survivors of the family went back to Spain after donating the buildings and land to the Catholic Church. The Church set up an orphanage to take care of the parentless victims of the plague and as a novitiate for nuns. The abbey had to become almost self-sufficient after most of household staff and field workers had either died or fled.

"The cloister of nuns was established in the building over our heads. Everything was going fine. The local natives were being converted to Christianity. The Church was pleased. The nuns were happy. Everybody was pleased."

Alejandro now realized that the subterranean tunnel doubled back to one of the abbey buildings.

Thereafter, Rivoli was brought to the abbey to revive the wine growing and initiate new crops.

"I was allowed to plant flowers and fruits from the old country. I had brought some beehives from my patroness. Everything was fine. I should have been happy. Why did I do it? I didn't mean to do it . . ." muttered Rivoli in an eerie tone.

What in the heck was he mumbling about now?

"I should have been satisfied, but I was the only man around. I would take great pleasure every night in drinking the wine that I had found in the old cellar. The Spanish family was already gone. It would have been a sin to let the wine go to waste."

Alejandro wondered if this deranged person was an alcoholic or just plain crazy. He was tempted to leave.

"About a year or two after my arrival here, I started talking to a young nun who was very attractive. She had big almond eyes. I had my eyes on her from the moment I arrived here. She was young. Her name was Sister Isabel. She became my assistant beekeeper at the abbey.

"At first I simply teased her like a father would a daughter. She would laugh. Then I started to give her a little bit of honeycomb every day from my beehives. I was enamored with her. She was a temptress.

"At the time I was experimenting in the development of mead wines. She would help me. She was always near by. I had taken a few books from the deceased apothecarist's belongings. The apothecarist had some ancient volumes of potions and prescriptions. I tried experimenting merely out of curiosity, mind you. Unfortunately, I became more and more reckless.

"One night I had imbibed too much of one of my alcoholic concoctions and I went into Sister Isabel's room. She did not resist me. I had my carnal way with her. I believed that even if she was a child of the devil, I would be willing to burn in hell forever for her.

"The next day I awoke with a hangover. I knew what I had done and I was so contrite. I couldn't tell anyone. I was afraid that she would confess to Mother Superior and that they would expel me from here.

"But lo and behold, to my surprise Sister Isabel came into my quarters the next night. She wanted to try one of the honey-infused potions that I had concocted. I gave her some.

Unfortunately, I drank more with her.

"I was torn between fear and passion. I wanted her, but I was afraid. I didn't have much to offer her. I gave her one of the other mead elixirs that I had brewed from the honey I had harvested from the beehives. That seemed to satisfy her.

"This then became a ritual, several days in a row. I was growing quite worried. I was afraid that we were going to get caught. I was also concerned that she might be losing her senses because she started acting strangely.

"Then one day while she was with me, she said that she had a terrible headache. I gave her some mead nectar, but she wanted something stronger.

"I had many canisters of drugs and elixirs that I kept from the ship's apothecary. She started to take small doses of some of the potions. I don't remember which. I mixed them with the royal jelly from the beehives.

"Instead of getting better, she got worse. Everyday thereafter, her condition worsened. She demanded more and more potions. She sank into deep depression. She seemed to be aging in front of my eyes. God forgive me!"

Alejandro shifted his weight. His leg was falling asleep.

"Finally, I decided that this was all wrong. I refused to give her any more elixirs. She screamed and went into a rampage. She flung everything about in my quarters. She ran out ranting and raving. I prepared myself to confess."

As Father Rivoli went through his incredible narration, Alejandro felt that the priest was a pathetic religious figure. But on the other hand, hadn't he and Chuy frequently become intoxicated. And on several occasions they had awoken to find naïve young girls in their beds. He knew it was hypocritical, but he had a hard time empathizing with the priest. Priests were supposed to representatives of God, not lechers.

"As I was walking to the chapel," Father Rivoli spoke on, "I saw swarms and swarms of bees. I ran back to my colonies. The hives had all been destroyed. I knew that it was she who had done this. She was a maniac.

"I went back to my room. I stayed there. I drank and I drank.

"A few days later I discovered that one of the abbey's gardeners had died of a bee sting. It seemed unusual but not impossible. However, the next day another death was reported. I was afraid to come out of my room. Instead I continued to drink. I drank to forget. I drank not to remember.

"The native workers started to die one by one. Another plague had invaded the villa. I stayed secluded in my room. I ignored the knocking at my door. I saw no one for weeks. I wallowed in my own shame and disgust. Finally, I ventured out. Many persons were dead. They had been buried without a proper funeral due to my weaknesses.

"Strangely, the nuns at first seemed to me to be unaffected. But soon they too started to act strangely. I noticed that several bottles of the . . ."

Suddenly, a slight creak was heard above the two. There was a hint of light.

"*Vada! Ape! Vada!*" the old man shouted.

Alejandro blew out his candle and threw the burlap sack over his head and shoulders. Slowly and carefully he started to retreat, walking backwards with his arms stretched out.

He heard clomping steps slowly approaching the cell. *Should I stay? I can try to figure out what is going on? But did the priest just warn me off?*

Eight, nine, ten, . . . Alejandro tried to remain calm.

He paused. He could not see in the darkness, but he

thought that a figure was drawing near to the cell of the prisoner.

"Talking to yourself again, Father?" laughed a wispy, feminine voice.

There was no response.

"Here is your food."

"Thank you, Sister Anna."

"My! You are polite today."

Alejandro surmised that Father Rivoli was trying to tell him about something. He left walking slowly and trying not to make any noise.

"Mother Superior has not been happy with you." This was last thing he heard.

The voices had faded. Alejandro was now out of earshot of Father Rivoli. His head was drenched in sweat as he reached the turn in the tunnel. From here he walked cautiously without the aid of a candle. He felt along the walls and used them as guides. The debris on the floor was often slippery and sharp.

Still perspiring in the cool, damp air, he finally succeeded in making his way back to the passageway entrance.

He left one of the sacks and the remaining candles inside the passageway. He took his clean shirt from the other burlap sack.

The fresh air hit him full in the face. It felt cool and invigorating. Alejandro inhaled again and again.

Alejandro dashed into the groves. He picked several plump orangish mangoes. He threw these into a sack but not until he had devoured a ripe, juicy one.

He walked rapidly up to the pond. He wanted to share his experience with Melissa. He wanted to tell her about Father Rivoli. He splashed water on himself and tried to clean up.

He waited and waited. But Melissa never arrived.

Slowly he made his way back to the abbey building. He left the fruit on top of the wooden table in the empty kitchen. Alejandro returned to his room and lay on his bed. He was exhausted and closed his eyes. *That man is crazy. But why had Sister Anna told Father Rivoli that Mother Superior was not happy with him?*

Does Mother Superior simply incarcerate people because they displease her? Am I in danger because of my actions with Melissa? Alejandro was now very worried.

CHAPTER 29

TRANSFORMATIONS

The night before, Alejandro had slept badly. His mind was agitated. He was confused about Father Rivoli and what had been said. He was worried that he might be in grave danger. He was anxious about when he might be able to leave the abbey. Melissa also concerned him.

There was a solid knock at the door. Sister Beatriz walked in briskly. He felt that he was still on the outs.

"How are you, my son?"

"Fine, Sister," he replied cautiously. He pulled on his ear lobes. He often performed this little ritual when he was tired. For some reason Alejandro thought it energized him.

"Are you taking it easy?" she asked in an inquisitive manner. "I pray that you are not trying to do too much."

"Yes, Sister."

"Very well."

"But I still would like to know when I can go home," he blurted.

"You have been told that we are isolated from the rest of the world. You need to be patient."

Alejandro remained mute.

"Mother Superior would like you to join her for dinner again tomorrow night," she skillfully changed the subject.

"Yes, Sister," he nodded submissively. His mind thought back. He had experienced terrible nightmares the last time he dined with Mother Superior. He had drunk too much.

He needed to be more circumspect. *Oh, well!* He surmised.

"I'll come to retrieve you."

"Yes, Sister."

She whirled around and left the room.

Alejandro finished cleaning himself up. He went downstairs to the kitchen where he ran into Marica.

"Good morning, Marica."

"Good morning," she motioned for him to sit down at the table.

She brought him some hot quinoa with honey. He drank some orange juice.

"Marica, how long have you been here at the abbey?"

She gazed at him suspiciously. "A long time."

He grinned. "A long time," he repeated.

"Yes, a long time," she asserted, but then she turned her face away from him and left the room as if she was in a hurry.

Alejandro finished eating. He grabbed some fruit and bread and exited the building.

Cautiously, he made his way down through the orchards, trying to make sure that he wasn't observed by anyone. The sun was hot with a cloud puff or two in the clear blue sky. The flowers sweated their fragrances as bees buzzed overhead.

Within a brief time, he was at the entrance to the underground passageway. He took off his shirt and packed it into the burlap bag. He drew out the candles that he had previously left in the other sack and lit one of them.

One, two, three, . . . He repeated the cadence of his previous journeys. Alejandro passed through the passageway almost tripping on one of the skulls lying on the path. Cautiously, he proceeded past the catacombs.

Finally, he came upon the cell of Father Rivoli.

"Father! I'm back."

"Yes, Señor Rubí. It's good to hear your voice," a sound echoed back.

"Are you okay?"

"Yes," said the frail being. "Did you bring any wine?"

"Sorry, no. Just some food." The wily hands reached from within the bars and seized the viands.

"That's good. They starve me down here!" he cried out.

Alejandro heard the priest smacking his lips as he devoured the rations.

"Garlic! Garlic! I need garlic!"

"Okay. I'll see what I can do. Do you need a blanket or anything else?"

"No, my friend, I'm way beyond earthly pleasures. I am suffering. My soul is dying. Neither cold nor heat affect this broken down temple.'

"Father, was that Sister Anna who came down here yesterday?"

"Yes. She is my caretaker," he heaved a sigh. "Or should I say my jailer."

"Did she know that I was here?" Alejandro was afraid of his forays being discovered.

"No. She is almost blind and can barely hear. Just like me," he chortled with a raspy cough.

"Yesterday you were telling me about the mysterious outbreak that hit this place. You said that it was maybe caused by bee stings?"

"Did you bring any wine? I'm very thirsty."

"Sorry, no. You were telling me about this plague."

"Ah, yes. One by one the inhabitants of the villa started to expire. The nuns were frightened. They were taking care of the dying. The buildings became quarantined. The food supplies were dwindling away." He mumbled as he recounted his story. The words were dripping in sorrow.

"My temptress came to me. I let her in my room. She looked at me. I looked at her. She was looking wrinkled and aged. In any event, we made love. I gave her what little food I had left. She wanted still more. She consumed the mead nectar and the royal jelly. She became crazed. She seized the powders, tinctures, and concoctions from the apothecarist's chest. She ran off with them. There was nothing that I could do to stop her! She dispensed them to her sister nuns. She thought that she could save them from the plague. Little did we know that this was a helpless situation.

"Father, why was she giving these potions or whatever to the sisters?" Alejandro could not understand what the priest was ranting about.

"She was so demented! She thought that she could prevent the nuns from dying. She made me crazy. She survived the plague. Or so, we all thought. She wanted to save her nuns. All I could do was to drink and drink and drink. I lamented in my room. I remained there for days."

"During these cursed times, once or twice the family members of the villa sought me out. One of the young sons asked me to administer the last sacraments, but I was incoherent. I couldn't. I failed them. I broke my sacred vows. I didn't perform the last rites for them! They couldn't go to heaven!" he rambled on until he finally broke down and began sobbing. It took Rivoli a few minutes before he resumed his narrative.

"Then one morning my seductress reappeared at my quarters and informed me that all of the abbey's natives were deceased. I wept for my betrayal. I was the cause of their deaths!"

Alejandro was caught between being bored and losing

patience.

"But that was just the beginning of the scourge!" he shouted. "Some of the nuns had also died, including Mother Superior! The previous one. The Spaniard. At the same time my enchantress was changing."

"I am not following. What do you mean, Father?" Alejandro interrupted.

"Metamorphosis."

"I still don't understand."

"Each day she became less human and more apian. Her body was aging rapidly."

"I still don't understand."

"My temptress now came to me every day. I just couldn't control myself. We would consume the mead nectar and royal jelly, and then make love.

"However, the intercourse became less and less frequent and more difficult. She was evolving. Her skin seemed to loosen and wrinkle and became yellowish. She became wider and rounder. Her eyes bulged and became darker. Then finally I became aware that she was an abomination, created by my concoctions and me.

"I refused to make love to her. She became livid with the rejection. She had me thrown into this cell. They haven't let me out for years. I'm too weak. I'm just ready to die."

"They do feed you, though?"

"Yes. But only the mead nectar and fruits. No wine."

"But why do they continue to punish you?"

"I'm not really being punished. I'm being held captive. I have been a failure for the most part. I was supposed to help them propagate.

"You are not saying that the nuns were using you to breed, are you?" Alejandro asked incredulously. "Why wouldn't they simply bring in new novitiates from the old country?" he questioned naively.

"They didn't want anyone to know their secret. Their sacrilegious transformations.

"Besides, my temptress was obsessed with me. Most of their blasphemous experiments to use me to reproduce failed. They tried potions. They tried conjugal visitations with native girls to arouse me. And finally, they tried deprivation and incarceration. But they rarely succeeded, no matter what they tried.

"Now they are becoming extinct. They are blaming me."

"Father, how long have you been confined here?" Alejandro broke in. *What in the heck was Rivoli rambling about? Transformations? Metamorphosis? Sounds too Kafkaesque.*

"Many years. I don't know."

"Did the temptress die?"

"No, my friend, this is why I am warning you. She is still alive. Sister Isabel. She is now the Mother Superior! Be vigilant! She will try to make you a love slave. You are in grave danger!"

"What?" Alejandro was dumbfounded. *Holy crap!* This couldn't be true. Yet, he pondered, it was consistent with some of the eerie happenings at the abbey.

"Trust no one. The possible exception is a native woman by the name of Marica, if she is still around."

"Father," Alejandro interjected, "there is a cook here at the abbey by name of Marica. She is about fifty years old." *Why her?* He deliberated. He was alarmed.

"That's probably her. She can be trusted. I fathered a daughter with her niece. That is, at least, that was what I was led to believe."

"Who is this child?" *Holy crap! This guy is insane! I don't know who is crazier, him or me!*

"I can't remember," the priest mumbled. "I'm getting tired."

"What was her name?" Alejandro pressed. "Maybe, I can ask Marica about her."

"Maybe, it's Melissa," came a faint reply. "I think."

Melissa! He couldn't believe it. *Holy crap! It can't be!* Alejandro's love was the daughter of this condemned priest. "Father, she's here at the abbey."

"Oh, God! No! That's impossible!" the priest cried out. "Oh, how much more punishment must I endure?"

"Would you like to see her? I could bring her," he tried to calm the priest down.

"I don't know, my friend. She probably doesn't know about me. She would hate me. Why is she even here?"

"Actually, Father, she believes that she was abandoned by her parents and has been raised as an orphan here."

"These nuns are so deceitful. God will strike them down," he coughed and then spit.

"Father, have you not asked for forgiveness yourself?"

"I have tried, but I fear not even God can pardon me for all that I have sinned. The prayer of this wretched dog can not penetrate the heavens."

"But, Father, our parish priest taught us that as Mary Magdalene was absolved, we too can be exonerated. A wrong confessed is already half-forgiven. "

"Yes, you are right. God has sent you to me to try to salvage my soul. It is often said that God does not strike with both hands. You have shown me the light in the darkness of this abyss of Dante's *Inferno.* Thank you. God bless you."

"You're welcome," Alejandro replied meekly. "Father, is there any way to escape from the convent? How far is the next village?"

"I don't remember."

"I can try to help you and Melissa escape from here."

"I'm too weak. I could not make it. It would be too dangerous for you." A mocking laugh could be heard coming from the cell. "God sometimes sends almonds to one that has no teeth."

Alejandro didn't understand what he meant.

"We could at least try."

The flame of the candle flickered as it burned down.

CHAPTER 30

DUPED

Alejandro was sweating profusely as he exited the subterranean tunnel. He ran his hand through his hair as he tried to collect his thoughts. Was the old priest delusional? The priest's incarceration. Maybe the captive was just plain crazy. Alejandro was feeling like he had been duped. How could he be a good lawyer if he didn't have any common sense and fell for every sob story?

On the other hand, very little had made sense to him at the convent. He himself was being held hostage, just like Father Rivoli.

His parents always believed what the nuns at the Ascension Elementary School said. If Alejandro was summoned to the principal's office, his mother and father would always take the side of the school. He was taught to respect and honor authority.

If Alejandro dared tell his parents that he was being held captive by a bedeviled nun/randy jezebel/bestial abomination, he would bring down the wrath of his father. Señor Rubí would shame him for slandering and disrespecting a religious prioress who had saved his life and who had given him shelter. He could imagine his mother weeping and praying to God about how it was her fault that her son had blasphemed against the Holy Church. Even his siblings would be too apprehensive to support him.

Chuy would tell him to just shut the f__k up. No use

in opening a can of worms. "It's none of your business," he would say.

But these nuns had imprisoned at least one person who happened to be a priest. They may have caused the death of who knows how many others. His moral compass told him that the right choice would be to tell someone about the mysterious secrets of the abbey.

Alejandro changed his clothes at the passage entrance where he had previously left the other burlap sack. He trudged deeply into the orchards and gingerly picked some low hanging fruit. He plucked mangoes and papayas and guavas.

He looked up. The skies were still sunny and clear. He took a deep breath. The air was fresh. He hated the stench of the subterranean tunnel.

His mind was still subconsciously preoccupied with the priest's tale.

Here I am a lawyer and my client has told me a seemingly outrageous fantasy. What has Professor Peña taught me? What should I do first?

Hmm. I might see if there was some sort of physical evidence. Oh, my God, I guess I could look at one of the skulls in the cavern. Holy crap! I wouldn't even know how to begin to examine a cranium.

He approached the buildings. The edifices were old and of a colonial style. The furnishings were at least a hundred years old. Or maybe even four hundred years. It would be too difficult to determine.

Upon entering his building, Alejandro emptied the fruit from the burlap sack onto the table in the kitchen. No one was present there. He withdrew into the hallway.

A thunderbolt struck him. He could talk to Marica.

Would she discuss such matters with him? Father Rivoli had told him that she could be trusted. She might be able to corroborate the priest's tale.

Nobody seemed to be in the chapel as he passed by. He returned to his room. His heart smiled. On top of his bed sat a sprig of lavender. This must be some sort of sign from Melissa. A token of love?

Alejandro sighed deeply with emotion. He fantasized about her. Her long raven black hair. Her penetrating violet eyes. Her smooth cinnamon skin. He wanted to taste her. To bite her. To have her.

I wonder what Melissa knows about Father Rivoli. Maybe I should ask her.

Then it dawned upon him. Could the lavender be a forewarning? Or was it a signal for him to attempt to see her again?

There was no note from her. Maybe she didn't know how to write.

Think! Think, man! Think logically!

It shouldn't be a caution. The lavender on top of his bed was too conspicuous. Maybe she would want me to meet her in the secret garden, near the fountain at the top of the hill. He frowned as he tried to guess the meaning of the floral sign.

Maybe I shouldn't think! I need to trust my emotions!
Quickly he freshened up a bit and bolted from the building.

Moments later he was climbing the stony stairs. As he trod by the fountain, he observed its intertwined design of masks and bees. *How was all this related?* He asked himself.

He reached the pool on the upper heights. The perfumed air assailed his senses. There was a rainbow of flowers about him. In the center of the clover bed, Melissa was posed on a polychromatic blanket.

She beamed lusciously at him as he approached.

"Hi, Alejandro," her ivory white teeth gleamed.

"Hi, my sweet thing," and he gazed into her doe eyes and kissed her. They fervently embraced each other. They were on Venus, millions of light years away from this planet. They were in another cosmos.

"What is happening to you? Are you okay?" he probed subtly.

"Yes, I'm fine. Marica has been keeping a keen eye on me."

"Melissa, are you related to her?"

"I don't think so," Melissa gave him a puzzled look. "Don't you remember that I told you that I was abandoned as a baby? The natives found me and the sisters raised me. Actually, Marica, come to think of it, has really been the one who has taken care of me."

"Has Marica ever told you about herself? Where she grew up? If she had any children?"

"No, not really. She has been a very private person. A very pious person. We are all very private at the convent. We devote our full attention to God and to the best interests of the abbey."

Alejandro thought that he could sense that she was a little defensive about Marica and was being protective of her.

"Why do you ask me about Marica?" she continued. "I have noticed that she has been very tense lately. Almost like she is afraid."

"Afraid of what?" he tried to probed further.

She moved away from him. "I don't know. When she and I talk, she looks around to see if anyone else is around."

"How do the nuns treat her?"

"All right, I guess. I don't see anything out of the ordinary.

"Alejandro, you sure are curious today. Is this what the outer world is all about? A preoccupation with the Inquisition?" she teased.

"No, I'm just a little bit interested, that's all," he shaded the truth.

Should I stop or not? I don't want to make her feel uncomfortable or disloyal.

"Kiss me then," she beckoned.

He reached over and grabbed her forcefully and licked her ruby lips. She giggled. He edged his way down her neck. She squealed.

"Who is Sister Anna?" he queried as he lips gently caressed her ear.

"She is one of the caretakers at the other building. She attends Mother Superior. She is a Spaniard. I would guess almost 60 years old. Why are you asking so many questions?" She bent over him and kissed him on the neck. Again and again.

"What?" He was drifting. "I don't know. I don't see her much." He kissed the nape of her neck. She tittered.

"Oh, she never leaves the other building. She is ancient and is blind in the sunlight. She seems very cold toward me."

"What do you know about Father Rivoli?"

"Who?" She pulled his reddish brown beard and feigned annoyance giving him a stern look. "Why are you so talkative?" Then she rolled over on top of him and pressed herself against him.

Alejandro sighed. *Go with the flow.*

The tenor sang of joy. The soprano counterpointed with love. There was a staccato of groans. The moans panted toward a crescendo. The duet spent the next hour consummating an aria of passion. The perfect opera.

CHAPTER 31

WARNING

It was early when Alejandro awoke the next morning. He could still smell the scent of lavender. He could still taste the essence of Melissa. His tongue slid from side to side, licking his upper teeth as he lay in bed fantasizing about her.

Finally, he decided to get up. Feeling a pang in his stomach, he hurried down to the kitchen to try to find Marica. She was not around.

After talking with Melissa the day before, he still had not learned about the mystery surrounding Father Rivoli. He really needed to confer with Marica.

Marica had left him a breakfast of quinoa with honey and currants. It was cold, but he ate it anyway. This was accompanied by his daily orange juice. He was hungry after his tryst with Melissa. He had not eaten dinner the night before.

Alejandro glanced around the kitchen. Where would Marica keep garlic? Inocente would have kept it in a little nondescript jar. In a cool, dry place. He didn't see any. Maybe Marica had a little herb garden behind the building.

He finished his breakfast and started toward the back door of the kitchen. He thought that this was an exit to the outside.

Suddenly, Sister Beatriz appeared at his side.

"Good morning, my son."

"Good morning, Sister," he replied, hiding the fact that

she had startled him.

"You are up early today," she gave him a giant smile. "How are you?"

"Fine. Better every day."

"Is there anything you need?"

"No, not really," he sheepishly grinned. "Just maybe a bath."

"That should be no problem. Remember that you are to dine with Mother Superior this evening."

"Yes, Sister," he had forgotten. Or maybe, he just wanted to repress the thought.

Sister Beatriz has positioned herself between him and the outside doorway. Alejandro wondered if she was blocking him. He judged that he shouldn't pursue his trek out the back door.

"With your permission, Sister," he departed from the kitchen and returned to his room. He gathered up the burlap sack and left the building. As he was leaving, he noticed that Rafaela was approaching from the direction of the orchards with a crate full of assorted fruits.

"Good morning, Rafaela," he gave her a cheerful greeting.

"Good morning, señor," she exchanged the salutation.

I wonder if she knows that I've been going down to the cavern. I'll have to be careful. I'll take a circuitous route there.

Alejandro set off in a different heading through the orchards. He was fortunate that there had not been any rain lately that could leave muddy tracks. He kept checking his back to see if he was being followed. There was no one around and only a swarm of bees near the flowerbeds.

He continued onward until finally, he discovered the tall iron gate that led from the bottom of the slope up to the abbey buildings. The entrance way looked impenetrable.

There was a huge metal chain with a large iron lock that secured the right of entry. He looked through the grating of the portals. Alejandro could see nothing but a massive green jungle on the outside.

He meandered to his left for about thirty or forty paces. The ocher-colored adobe wall that encompassed this domain averaged between three to four meters in height. There were tall cottonwood trees that grew along this section of the wall. Alejandro contemplated that if he wanted to, he could scale a tree and then jump over the protective walled barrier.

He strayed back through the orchards. As he did so, he picked some papayas. After becoming disoriented a few times, he eventually found the rose-covered mound.

Alejandro backtracked and picked a few very ripe mangoes. Then he returned to the wooden door that led to the underground tunnel.

He scouted around. It looked like everything had remained untouched. He took off his shirt.

Alejandro seized a few candles and tried to light one with his lighter. The lighter sputtered at first, but at last fired up.

One, two, three, . . . Carefully, he started down the passageway. The same rhythmic cadence. Down the tunnel he trekked.

About ten minutes later, he arrived at Father Rivoli's cell. His hand covered his face to minimize the stench.

"Father, I'm here," he whispered in a soft tone.

There was no response, only silence.

"Father, are you there?" he called out a little louder.

There was further silence.

He held the candle to the metal bars of the cell. He moved the light from side to side. He could barely discern a bulge on the floor.

"Father!" he exclaimed.

A feeble voice whispered. "Yes. Yes, I'm here."

"Are you all right?"

"Bene," the priest responded without conviction. He coughed and it sounded like he spit out some sputum.

"Here, Father," Alejandro offered him the ripe mangoes and papayas. Two withered stems of hands slowly reached out and took the offering. Alejandro could barely make out two yellow beady eyes and a toothless mouth. The priest seemed to consume the fruit exceptionally slowly today.

"What is the matter, Father?"

"I'm going to die. Maybe today. Maybe tomorrow. Not much longer."

"Don't say that, Father. Please don't despair!"

There was another cough. "I'm not forlorn. I'm actually at peace. The Lord is hearing my prayers. I'm asking for forgiveness. To be forgiven for all my sins!"

"I'm pleased, Father. Quite pleased."

"But you are in grave danger. When I die, they will make you assume my place. The future does not portend good tidings for you if you remain here."

"Father, I still don't understand. Why would they (whoever they are) lock me up like you?"

"Oh, God, I have the curse of Cassandra. I can see into the future, but I can't change it. Do you really not understand? Have I failed to warn you of the ominous peril?" The old man choked.

"Tell me, Father, what is wrong?" Alejandro was getting more and more worried. More ranting and raving?

"This place is evil. This place is a blasphemy! This place is an abomination! God will smite it down for its depravities. Drunkenness! Debauchery! Carnal knowledge!"

Alejandro noted that Father Rivoli was spouting words similar to those that Mother Superior had utilized at the funeral of Sister Sophia.

"You will be the drone."

"Drone? What drone? What are you saying?"

"You will have to take my place. The Order needs to survive. They need you to survive. They need you to breed so that they can regenerate and survive."

"Order? What order?" Alejandro was alarmed. "Breed? What breed? What are you talking about? I don't understand a word that you are saying!"

"Yes, I know. I have not been able to service them in the propagation. They have almost all died. Only a few remain. There is not much time left for them."

"I still don't understand. You don't really mean sleeping with the nuns?" Alejandro felt embarrassed. He thought that Father Rivoli was now expounding on his own sexual relations with the nuns. How ludicrous!

I am feeling guilty for tolerating such impure thoughts. I've probably committed a mortal sin for such evil thinking.

"No! No! I did not sleep with just anyone. I used to lay with Mother Superior, my temptress. Later, I became her drone."

"Father, are you saying that you were forced to have sexual intercourse with Mother Superior?"

"Yes, at first I seduced her. Then later, I was her drone."

"But yesterday I thought you said that you had slept with a native woman and that Melissa is your daughter."

"That is what I am also trying to tell you. You must escape from this hell. You must take Melissa away from here. Promise me!"

Alejandro now thought that the priest was a schizophrenic

fool. "Okay, Father, I promise." What difference would such a pledge make to such a lunatic?

Father Rivoli continued with his narration about the gruesome and vulgar details of his captivity and the forced attempts at copulation. Alejandro listened silently in disbelief and horror. Alejandro on the one hand wanted to be supportive of this poor old soul. But how could he believe Rivoli's ludicrous story?

Alejandro's father's cousin was a doctor. A medical and psychological examination might indicate that the priest was suffering from malnutrition. His hysteria was a byproduct of such an infirmity. Or maybe it was from alcoholism?

None of this made sense.

Father Rivoli's voice seemed to grow feeble. Finally, he ceased talking.

"Father, are you all right?"

There was no answer. And then unexpectedly there was snoring from within the priest's cell.

I have a million questions? Where do I begin? I need to find some answers. Quickly!

Where did the stairs lead? He climbed up the steps from Rivoli's cell. He ebbed back to the left from where he thought that Sister Anna had come the day before.

One, two, three, . . . with circumspection he advanced in this new direction.

He ambled about fifty paces over a smooth, dirt surface. The atmosphere became warmer and warmer. There was an olfactory mélange of gardenia, roses, and cloves. Old timber beams supported the walls.

The surfaces of the walls felt sticky to him. He raised the candle and lowered it, then raised it again. Then he moved it from side to side. He discerned six-sided shelves within huge hexagons. The larger forms measured over three meters across.

His hands explored the openings. There was a waxy, viscous substance that sealed some of the internal shapes. This was not a wine cellar. This was not a nook for aging cheese.

Looking around he discovered small baskets of yellow powder in some of the cavities. The features looked familiar, but he couldn't recollect what they were.

He went further down the tunnel and almost tripped upon a wooden staircase leading upwards. He had tallied about another fifty paces. Could this lead to Mother Superior's quarters?

Alejandro was tempted to ascend the stairs. But he thought that he might get caught. There could be additional danger to Father Rivoli.

He decided to retrace his steps. *One, two, three,* . . .

At the count of one hundred, he had returned to Father Rivoli's cell. There was now only calm.

"Father, I'm leaving."

There was no reply.

He repeated his intent to leave. Still no response came forth.

Attentively he tried to perceive any sound or movement. There was none.

Was Rivoli sleeping or was he dead? Alejandro decided to leave.

One, two, three, . . .

About fifteen minutes later, he came to the entrance of the cavern. Alejandro was exhausted and drenched with sweat. He changed back into his clean shirt.

He wiped some of the dirt and stickiness off his hands.

He needed desperately to bathe.

Alejandro's hunger forced him to eat some of the remaining fruit that he had picked earlier.

Cautiously he hiked up the slope, taking a roundabout way to avoid being seen.

CHAPTER 32

MAGIC MUSHROOMS

Alejandro decided to walk up to the pond. It was early afternoon. The sun was hot and the air a little humid. A while later he arrived there. Melissa was not around. Maybe she had already finished washing clothes, he thought.

Alejandro splashed water on himself at the pond. His soul was tired. What Father Rivoli had told him couldn't be true. It was an aberration of nature. It was heresy. It was probably dementia.

Slowly he trekked backed to his building, sighing deeply. He went to the kitchen and dropped off the few mangoes that he had remaining.

There was a glass of orange juice and some bread on the table.

Marica was still not around.

Alejandro inhaled the liquid and ate a little of the roll.

He left the kitchen and walked by the chapel. He heard a humming sound. There were nuns seated in the pews.

At the top of the stairs, he speculated that a bath might be ready. He was confident that Sister Beatriz would ensure that he was presentable for his dinner that evening. He opened the door to the storage room. He saw that there was water already prepared. He sprang over and dipped his hand in. It was on the cool side. But it really didn't matter.

Alejandro dashed back to his bedroom. There were clean clothes on top of the bed. He clasped them securely and went back to the bathing room.

Hastily, he disrobed and slowly slid his naked body into the small tub. He was chilled. Shivers ran up and down his body. He put both of his hands into the nippy liquid so as to acclimate himself to the water's temperature.

After a little quivering, he was finally partially submerged. With a bar of Castile soap, he lathered himself. He washed his hair and beard. He felt a little better even though there were goose bumps blanketing his nude body.

He sat for a long time trying to forget his encounter with Father Rivoli. His body trembled and he was still tired.

He quickly arose from the tub with his teeth chattering and dried himself with a large white towel. He put on the clean clothes and traipsed back to his room. He decided to crawl under the blanket on top of the bed without disrobing.

What should I believe? Everything seems so unreal.

Images floated through his mind. It almost seemed like the fairy tales that his mother told to him when he was four years old. There were monsters and ogres and witches. Parents always thought that these fables were cute and innocent, but in truth, they were filled with sorcery, death, and mayhem.

There were curses. There were evil spells. There were slimy and loathsome creatures. Thumbelina . . .

Toad princes swam by. Haggish sorceresses cackled over their vile brews. Fiery dragons attacked the peasants.

There was a sharp rap at the door. Alejandro awoke with a start. Sister Beatriz came in.

How long was I asleep?

"Are you ready, my son?"

"Yes, Sister."

Ready for what? He was still drowsy from his nap. *Oh, tonight is another dinner with Mother Superior.*

He groggily climbed out of bed and tried to comb his hair with his hand.

Sister Beatriz escorted him from the room and together they strolled over to the other building.

"How was your day, my son?"

"Fine." His mind was still clouded. Did she suspect anything?

"How was your bath?"

"Fine," he was wondering what she knew about his day. "Thank you."

"You're welcome, my son."

Alejandro was becoming more alert and awake now.

As the two proceeded toward Mother Superior's building, Sister Beatriz asked Alejandro if he knew anything about botany. He replied no. He postulated that the question was a bit odd, but assumed that she was trying to make pleasant conversation. She was, at least, more at ease than she had been a few days before.

"Sister, how often do new nuns arrive here?" he rejoined.

"Unfortunately, my son, we haven't had any come for a long time."

"Do they come from Spain or Italy . . ." Damn! He had let it slip from his mouth. "Or Portugal or France?"

F__k! I hope that I have not given Sister Beatriz the notion that I have been speaking with Father Rivoli.

"Like I said, we haven't had any new arrivals for eons. Well, here we are, my son." They had reached the foyer and progressed into the formal dining room.

Mother Superior was seated at the large oak table. It looked like she was reclined against puffy red cushions. She was conferring in inaudible tones with Sister Teresa. She stopped and raised her head toward the two visitors.

"Welcome, Señor Rubí," Mother Superior greeted him.

"Good evening," he smiled charmingly.

"How has been your stay so far?"

"Fine. Thank you." He watched her like a hawk. He wanted to be alert. Was she really a licentious temptress or just an old hag nun like he had at the Ascension Elementary School? He would be vigilant.

Mother Superior glanced at both Sister Beatriz and Sister Teresa. They immediately left the room.

"Please be seated."

He sat down and pulled in the wooden chair. There was no seat pillow and it felt hard against his backside.

Mother Superior said grace with Alejandro mouthing an "amen" at the end.

Sister Teresa reentered the room and started to fill his nectar glass.

"Oh, no, thank you." He remembered the terrible experience he had the last time he had imbibed with Mother Superior.

"Just a little?" Sister Teresa offered.

"No, thank you, I'm not used to drinking anymore." He gave her a childish grin.

The nun looked curiously at Mother Superior who nodded her head affirmatively.

"What would like to drink?" asked his hostess.

"Just juice, please."

Moments later, Sister Teresa brought him a glass of orange juice. He gulped it down without really tasting it.

"My son, how would you feel about staying a little longer around here? We need some assistance in bringing the abbey back to its full promise."

"I'm sorry, Mother Superior, but as I have told you

before, I need to go back home to my family. And I have a job, I hope, when I return."

Why did she ask that question? Is this what Father Rivoli was talking about?

"Yes, I know. I know that Providence has rescued you and we are grateful to you for coming into our lives."

Sister Teresa served him a bowl of mushrooms and spinach swimming in a steamy broth. It smelled wonderful.

Alejandro dipped his bread into the soup and sopped it up.

Mother Superior did not discourse much. She seemed simply to be studying Alejandro.

As for Alejandro, he was just famished. He devoured everything.

After he finished the main courses, Sister Teresa brought in the gelatinous dessert terrine that he had consumed the time before. He took a nibble. He recalled how it tasted previously. He was ambivalent.

"Mother Superior, excuse me, but I think I'm quite full tonight."

"Yes, Alejandro. I see. You have been under much stress lately," her wrinkled face said grinning. "Melissa is a mere child. She doesn't understand temptation. We must protect her. Disobedience is not tolerated here at the abbey . . ." Mother Superior began to rail against Melissa.

Alejandro felt his blood inflame. He was getting hotter and hotter. *Who was she to malign the girl that he loved? The young woman that he swore to himself to protect.* At several instances he wanted to interrupt her and defend Melissa's honor.

But to what end? Be calm. Be calm. I'm here to win the war, not to lose a futile battle. Professor Peña had taught his law students to be patient. To be calculating. To strike at the optimal time.

The legal scholar cautioned them not to think nor act with their stomachs, their hearts, or their genitalia. The class would burst out in laughter and point to one another. They were urged to think with their brains.

Chuy would suggest that he had two brains and they would laugh.

"Melissa does not seem suited to becoming a nun. Maybe she could marry a local native, but she has so very little in common with the Momos. If only there was a suitable solution. What would you suggest, Señor Rubí? You are quite erudite. You seem to have some affection for this young stray."

Alejandro was pensive. Was she trying to bait him? He smelled a trap. It was like he was in the chess game of life.

"I don't know, Mother Superior," he played his "naïveté'" pawn. He did not want to seem too anxious. He did not want to commit his game pieces too early. "Perhaps she could accompany me when I return to Mexico City," he suggested with an impish smile. "There are convents and boarding schools there. I'm sure that my parents would do their Christian duty as far as Melissa is concerned."

"Impossible!" she blurted. *Was this an overreaction or had Mother Superior overplayed her strategy?* "I could not permit that innocent child to enter the insidious world of man! She would be taken advantage of. What would your Christian duty entail? How could she be protected? She couldn't survive out there. Can't you comprehend that? None of us can. No, it wouldn't work," she tried to calm herself as she stared at the table in front of her.

Alejandro realized that her tirade revealed many strata of feelings and schemes. She is trying to lure him into remaining at the abbey. Melissa was being used as the pawn of "enticement".

He unconsciously frowned. His forehead started to erupt with beads of sweat. There was moisture creeping under his eyes.

Oh, f__k! My head is swirling!

Alejandro's head bobbled up and down like a float in an incoming tide. His eyes drowsily closed. There was a sigh emitted from his larynx.

Oh, man! I'm feeling strange.

Slowly he tried to open his eyes. Alejandro was in total oblivion. He felt a tingling on his body. At first it felt like tiny pin pricks. Then he imagined that there were little spiders with hairy legs climbing all over him. His breathing accelerated.

His back ached. He couldn't move his arms or legs or any other part of his body. He seemed conscious, but could not react to the intrusive stabs.

Alejandro thought he perceived a thick liquid being decanted all over his body. The atmosphere was being aerated with a putrid sweet smell. Very floral. He felt a lump in his throat. His esophagus was spasmodic. He wanted to lurch forward and vomit. He couldn't move his limbs.

He sensed some sort of brush spreading the fluid to and fro. He wanted to scream, but he couldn't.

The universe was silent, save for the fitful movements on his body.

The ambrosial syrup entered his mouth. The honeyed flow soared his mind into a psychedelic consciousness.

Blood pulsated through his body. Air molecules filled his bronchial cavities. Synapses were exploding like atomic bombs, a trillion times a second.

His irises flared. Red turned into blood. Yellow turned into the sun. Blue turned into the sky. Violet turned into spirits.

He could see the universe. He was the cosmos.

Who am I? What am I? Why?

CHAPTER 33

TEARS

The room was bright with sunlight. Alejandro's head pounded from within. He slowly opened his eyes. He found himself on top of the bed in his room, disheveled in his clothes.

What in the heck happened to me?

His kidneys ached. These organs sent sharp pains throughout his lower back. His thighbones felt extremely heavy. He hadn't felt this bad since he had influenza a few years before.

What bizarre dreams I had! There was a beautiful vamp that was trying to seduce me. As she approached me, she was transformed into a monster that looked part woman and part bee. This frigging abomination was sliming me with a long tongue. Ick!

What in the heck had he eaten? He had avoided the mead nectar intentionally last night. Did he have an allergic food reaction? He could and did eat everything. Or maybe he was being drugged?

He inhaled deeply. *Maybe Father Rivoli was right. I just need to leave this place.*

For the remainder of the morning he rested on top of his bed trying to recollect what had occurred the night before. Something sinister was occurring, but he couldn't figure out what it was. There was no plausible explanation for his dream or for how he felt. What was the purpose of the ritualistic dinner? He no longer trusted Mother Superior or anyone, for that matter. That's what Father Rivoli had advised him.

Finally, in spite of the threat of vertigo, he rose and voided himself at the chamber pot in the corner.

Should he try to eat something? Neither Sister Beatriz nor anyone else had looked in on him that morning. Food did not seem appetizing. But maybe some hot tea and dry toast would settle his stomach.

He exited his room and gingerly walked down the stairs to the kitchen. He felt nauseous and he held his hand over his stomach.

There, Marica was humming merrily to herself. She seemed to be preparing a large meal for the nuns.

"Good morning, Señor Rubí" she greeted him with a smile. She had a different temperament from the last time he saw her.

"Good morning, Marica," he slumped into the chair next to the large oak table.

She continued to chop up some vegetables with a large cleaver.

"Are you hungry?" she looked around to observe him. "What would you like to eat?"

"I'm not really hungry," he gave her a forlorn look. "I'm not feeling that great."

"Nonsense. You have to have something in your stomach. Don't you know that all pains with bread are less," she was trying to comfort him. "I know that you didn't have any breakfast yet this morning. Now, what would you like?"

"Maybe some hot tea, please," he asked in a boyish tone. "And some toast."

"Done," she declared as she swaggered to the overhead cupboard to get a cup.

"The dinner with Mother Superior did not sit well with me. I'm probably not used to the food and water from these parts. Maybe I have a bacterial infection or a parasite."

Marica did not react. She simply kept silent. She continued to toast some bread for him.

"Oh, excuse me, Marica, you don't cook for Mother Superior, do you? I don't mean to offend you."

"No, señor. Sister Teresa is the only one who is permitted to cook for Mother Superior."

Alejandro had cast his fishing line into the lake. The fish has seen the bait. Reel it in slowly, Alejandro thought. Don't scare the fish.

"Marica, you told me that you have lived here a long time. I assume that you came here from a local tribe."

"Yes, but that was a very long time ago. I don't remember much."

"The local natives are called Momos, aren't they? Are you from their tribe?"

"Yes. I was brought here when I was young."

"Do you know why you were brought here?"

"The nuns needed help. My father gave me to the convent to work." She gently placed the cup of tea in front of him with the toasted bread. "Do you want some fruit preserves or honey?"

"Yes, I'll take some fruit preserves please," he broke off a piece of toast. "Did your father want you to become a nun or did he intend that you become educated?"

"I don't remember. It was a long time ago. I never learned to read or write." She placed a bowl of strawberry preserves in front of him. "I just heard that my father was some type of medicine man."

"Did you ever visit your father and family?"

"I was told that my father died several years ago. The only family I have now is . . ." she stopped. She knew that she had probably shared too much about herself already.

Timing. Timing. Time to jerk the line. "Is Melissa related to you?" he inquired as he penetrated deeply into her squinted dark brown eyes.

Marica glanced around and then said with hesitation, "Yes." It seemed that a giant weight had been lifted from her shoulders. Her secret was out.

"Is Melissa your niece's daughter?"

"Yes, but how did you know that?" her face gave him a surprised look. "She doesn't even know about this!" She was exasperated. Marica was trying to read his mind.

"Marica, who was Melissa's father?"

It was as if he had struck her with a fatal blow. The color left her face. Her stealth was about to be unveiled. She fought back her fears. She remained mute.

Alejandro sensed that the woman felt threatened. He needed to proceed with caution. He didn't want the fish to jump off the line.

He put his head in his right hand and supported his right arm with his left palm on top of the table.

"Melissa believes that she was abandoned as a child by the natives and discovered in the hills by Father Rivoli. That is not true, is it?"

"No," she replied in sotto voce. Her eyes started to well up.

"Melissa doesn't even know that you are her great aunt, does she?"

"No, señor," she looked away and broke into sobs. She lifted her apron up to her face to cover the deluge of tears. "I'm so ashamed!" she keened. "I should have told her the truth. But I was afraid for her."

Alejandro sprang up from the table and put his arms around her. He wanted to console her. Her chubby cheeks rested against his chest. He had caught the fish. But what did he do now?

"Marica, Melissa loves you. She knows that you are the one who raised her all these years."

She sniffled.

"Why don't you tell her? I know that she will be very happy."

"Do you think so?" she voiced what her heart had been searching for all those years. She was in a human dilemma. She no longer wanted to remain silent.

"Yes, of course," he said confidently.

"I don't know. There are some things around here that go unspoken. I don't want to run afoul of the nuns."

Timing. Timing. Time to net the fish into the creel.

"Like what happened with Father Rivoli?"

Marica gasped. Her body started to weave. She had almost fainted from the shock of having the curse of the abbey being exposed.

"Who told you about him?" she inadvertently blurted. She could not feign ignorance any longer.

"I have talked to him."

She withdrew from him and sat herself down at the table with her arms sustaining her head. She pushed back her hair several times.

"Marica, he told me that I could trust you. Is that true?"

"Yes. Unfortunately, it is," she wiped her eyes with the heel of her hand. "I'm surprised that he is still alive after all of these years. I only hear bits and pieces of chatter. The nuns are oblivious to my presence. They think that I am a dumb and ignorant native. They are supposed to observe certain periods of silence throughout the day. Sometimes they don't. At times they even gossip when I'm around."

Her barriers seemed to have come crashing down. Alejandro now decided he had to roll the dice to see what fate had in store for him.

"Marica, I have a very important question to ask you? You would be doing me a great favor if you told me the truth."

"Yes," she replied waiting for the unexpected.

"Am I in danger here at the convent?"

"Yes," she stated without an ounce of hesitation.

"Are the nuns going to permit me to leave the convent?"

"No," she continued.

"Is Melissa safe here?"

"I don't know. I want to think so, but I am uncertain," she started to sob again.

"Marica, then you know that I must leave here. You understand. I know that I can trust you. You need to trust me. I vowed to Father Rivoli that I would protect Melissa from the evil forces around here. I will make you the same promise. I swear it.

"Right now I will be going to the pond where Melissa washes clothes. I need to meet with Melissa and talk with her."

Marica was listening attentively.

He stuttered, "I will ask her if she wants to join me in my escape from here."

Her eyes closed. Her heart was breaking. Her eyes were swollen with tears of pain.

"Thank you, Marica," he rushed over and pecked her forehead.

As he departed, she shouted, "may God be with you."

Sister Beatriz was leaving the chapel as Alejandro passed by hurriedly. They exchanged hurried salutations.

As he walked outside of the building, Sister Beatriz walked toward the kitchen.

CHAPTER 34

MISTRUST

Could Alejandro really trust Marica? He wanted to, but what if Sister Beatriz found the old woman crying in the kitchen? That could arouse the nun's suspicions. He was apprehensive. *I'm not going to trust anyone.*

Alejandro hurried along past the fountain and up the path that led to the pond. He heard the gravel under his feet as he forged ahead. Rafaela was nowhere to be found. The air was hot and smelled peppery. The bees were swarming over the honeysuckle.

At last, he reached the pool. Melissa was not there. He threw some water on his face.

The adrenaline rush in conversing with Marica had cured his headache.

How was he going to escape? Wasn't he afraid for his own safety? What was that the real reason that he wanted Melissa to accompany him? His mind raced. *I need to get home!*

Alejandro reminisced about his family. He missed them dearly. They most likely thought he was dead. Who could advise him what to do? What was the path of truth? Alejandro could not hide from his own conscience.

His father would always recite dichos to him to help in making a decision or to impart wisdom. In this case, he might articulate the proverb that a soul alone neither sings nor weeps. However, Señor Rubí might also say that love is blind to reason. *Where there's life, there's hope,* Alejandro thought.

A while later, Melissa came rushing to the pond. She was panting from trying to reach him. Her cheeks were flushed. Her hair was disheveled.

"Alejandro!" she threw her arms around him and embraced him tightly. It was like she never wanted to let him go. She pulled him closer.

He kissed her full on the mouth. He felt her heart beat against his chest. Her sweat whetted his appetite.

"How are you, my love? You look worried." He sat her down at the edge of the pond. "Is anything wrong?" He gave her a reassuring smile. He held her right hand in both of his.

"Marica. Marica just told me that I'm her niece's daughter," she murmured out of breath. "I don't understand what is going on around here. Everybody has been lying to me."

He squeezed her hand. "Marica was just trying to protect you. She loves you."

"What is she protecting me from?" she exclaimed in a piqued tone. "Does she think that I am still a little girl? Does everyone want to treat me like a child?"

"From the nuns," he blatantly replied.

"What!" she exploded in shock. "What can they do to me? They're old and blind."

"All is not what it seems to be. Let me share a few things with you. Hear me out."

Alejandro recounted his bizarre visits with Father Rivoli She was very attentive while he gave her the sordid details.

"Father Rómulo Rivoli was born in Valencia in 1927. In addition, to being a priest, he was trained as a chemist and vinoculturist. He came to México to help cultivate ecclesiastical wines . . ."

Melissa did not interrupt the commentary, but her mouth gaped open with astonishment.

"He arrived at the abbey here to help the Spaniards grow grapes. He had carnal knowledge with Mother Superior . . ."

"Alejandro! For heaven's sake, what are you saying?" Melissa jumped up. She stared intently at Alejandro.

"I'm just telling you what he told me."

"It's too crazy. I don't believe it!"

"I didn't either," he put his hand on her shoulder to try to calm her down. "But it explains some of the strange things around here."

He told her about her own background. He related that her own mother was a Momo and that she died giving birth to Melissa. However, Father Rivoli suspected that Mother Superior was the cause of her death.

"Stop!" Melissa pounded on Alejandro's chest with her clenched fists. "I don't want to hear anymore. I can't believe any of this!"

"And Father Rivoli is your father," he rapidly added.

"What! I don't believe you. You're crazy!" she was agitated. Her mouth was twisted with revulsion. Her body was squirming. "Where is he? I want to see him! I don't believe he's alive!"

"Wait! There's more."

He continued to narrate about the metamorphosis of Mother Superior and the nuns into nonhuman forms.

Melissa's face was frozen with ire. She was fidgeting with anger. She glared at Alejandro with hateful eyes. Her hands were clenched.

"You're speaking blasphemy!" she shrieked as she pulled away from him. "Shame on you!"

"If only it weren't true," his head hung down before

her. "Do you know about the dinners that I have had with Mother Superior? She has tried to poison me or seduce me!"

He raised his head. He spoke excitedly, because he was losing patience at her resistance.

"I don't believe you. You're crazy. You are discrediting my belief in God and in my religion. I can't understand why you are saying these things." She wanted to run from him, but she didn't.

"You don't have to believe me, Melissa. But as my father would say, the devil lurks behind the cross."

He pulled her hand back into his. He could sense that she wanted to resist. She was shaking her head from side to side. Her eyes stared outward in disbelief.

"My love, there is one way to find out the truth. Ask Marica."

Melissa did not respond. Her gaze sunk into the depths of the pond. She put her other hand in the water and skimmed the surface creating little waves.

"Melissa, the reason that I needed to meet with you so urgently is to ask you to escape with me from this place."

Still no reply was forthcoming.

"I plan to leave from here tomorrow around early afternoon. I want you to come with me."

The lull persisted.

"If you want to join me, meet me here at midday." He did not ask for a commitment. He was just laying out a plan. He was being matter of fact. Yet he knew in his heart that trying to overpower her would not be fair. Her look told him that she was vulnerable.

He looked at her intently. "Listen, I really want you to come with me."

Melissa continued to stare into the water.

"We'll need some food and water. I can gather some fruit from the orchards tomorrow morning.

"And, let's see, we'll require some candles. I still have a few. I'll have to get a few more. We might also need a blanket. And I need my old clothes. The ones I had when I arrived. Do you know where they are?"

She instinctively bobbed her head up and down. Her face was expressionless. There were tears flowing down her cheeks.

"What else?" *I don't know. I wasn't a good "Scout of México",* he thought to himself. "What else do you think we should bring?"

She turned slowly toward him and said despondently, "I don't know, Alejandro. You say that I have a father imprisoned here at the abbey. You say that the nuns are plotting against you. You say that I'm in danger. I haven't seen any of this. I'm fine here." She was filled with apprehension.

"Do you trust Marica? Just ask her. If she says that what I have told you is true, then come with me. If she says otherwise, then I'll have to escape by myself." He hoped that he hadn't overplayed his hand. He hoped that Marica's blood relationship with Melissa would not water down the bond with his lover.

"Alejandro, I'm afraid. What will happen to me if you leave? You tell me that I may be in danger from the nuns. Why? What have I done?

"And what will become of me if I go with you? Who will care for me when you have gone to your family?

"You are asking me to risk everything for you. Will I suffer forever for a few moments of love?

"I love you, Alejandro, but I'm afraid."

"I love you too. You must know that I promised Father Rivoli to take you with me. I made the same vow to Marica.

My family will look after you."

He paused and then continued looking straight into her violet eyes.

"Unfortunately, I would like to rescue Father Rivoli, but he would never make it. He is so frail."

Melissa started to sob. She was distraught.

His heart was breaking.

"Alejandro, I must go. I have so many things to think about." She rose and started to move away from him.

Alejandro grabbed her. He kissed her hard on the mouth. More tears flowed from her eyes.

"I love you, Melissa."

She pulled herself apart from him and started to hurry away. She paused and glanced back at him.

"I've heard that the Momos might be arriving here within the next few days."

She dashed away leaving Alejandro alone to weather the tempest. He tried to contemplate the stratagem for his escape, but his mind was clouded. *What would the nuns do to Melissa if she remains in the abbey? I am sure everyone knows about our love affair, he thought.*

CHAPTER 35

CAPTURED

The day dawned with intense sunlight. The room was bright. This caused Alejandro to rise early that morning.

After a few splashes of water on his face and beard, he went down to the kitchen to see if Marica had talked to Melissa. Sadly, he found himself alone.

There was quinoa with bananas on the table. The dish was still warm. It was covered with a colorful cotton napkin. There seemed to be more bread on the table than usual, but he thought nothing of it. He drank his orange juice without tasting it and hastily left the kitchen.

From the empty chapel, he seized six full-sized candles and tucked them in around his waist.

Alejandro went back to his room, grabbed the burlap sack, and departed again.

He needed to be cautious. He walked toward the fountain. He saw Rafaela on the hillside. She probably had not seen him. He proceeded down through the orchards. He could hear the bees buzzing around. He picked oranges, apples, and bananas. Using a circuitous route, he wandered through the trees. He was cautious since he did not want to be pursued. There was no need to take unnecessary risks now.

The air was breezy, but the day was starting to warm up. Sweat rolled down his forehead. When he thought it was safe, he made his way to the rose-covered mound. He opened the old rickety wooden door and quickly entered the abyss.

As was now his custom, Alejandro took off his shirt. Although now, it probably didn't matter. He seized three candles and left the remaining ones in the sack with the fruit.

With his trusty lighter he lit the first candle and started down the passageway of obscurity.

One, two, three, . . .

He felt better today, although his mouth was parched. *I'll have to eat an orange or two when I get back.*

Plodding along in the tunnel of darkness, he arrived at the large chamber. He continued along the shaft up to the prisoner's cell.

There was an air of tranquility as he approached the priest's confines.

"Father, I'm here."

There was no sound from within the keep.

He neared the bars.

"Father, I'm here!" he repeated in a louder tone.

Only silence answered him.

He poked the candle half way through the grating. He saw a pile in the far end of the cell.

Alejandro squinted, but it was difficult to penetrate the blackness.

"Father, I've . . ."

A swooshing sound came from behind him. Something smashed against the back of his legs.

He cried out in agony as he fell onto his knees. As he turned around, he saw what seemed to be the semblance of an old wizened nun. But it was too dark for him to be certain.

With his left hand he tried to raise the candle. Was it Sister Anna?

"The light!" there was a scream.

The candle was knocked out of his grasp and fell to the

dirt floor. He saw the dark form move toward the dropped candle and stomp out its brilliance.

It was now pitch black.

He tried to upright himself.

Bam! He was struck in his solar plexus. He was knocked semi-unconscious. Several times he was kicked, but he didn't budge.

The cell door was opened. It creaked. Alejandro was dragged by his head and bearded chin into the keep.

He exhaled with a moan of pain.

"Caught you, my sly one, didn't I?" she cackled as she exited the cell. The door clanged shut.

"You thought you were so smart feeding this poor dog. But mango stones and candle wax betrayed you. Just like he betrayed us. Let's see what advice he can give you now.

"Just remember, you are now ours. You belong to us. Ha-ha-ha!" Sister Anna scornfully shrilled.

His mind was barely coherent. He could not comprehend all of her ranting and raving. Thereafter, he heard the shuffling of feet leaving his presence and going in the direction of the stairs. The stirrings down the tunnel faded into silence.

The air in the cell was foul with a heavy urinary odor. Alejandro tried to move around but his body ached all over. He persisted and rolled over. He groped around with his hands.

The dirt floor was randomly covered with liquid excrement and straw. Then he found the corpse.

"Father, are you alive?" he cried.

Alejandro shook the loose-limbed figure. It weighed next to nothing. Father Rivoli was dead.

At least Father Rivoli no longer had to suffer in this pit of hell. Alejandro's father would say no person is happy until he is dead. Maybe this was now true for the ancient priest.

Alejandro tried to mourn for the recently deceased man, but he couldn't. He didn't feel the soul-aching sorrow of losing a dear one. Instead, he experienced relief. This was like the sympathy of euthanasia for a patient with a terminal disease.

How was he now going to tell Melissa about her father? At least she did not have to bear the woeful sight of this poor soul.

However, the point was moot. How was he going to tell her anything trapped in this hellhole?

He laid his hurting corpus back down. Alejandro was weary. His body was still in shock.

When he was a boy of ten, his mother had read him a story about a prisoner who after many years of being incarcerated dug himself out of prison or something like that. Or was it that the prisoner hid in a canvas body bag meant for another?

Sooner or later someone would have to come back and retrieve the priest's body. Could Alejandro exchange places in order to save himself?

What would happen if he were carried off? Where would they dispose of his body? There was no ocean outside of this Château d'If. There would be no funeral pyre because supposedly this was a Christian place.

He was concerned. Perhaps he would be buried. Buried alive!

Alejandro's mind wandered in a nightmarish state. His acute faculties were abandoning him. His head throbbed.

He fell into a stupor. He dreamt about being buried alive with the stench of the priest's corpse. His arms flailed in this trance. He tried to push himself away from the decaying body.

There was the sound of movement from within the tunnel. There seemed to be two voices conversing in low tones. However, the words resonated throughout the passageway. The speech was undecipherable.

Two figures approached the cell. A key went into the door. The gate slowly creaked open.

Alejandro had been awoken by the voices.

Could he make his escape? He could probably find his way out, even in the dark.

I am in too much pain to run. I'll just pretend that I am still unconscious. Was it better to be a live dog or a dead prince?

CHAPTER 36

INFERNO

"Is that ingrate still unconscious?" inquired a husky voice. It sounded like it was Sister Anna who was asking.

Alejandro grimaced as he received a sharp kick into his side. Fortunately, he had prepared himself for something much worse.

"He seems to be," another voice added.

The nuns approached Alejandro.

"Let's tie our prize stud up. Be careful not to damage the precious merchandise. Ha-ha-ha," crowed Sister Anna.

"Maybe I should check him out. We wouldn't want to give Mother Superior blemished goods, would we?" The second nun joined in the titter.

Alejandro's hands were forcibly grabbed. He tried not to tense up. He let his wrists go limp as they were being bound in front of him. They let his hands drop all of sudden.

At the next moment he heard a commotion next to him.

"Sister Teresa, lift up the old man's body while I slip the sack over this human dunghill."

Alejandro heard the pair trying to maneuver the corpse of Father Rivoli. Alejandro flinched when he was stepped on inadvertently as the two nuns lifted the dead body.

"Let's dispose of the flea-infested body first."

"Where are we going to take him?"

"Just down the passageway. We can put him in one of the empty catacombs."

Very clever, Alejandro thought. Their strategy would not raise any suspicion from the other nuns in the abbey. *Well, so much for the rescue of Edmond Dante.*

He heard the body being dragged across the cell floor and out of the door. *I'll try to sneak out now,* he decided as he *started to move.*

"Let's lock the door."

Another setback. The two nuns were not taking any chances.

The voices of the two bearing their load down the passageway gradually faded away.

How many other bodies had been disposed of like this?

Well, it could worse. I could be stuck forever with Father Rivoli's festering corpse in this stygian underground cemetery.

What do they have planned for me? They are certainly going to keep me in confinement, but why tie my hands? My father used to tell me that misfortune comes in triplets.

Alejandro struggled to loosen the bonds.

Shortly thereafter, the two familiar speakers could be heard returning. Their conversations became louder and louder.

There was a key inserted into the lock of the cell door. It clanged. The door swung open with a creak.

Alejandro had assumed a fetal position. All of a sudden, coming without warning, he heard a swoosh.

He was doused with a bucket of water. It was cold. He almost choked. He didn't know whether to be afraid or angry.

"Wake up! It's time!" barked one of his custodians.

Time for what? Mealtime? He hadn't eaten for a while and he was famished.

"Get up, I said!" he felt two sets of arms lift him partially off the ground as if he were a feather. He was surprised at their relative strength. He couldn't be that light.

Without resisting, he stood upright. Now he was being escorted with the nuns' arms entwined with his. His bound hands protruded directly in front of him.

They left the cavernous chamber and went to the right in the direction of the stairs. After numerous paces, the trio reached the foot of the stairs.

One of the nuns released his arm and followed slowly behind Alejandro and the other captor as they started to climb the stairs.

"There are stairs here. Be careful. We don't want you to injure yourself." This time there was no laughter.

Alejandro tried to recollect the count of the stairs. *Fifty?*

"And you have to be in perfect condition," croaked Sister Anna.

One, two, three, . . .

They ascended about thirty steps.

He stopped to catch his breath. He needed to maintain his alertness. Okay. Rest.

They started up again. Finally, they reached the top of the stairwell. One of the nuns unlatched a wooden door.

As the portal was flung open toward them, Alejandro was momentarily blinded by the relative brightness. It was not daylight. It was more like a dimly lit atmosphere. The air seemed a little fresher.

They walked along a narrow, but ornate, hallway. Alejandro did not recognize anything. They veered to the right and went up a Persian-carpeted flight of stairs. Alejandro surmised that they were on the second floor of the second building of the abbey. This building was distinct, but probably had a similar floor plan to his abbey residence.

At the top of the stairwell, they continued to the left

and walked toward a large wooden double door. Here were neither windows nor curtains in this corridor. There were only large Spanish tapestries suspended from the walls.

Sister Teresa knocked on the door.

"Enter!" came a gruff bellow from the other side.

Sister Teresa opened the door and entered. Sister Anna pulled Alejandro in by the arm.

Directly in front of him, despite the dull lighting, he could discern Mother Superior sitting upright in her canopied bed. The atmosphere was stuffy and the furnishings looked ancient. There was a musty odor in the bedroom.

"Señor Rubí, you are welcome, in spite of the strange circumstances of your arrival here." She had a solemn look that dissolved into a fiendish grin.

Both nuns now held his arms firmly. His eyes were getting accustomed to the faint luminosity.

"Our abbey has been lacking someone like you for a long time. You will have a pleasurable experience here."

"I demand to be released!" he shouted emphatically. *The best defense is a good offense,* he thought in desperation.

"That is impossible! You are needed here." His two custodians tightened their grip on him.

"Needed for what?" he brashly shouted, trying to lean forward.

"Bring him to me." The two nuns shoved him to the side of the thickly covered bed. Sister Teresa pulled aside the lace netting.

Alejandro could make out the haggard face of Mother Superior with the bed covers up to her chest. Her arms were sleeved in bulky black flannel.

"We need you to help us survive."

"Who are 'we'?"

"Why, our Order, of course," he could see the snide countenance on her wrinkled face as she responded.

"And what if I refuse?"

"You can't. That old priest is no longer available. You have to take his place. You do understand that there are no other options available to you."

"What if I want to leave this place and take Melissa with me?"

Mother Superior gave a scornful laugh at his bravado. Alejandro was trying to remain in control of himself.

"You can have that ungrateful bitch, but you both must remain here. The little whore could not survive in the outside world."

"I want to marry her."

"Who would marry the two of you?" she said smugly.

"Her father, Father Rivoli!" he blurted without realizing what he had said.

Mother Superior shrieked. Her arm flew through the air and struck Alejandro full on the face. He was knocked to the floor. He felt a warm liquid dripping from his nose.

"Sister Teresa, get some soap and some towels. Make it lye soap. This young man needs to be purged of his insolence, not to mention his rancid smell. You should have cleaned him up before you presented him to me."

"Yes, Reverend Mother. We're sorry," Sister Teresa pulled up her gown and scurried out of the room.

Alejandro could feel the heat of pain from the slap on his face. He felt the drops of blood against his bare chest.

I need to act fast. What can I do?

His back was toward Sister Anna. He inconspicuously torqued his body and stuck his bound right hand into his pocket. He felt for his lighter. Where was it? He stretched further. He strained. There was pain. Finally, he found it. Carefully, he extracted it.

He tried to flick his lighter. It failed.

"What are you doing?" yelled Sister Anna.

He tried the lighter again. It sputtered.

"Stop him, Sister!" wailed Mother Superior.

He tested the lighter a third time. It flared up. He turned partially sideways and directed it toward Sister Anna.

Sister Anna shrieked. The light was blinding her. In a panic, she tried to subdue him. She sprang on top of him.

She collided with him, knocking him down. The lighter was thrown underneath the bedding.

The old linens spontaneously caught on fire. Flames flared up onto the bed covers.

"Help me!" howled Mother Superior, as she tried to lift herself out of the bed.

Sister Anna turned around and desperately threw herself on top of the blaze on the bed. She fell over the leg of Mother Superior, who had become immobilized. Sister Anna's habit became engulfed in flames. The canopied bed was also on fire. Smoke was billowing everywhere.

Alejandro rolled over, sprang to his feet, and clumsily made his way to the door.

He heard choking behind him. The grey smoke was spewing everywhere.

He escaped out the door. He didn't look back.

CHAPTER 37

EXODUS

Alejandro struggled down the stairs. He was still gagging from the smoke inhalation. At the bottom of the flight, he saw the foyer that he suddenly recognized that led into the dining room. He crossed the entryway and escaped out of the front door. The sunlight hurt his eyes even though it was late afternoon.

With his bound hands cupped over his eyes, he glanced all about him. He took several deep breaths trying to clear his lungs. Alejandro saw no one. He started to scurry across the stone pathway, past the fountain to the first building.

"Melissa!" he yelled as he entered. "Where are you, Melissa?" He made his way to the kitchen.

Marica was there. Her eyes looked at him in horror.

"What happened to you?" she asked in amazement.

"I must find Melissa," he ranted.

"Sit down. Calm yourself. Let me clean you up," she said with a frown.

"I haven't got time." But he sat down anyway.

Marica approached him slowly. She held a butcher knife. She looked at him intently.

"Show me your hands."

He obeyed her. She cut the twine loose.

"Thank you."

He started to leave, but she motioned him to stay. Alejandro sat still. She grabbed a towel and wet it with water.

She wiped the dried blood from Alejandro's nose and chest.

"You're welcome. Try the pond. I think you should clean up though. You smell like a pig sty."

Underneath the grime, his cheeks reddened from embarrassment. He paused for a moment. He then stood up and gave Marica a peck on the cheek.

He rubbed his sore wrists as he dashed out of the building. He smelled smoke in the air. Little ashes were flittering in the air.

Alejandro hastened toward the pond. *I wonder if she is there. She may have come and left.*

He went huffing and puffing up the path.

Then Alejandro spotted her by the pond. She in turn spied him.

"Melissa! Melissa! You're here!"

The two ardently embraced as if two trains had collided. He started to kiss her on the neck, but she pushed him away.

"Where have you been? I have been waiting here for a long time!" she demanded, her voice edged with anger.

"I was being held prisoner," he started to explain as if he was giving a deposition in a lawsuit. Then he caught himself. "It's a long story. I'll tell you the whole story later," he sighed.

He tried to kiss her again, but she resisted him.

"I'm not sure that I can believe what you say to me," she posed, "but I can tell you one thing for certain." She grabbed him by his beard.

"You smell like smoked garbage. You need to clean up," she implored.

Alejandro knew that wallowing in the stench and waste in the priest's cell had made him a pariah to her.

Without giving her notice, he drew back from her and jumped into the pond. The water splashed her a little. The undulations lapped against the edge of the pond. Melissa smiled at him.

Alejandro submerged himself totally several times in spite of the water being cold. He started to shiver.

"Do you have anything for me to use to dry myself, my love?" he asked of her.

"I didn't bring a towel. How about your old clothes? They should work for now. It's the best that I can do."

"Fine."

Melissa proceeded to a burlap sack and pulled out some folded clothing. She brought them back to the edge of the pond. Here she dipped her hands in the water and wiped off the remaining slimy smudges on him.

Alejandro climbed out of the pond. Shivering from the cold water, he took off his pants and sandals. He stood stark naked in front of Melissa.

She handed him his old torn shirt. With great difficulty he put on his old, holey jeans and sneakers.

"Now you can kiss me."

He pulled her closely and began to kiss her.

"I'm so glad to see you again," he murmured in her ear. "I thought that I might never see you again."

"Me, too."

"Are you coming with me?"

"Do you want me to?"

"Yes."

"Then I will."

"Do you want to hear my story?"

"I don't know. Marica told me some of the same things that you did. But I'm still not sure. This is so unbelievable," her face scowled.

Alejandro did not respond.

"By the way, Marica baked some extra bread this morning and she encouraged me to take it," she added.

She was so beautiful. Despite her young age, she seemed to have the wisdom of a woman. Her voice was determined and deliberate as she spoke. She had decided to accompany him on her own.

It seemed that Marica was trying to help the two lovers.

"Did you bring water and everything?"

"Yes, they're in the sack."

"Great. Thank you, my love. You have made me the happiest guy in the whole world."

He took her by the hand and grabbed the sack. They walked quickly back toward the fountain. They could see anthracite smoke rising on their left, down the hill and could smell the acrid air.

As they approached the fountain, they saw someone coming toward them. It was Sister Teresa. Her clothing had been charred. She was carrying a basket.

The two lovers stopped and looked to the left. They could see that the second building was now ablaze. Dark smoke was billowing from the inferno. Little ashes were afloat everywhere.

The nun suddenly spotted them. She tried to block their way.

"Mother Superior is dead!" She pointed to Alejandro with her blackened hand. "You killed her!"

Alejandro could see that her lined face had been seared. It almost seemed that it had melted away like candle wax.

"Sisters! Come quick!" she shrieked as she dropped the basket.

The basket held some hexagonal-shaped containers that looked somewhat familiar to Alejandro, but in the midst of the excitement he couldn't remember where he had seen them before.

Alejandro put his body between Sister Teresa and Melissa as the nun tried to grab the pair. He remembered how many times the nuns at his elementary school had subdued him and his classmates when they misbehaved.

"Sisters. Hurry!" she screamed.

Filled with adrenaline, Alejandro yanked Sister Teresa's arm hard at the same time that the nun was reaching for him. He heard a soft snap and an ungodly wail from her. Her arm fell limp at her side as she fell to the ground writhing in pain.

Melissa was staring at him. She looked down at Sister Teresa. The contents of the basket were strewn all over the ground. Instinctively, Melissa swooped forward and picked up the loose containers. She began to cry. She was shaking her head. She looked at Alejandro.

"What have you done? What is happening?"

Alejandro forcefully seized her by the shoulders.

"Let's get out of here!"

She sniffled. She did not try to resist.

"Help me, Sisters!" Sister Teresa continued to cry out in pain, trying to summon the other sisters. "They're trying to escape!"

Alejandro knew that they had very little time left. They had to flee immediately. But he had to take precautions. His first impulse was to proceed to the rose-covered mound expeditiously. He now had to protect Melissa. He had promised Father Rivoli and Marica. He had also vowed to himself.

The two wandered in a serpentine fashion through the orchards. On the way they both picked a couple of ripe mangoes.

Alejandro and Melissa went on until they could no longer see the buildings or smell the smoke. They finally reached the entrance to the subterranean passage way.

"This is the door to the underground catacombs that I've told you about." He opened the wooden portal and seized the burlap sack that he had left earlier that morning.

"Is this the way to where father is?"

"Yes."

"I want to go see him," she implored.

He reached around her and hugged her fervently.

"You can't. He's dead," he whispered.

She gave a whimper. Her tears fell on his neck.

"I'm so sorry, my love. I wish that you could have known him. He was at peace with God when he passed away." He gently kissed her on the neck.

It would be futile to rescue his body. It would be too dangerous. How could he find the body lodged somewhere in the catacombs? They needed to leave as soon as possible.

Alejandro touched her right arm and pointed her to the left of the mound. The vegetation was lush. They progressed and soon reached the wall that surrounded the abbey.

They followed the perimeter to the right. Alejandro was carrying both sacks over his shoulder. Melissa wondered where he was leading them.

"Are we going to the main entrance?" she inquired.

"We can't. It might be guarded."

They continued on for a while. Then Alejandro halted.

"There," he pointed.

"There? Where?"

"The tree. You can climb, can't you?"

"Of course."

They proceeded to the tall cottonwood that abutted the

wall.

Alejandro put down the two sacks and climbed up to the third branch.

"Hand me the sacks, please."

She complied and passed him the burlap sacks one at a time. He carefully tucked them securely in between some limbs.

Then he reached down and pulled her up. She negotiated the tree like a squirrel. Branch by branch they gingerly ascended, making sure that the sacks were always secure before they continued.

As they approached the top of the wall, Alejandro raised himself and peered over. He calculated the drop to be between three and four meters. One of them could break a leg or twist an ankle, he feared.

He seized the two burlap bags and dropped them over the side.

"Melissa, grab onto my arms. Hold on tight. I'm going to lower you down."

"Are you sure?" her violet eyes asked.

"Yes."

She crawled over the top of the wall. Alejandro made sure that his legs were anchored around a tree limb. Slowly, she descended using her feet to walk down the wall while Alejandro supported her. She became parallel to the wall and was dangling about a meter off the ground.

"When I count three, I'm going to let you go. Okay?"

"Okay."

"One, two, three," he released her.

She dropped down and with a thud landed upright with her knees bent.

"Are you all right?" he called down.

"Sure. Now let's see you try it," she taunted.

I hope that I'm not the one that's going to get hurt.

He pulled his legs over the adobe partition and started to lower his body downward.

The top of the wall was rough and his hands were getting chafed.

Go slowly, he thought. *The first elbow down. Now the second.* He was hanging on by his fingers like a spider on a web. He had skinned his chin a little, but his beard had saved him.

He was a little more than two meters above the ground.

Here goes nothing! One, two, three.

Into space he fell with no one to catch him. He hit the ground hard, and fell backwards hard on to his rear end.

Alejandro hesitated in getting up. He inventoried his body. He rubbed his butt. No broken bones. He was all right.

Melissa gave him a big grin.

He kissed her.

They picked up the sacks and started hiking through the jungle.

CHAPTER 38

THE SUCCESSOR

Marica was surprised when she observed Sister Agatha and Sister Clara suddenly enter the dining room. They had not seen her as they passed. The wooden doors were slightly open, and the native woman could hear the conversation between the two nuns. It seemed that the two nuns had tried to rescue their religious comrades from the fire in the other building, but had not succeeded. The conflagration had been too great and the smoke had hindered their attempts. In the end, Mother Superior and Sister Anna had expired in the blaze.

Moments before, Marica also heard Sister Clara mention that Sister Teresa had also succumbed, due to a fatal attack by Alejandro. Marica could not believe her ears and strained to hear more. She leaned closer to one of the doors, but kept very still so as not to get caught eavesdropping.

"Sister Clara, please make arrangements for a little wake in the chapel this evening," directed Sister Agatha to her assistant.

Marica was shocked to hear that Mother Superior and two other nuns were dead. But she was also surprised that Sister Agatha was speaking. She had rarely heard Sister Agatha say anything. She was light-skinned with a slight built. Although the Order of Our Lady of the Flowers did not require the nuns to adhere to a vow of silence, Sister Agatha had always done so.

"Yes, Sister," curtsied her subordinate.

"Sister Teresa was the only one not burned in the fire, so please take special care of her corpse. We owe Sister Teresa much for trying to rescue the royal jelly during the fire."

"Yes, Sister."

"And let's conduct a memorial service for Mother Superior and Sister Anna at the wake this evening," add Sister Agatha. "There is no way we can retrieve their bodies now."

"Yes, Sister," nodded Sister Clara who was fair-skinned and slender. "Then we will only have a burial ceremony tomorrow morning for Sister Teresa."

"That's correct, Sister Clara. Very well. Please have Rafaela make the proper ground preparations."

"Yes, Sister."

"Anything else, Sister Clara?"

"Yes, Sister," eagerly asserted the subordinate. "As Sister Teresa said in her dying words, we need to select a new Mother Superior."

"Well, Sister Clara," mulled Sister Agatha. "I thought the obvious choice would be me. I am now in charge of the entire abbey and have the most experience."

Marica knew that since Sister Agatha was in charge of the first building and also supervised Sisters Clara, Beatriz, and Consuelo, she would want to take charge of the entire abbey.

"With due respect, Sister Agatha," the subordinate looked her straight in the eyes. "Maybe we should consider a younger candidate, especially if we want to ensure the continuation of our Order. We need to maximize our survival."

The older nun could insist that she be the successor, but what Sister Clara said made sense. She needed to be altruistic for the sake of the sisterhood.

But Marica knew that Sister Clara had her own ambitions.

She had observed Sister Clara over and over again, acting officiously with some of the nuns and especially with Rafaela. Something was brewing, thought Marica.

"Very well, Sister Clara," capitulated Sister Agatha. "We shall have a democratic election for Mother Superior's successor tomorrow after Sister Teresa's burial."

"Yes, Sister," replied the other without showing the disappointment in her face.

"In any event, what happened to the royal jelly that Sister Teresa salvaged for us?"

"I think that most of it was spoiled by the heat of the fire," advised Sister Clara. "There was supposed to be a reserve supply. Marica has been using some to feed Alejandro. I hope that ignorant native still has some of it."

Marica bit her lip. She hated when the nuns said unkind things about her, Rafaela, or Melissa.

"Sister Clara, that is a bit unkind."

"Yes, Sister," insisting that she had a point, Sister Clara gave a scowling look to the other nun. "But it was her niece that upset our community here at the abbey."

"As you know, Mother Superior was aware of everything that went on," Sister Agatha asserted. "We had to make sure that the male was virile. Our survival depended on it."

"Yes, Sister," said the subordinate who refused to retreat. "I still think it was wrong to have a man control our destiny."

"Unfortunately, Mother Superior needed a drone to reproduce. We must accept that fact."

Sister Clara grimaced in disgust.

"Two more things, Sister Clara. We will also vote on whether or not to move from here. New queens usually relocate," her forefingers crossed. "And also, have Sister Beatriz locate Alejandro and bring him to me."

Sister Clara did not want to the Order to move and was about to respond when they were interrupted. They heard a noise behind them and turned to face it.

"Sisters, may I bring you anything to eat or drink?" inquired Marica who had just walked into the dining room.

CHAPTER 39

THE SHELTER

Melissa and Alejandro had been snaking their way outside the abbey walls toward the main gates. The trees diminished into thick foliage. They paused behind an oleander bush and observed the entryway. There was no sign of activity.

Looking from side to side, the two scanned the area in front of the gates for a few moments until they noticed what appeared to be a trail. It led away from the abbey. That's what they had been searching for.

They continued to traipse silently down this narrow clayish path that bisected the sylvan jungle. Sometimes they would have to detour in order to avoid obstacles like fallen trees or ditches that nature had dug through decades of erosion.

Was this the right course? My father used to say that the beaten path is the safest. But how about in the case at hand? He wondered. He didn't want to wander aimlessly in the jungle for hours.

The lovers trekked on for a long time without saying very much. They were nervous, but glad to be away from the abbey.

"Do you know where we are going?" she asked somewhat apprehensively.

"No. I just hope that this path runs into a village or a plantation."

The trail was a coral-colored mixture of shale and clay.

The verdant vegetation was dense on both sides. There was a peppery smell in the air. The surroundings were silent.

"Alejandro."

"Yes, my love," he switched the burlap sacks from his right shoulder to his left.

"Are we going to be all right? Should I be afraid?"

"No, my love, we're fine. You have nothing to fear. I promise." *What else can I say to her? I don't know what the f__k I'm doing. I don't know where the f__k we're going. I only know that she and I could no longer remain at that shithole of evil. I will protect her.*

"My dear, it will be dark in an hour or so," he said softly. "We'll need to find a place to spend the night. Are you hungry?'

"No," she said hesitantly. It seemed that she was still fearful. She had never been outside the premises of the abbey. Inside she was afraid, but did not let on.

Sweat was beading up on Alejandro's forehead. He tried to wipe it away. He was getting fatigued. He was not used to this much physical exertion.

"Are you thirsty?"

"No," she replied.

"Let's take a little break anyway." They stopped by an old fallen eucalyptus tree trunk. He reached into the sack and took out the water flask. He gulped down a few swallows. He handed it to her. She took a small swig.

"Are you feeling okay, Alejandro?" she looked at him with concern in her eyes.

"Yes, my love. Let's go."

Alejandro's right hand found her left hand. They continued their journey stealing glimpses at one another along the way. The trail meandered through the small hills.

The vegetation became wilder and wilder. Every so often the trail disappeared. They would have to venture one way or another before proceeding forward.

Alejandro started to whistle. She started to giggle.

"It's funny. I have never heard you whistle before," Melissa beamed.

He smiled in return. He was elated. They were free at last.

The sun was descending. The heliotrope-colored skies were starting to hail the night. The shadows now were elongated.

Alejandro had been scouting for a place to settle down for the night. He thought that they should bivouac off the trail. Someone from the abbey might be following them. *Would someone be pursuing him? Or her? Maybe both.* Alejandro did not want to assume any risks.

He thought that he heard running water. He saw what looked like a break in the foliage.

"Melissa, let's go this way." He grabbed her hand and led her to the left.

They veered off the main path and toward the sound of a babbling brook. The gurgling got louder as they trekked forward. He broke little twigs along the way so that he could easily find his way back to the trail.

Alejandro was in front of her, shielding her from the branches. The way was tight and difficult to carry the sacks through. The boughs rubbed up against them as they passed by.

The sound of the stream ahead seemed to strengthen as they advanced. They had walked about a hundred paces when they finally reached the water.

Melissa seemed ecstatic. He dropped the sacks. She took off her sandals. He did the same. They slithered into the shallow waters. It felt invigorating against their hot and sweaty bodies.

They drifted further into the middle of the stream. The depth was just over a meter. The current was lazy.

Alejandro all of a sudden sat down creating a slight splash. He submerged his head for a few moments and came up spitting water at Melissa.

She screamed playfully and splashed him. He chased her in his squatted stance. She skillfully circled around him like an eagle soaring over its prey.

Alejandro caught her hand and dragged her close. Her smile penetrated his heart. The water glistened on her cinnamon skin. The sun was setting.

She looked at him and kissed him fully on the mouth. The two lingered for a few moments.

He felt pressure being exerted on him. Melissa was pulling him upwards. She wanted to return to terra firma.

"Alejandro, we better eat something now. It will be dark soon enough."

Alejandro took off his wet shirt and hung it on top of a palo verde branch. His body sprouted goose bumps. Meanwhile, Melissa took out a multicolored blanket from one of the sacks and laid it open on some uneven ground. This unfortunately was the only spot where it was feasible to retire.

It was now twilight. She opened one of the burlap sacks and took out some food. For the next few minutes they gorged themselves on mangos and bread with honey.

"Wait a moment!" she halted his eating and grabbed a hexagonal canister that she had taken from Sister Teresa. She opened it and spread the contents on the bread. She offered Alejandro a piece. He readily accepted it.

"What is this stuff?"

"I think it is some sort of jelly."

"Marmalade?"

"I don't know. It's just the stuff that Marica has been feeding you to make you better."

The two finished the solid food.

"Hey, Alejandro," she pulled a gourd out of the sack. "I have a surprise."

For the next ten minutes they imbibed the mead nectar. They were laughing and giggling.

She lay down on the blanket and stretched out. He reclined next to her.

"Are you cold?" she asked him.

"No, not really," he lied. "How about you?"

"Perhaps, a little."

"Me, too," he confessed.

"Shall I warm you up?" she grinned.

"Sure," she ran her hands caressingly up and down his back.

"Alejandro, your pants are still wet!" she exclaimed in a vixen tone. "You should take them off."

He obeyed her without hesitation. She had draped part of the blanket over herself. She was almost completely covered up.

Alejandro reposed himself next to her. She was on her side. His arms reached out and encircled her slender waist. She was naked. He brought her near.

Alejandro pecked her on the lips. They tasted like honey. He licked them.

Then he kissed her cheek. Then her eyelids. Then her forehead. He could feel her fever.

Melissa leaned into him resting on his arms and kissing

his neck.

The crescent moon was aglow. Venus was on the horizon. The myriad of stars began to illuminate their love scene. Orion was ready for the hunt.

Alejandro sensually rubbed her shoulders. She trembled. He felt her. He fondled her. He mouthed her. He lipped her. Back and forth. In circles. Up and down. He was no longer chilled.

"Oh, Alejandro, I'm so happy to be with you," she moaned as she stroked his beard.

"Me, too, my love."

His hands felt about her body. Her nipples grew hard. She dug her fingernails into his back.

He felt her bottom. Nice and round.

She, in turn, explored his body. He continued to search hers. Both were touching. Caressing. Kissing.

Alejandro wanted her. She wanted him.

The comet grew larger and larger. The earth stood still. Mercury could feel the heat of the heavens.

She put her leg between his lower limbs. He massaged her thighs. He rubbed her up and down.

The comet was piercing the Milky Way.

She took him.

The comet entered Venus' atmosphere. A world of ardent steam.

She bit him on the lip. He yelped. The two lovers undulated like stars twinkling in the heavens. The universe was in harmony.

The Milky Way exploded into a million points of light.

And Jupiter seeing their deep love, placed them in the heavens.

CHAPTER 40

MOTHER SUPERIOR

Marica placed the platter of bread in the middle of the dining room table. She had already served the nuns their orange juice after they had said grace. She then retreated into the kitchen.

It had barely dawned and the nuns were back from their morning prayers. The darkness of night was quickly disappearing.

A bell rang. The nuns drew to attention.

"Sisters, there will be a delay this morning in the burial of our dearly beloved Sister Teresa," announced Sister Clara from the middle of the table.

The other nuns looked a little surprised, but they were used to disruptions to their daily schedules.

"I am sorry to report that Sister Agatha passed away suddenly last night. As you know, we were unable to extract the other bodies from the burning building due to the enormous damage and the still smoldering rooms."

There was a collective groan of surprise and sadness.

Sister Clara bit into a roll before anyone could ask her any questions.

Marica reentered the room with another platter of bananas, papayas, and guavas. She refilled the juice cups.

"How did Sister Agatha die?" inquired Sister Consuelo.

"She was slashed to death," replied Sister Clara nonchalantly. "Rafaela is busy preparing a second burial ground."

Marica almost dropped the jug when she heard this. Just the night before, she had overheard the discussion between Sister Agatha and Sister Clara about the necessity of electing a new Mother Superior. Sister Agatha had seemed to have the inside track. *What had happened to Sister Agatha? Who had mutilated her?* Marica wondered. *Something was drastically wrong.*

"Is El Sombrerón here again?" cried out Sister Consuelo in a panic.

There was an undercurrent of alarm among the others.

Sister Clara did not respond. She simply waved her hand and looked over to Sister Beatriz.

"Sister," Sister Clara continued. "Have you seen Alejandro today?"

"No, Sister," Sister Beatriz timidly responded. "I looked for him all last evening. I couldn't find him. He did not come to his room last night."

"Has anyone seen the boy?"

All the heads nodded in the negative.

"After this morning's burial service, I want everyone to search this building and the grounds for Alejandro. You may have a couple of the Momos assist you," directed Sister Clara.

A hand shot up from one of the novices. "The Momos are here?"

"Yes, Sister Consuelo," Sister Clara acknowledged her.

"The Momos arrived this morning at the front gates with our supplies," she advised. "We are still in the process of accumulating our goods to trade with them."

Marica was concerned about how quickly things were moving. *Was it foul play that she sensed?*

"We probably shouldn't let them enter the premises while

there is disorder here," Sister Clara was contemplating out loud. "And yes, Sisters, we still have some important decisions to make before we can resume our activities."

There was pause and total silence blanketed the room. The nuns sat motionless.

"Sister Beatriz, after this morning's burial service," broke in Sister Clara, "I want you to leave the abbey in case Alejandro has escaped. Take some of the Momos with you and make sure to bring him back here if you find him."

"Yes, Sister, as you say," replied the other.

Marica was now getting more worried. *Were they going to accuse Alejandro of Sister Agatha's death?* She knew that Alejandro had fled the abbey long before Sister Agatha's conversation with Sister Clara. She was glad that they had escaped. Melissa would be safer.

"Sister Consuelo, you will arrange the normal trading with the other Momos. Marica can assist you. She knows what to do.

"However, before we can proceed, we need to make some very important decisions," Sister Clara looked at the other sisters. "We need to select a successor Mother Superior. Theoretically, I have the most seniority and could claim the position. However, we must all do what is best for the Order. I am willing to have us vote on it. Any objections?"

"I'm too young," blurted out Sister Consuelo nervously. "I'm still a novice. I'm not ready. I couldn't do it."

Sister Clara turned her head toward Sister Beatriz. "What about you, Sister?"

Sister Beatriz's eyes dropped. "With all due respect, Sister Clara, I think you should be the next Mother Superior. Don't you agree, Sister Consuelo?"

The young nun nodded her head in approbation.

"Very well, Sisters, I will accept." Sister Clara had been correct in letting them decide the matter democratically. In reality, they had very little choice in the matter.

"The second issue that is also very vital to our survival and propagation is the site of our Order. Normally, the new Mother Superior moves from the old location to a new one. We could have the Momos assist us in finding a new spot somewhere in their territories or we could stay in this building. The other building is beyond repair and it would take forever to rebuild."

"I really don't have an opinion," submitted Sister Consuelo. "I am fine wherever."

"Sister Clara, what . . . I mean Reverend Mother, what would be the best location for you to fully assume your duties and responsibilities as soon as possible?" meekly inquired Sister Beatriz.

"If you all don't object, I would like to remain here. The other building is not viable and we will have the Momos clear the debris. Sister Consuelo, talk with the Momos and tell them what we want. Remember to have them camp outside our gates until they are finished."

"Yes, Sister . . . I mean Reverend Mother."

"Don't worry. It will take time for all of us to get accustomed to our new direction. Anything else that we need to discuss?"

The other nuns nodded their heads from side to side. In a few minutes they had left the dining room to ready themselves for the burial services.

Sister Clara remained in the room. Marica came in to clear the dishes.

"Marica," addressed the new Mother Superior. "I have good news for you. We are going to remain here at the abbey.

Just in this building. We will not have to move anything."

"Very good."

"I will need you to prepare me a special diet every day," she said in a condescending tone. "Remember the product that I asked you to take special care of? The royal jelly."

"Yes, Sister."

"How much is still good? How much is spoiled or contaminated?"

"About half is still good."

"Please keep it safe." she was patronizing to Marica. "The survival of our Order depends on it."

"Yes, Sister."

"About a cupful each day, should do. Mix it in with my regular food."

"Yes, Sister."

"And Marica," added the new Mother Superior. "The Momos will be taking Melissa back to their village. She can no longer live here. She is a major distraction."

Marica looked fixedly at the speaker.

CHAPTER 41

DELUGED

The sun had risen like a morning song. It was a bright day. There were little puffs of clouds floating overhead. The breeze was gentle. There was a slight scent of wild sage in the air. The sounds of birds echoed in the distance. The dew rested all about them.

Alejandro's arms were wrapped around his morning star with the blanket covering them both. The duet had spent most of the night touching the other's body and soul.

The passion had expended their energies. The afterglow of their love had melted their spirits together.

Melissa awoke first. She still lay next to him. She stared at his face with its closed eyes. She was happy. She was in heaven. She listened to his heavy breathing.

Carefully she got up, trying hard not to wake him. She was famished. She grabbed one of the sacks and took out some fruit. She munched on a mango.

Alejandro rolled over. His arm blindly reached over. His fingers touched her and lazily caressed her back.

"Good morning, my love."

She bit off a piece of her mango and placed it gently into his mouth. He chewed it.

"Thank you," he smiled.

He drew close to her.

"Ready for more?" he tantalized.

She withdrew bashfully.

"I'm going to clean up a little," she got up. "I'm going to walk up the stream a little way. I'll be back soon."

She pecked him on the cheek and took her clothes and a few things from the bag. She left and trekked to the right. In an instant she disappeared from his sight.

Alejandro found the fruit and bread. He ate with gusto.

Never in his short life had he been so much in love. His experiences with the opposite sex in law school were dismal at best. Chuy would taunt him. His best friend would joke that if he didn't have bad luck, he wouldn't have any luck at all.

Alejandro hoped that his parents would be pleased with her. He needed to figure out how to tell them a sanitized version of what had happened.

He had to urinate. He rose and put on his pants.

He thought that he should wander downstream, so as not to invade Melissa's privacy. Cautiously, Alejandro ambulated barefoot over the pebbles in the shallow bottom of the stream.

At about twenty-five meters away, there was a tall cottonwood tree. He exited the water and voided himself as was nature's way.

He slowly started his retreat.

We probably should leave as soon as she returns.

The skies were getting darker as clouds seemed suddenly to be gathering overhead. He could feel the prickly heat rising. He finally made it back to their point of origin.

Splash. Splash. Splash. He could hear Melissa's feet splattering.

Within the next fifteen minutes, they had picked up their belongings and tossed most everything into the two burlap sacks.

"Are you ready?" Alejandro asked.

"Which way are we going?" Melissa inquired.

"Back to the road, the way we came last night," he had a puzzled look on his face. He had broken little boughs and bent grasses on their way to this bivouac to guide him from the main path. "Why do you ask, my love?"

"If we go back to the main path, somebody might see us."

"That could be a good thing, my love."

"But what if it isn't?" her face was sad. "I don't want to be punished."

"You won't, my love."

"Couldn't we just follow this stream? There should be a village on it, don't you think?"

"Why not?" Then the two set off downstream.

They felt drops as they approached their first rows of eucalyptus trees. Moments later there were sheets of rain descending upon them. At first, they used the burlap sacks to protect them, but they became saturated after a very short period.

The pair stopped in a clearing underneath the convergence of three tall and leafy sycamores.

"Alejandro, can we please wait here until the rain stops?" implored the girl. "I'm not feeling well."

He grunted in assent. He was soaking wet and his clothes were muddied. He really just wanted to keep moving. He was getting crabby. Alejandro set one of the bags underneath them.

For an eternity, the deluge continued. Melissa leaned against her hero until she fell asleep.

The storm finally ceased and the sun peeked from behind the clouds. Steam rose from the vegetation around them.

Alejandro's body ached from not being able to move because his arm had been pinned underneath her.

He was hungry and most of their stores had been depleted. He maneuvered himself carefully from out of her grasp. He laid Melissa's head softly on top of the sack.

He grabbed the other bag and walked further downstream. His heart was happy and he sang to himself. At times he would be forced away from the brook, but he always kept it within view.

Fifty paces in front of him were a dozen avocado trees. He felt the fruit on the branches. They were as hard as rocks. Alejandro then picked one up from the ground. It appeared to be ripe. He threw it into the sack.

He thought he heard a noise from far off. He scavenged five more avocados.

Alejandro didn't know how long he had been gone, but he thought he should start walking back.

Moments later he heard a cry coming from the direction where he had left Melissa. He picked up his pace and started to hurry.

"Alejandro!" He could discern the frightened scream.

He started to run, rushing into thorny bushes and stubbing his toe. *Was she having a nightmare! Was she afraid because she was alone? Was she frightened because she thought he had abandoned her?*

Alejandro dropped the sack and was making his way as fast as he could. He slipped twice on muddy rocks and painfully recovered the pursuit. *Shit!*

"Alejandro!" the sound of terror was repeated.

Where is she? He started to panic in his exhausted state.

Then he saw a figure dash past him in front of the sycamores.

"Alejandro!"

He rushed forward with reckless abandon.

Whoosh! He felt his body being catapulted into the air. "Alejandro!"

CHAPTER 42

MARICA'S TALE

"Marica," Rafaela huddled close to the heavyset cook in the kitchen, "I'm afraid. I don't understand the terrible things going on here."

"I don't either," Marica tried to comfort her colleague. "I don't think that it is safe for any of us during this time."

"Did El Sombrerón kill Mother Superior?" There was panic in her voice. "Sister Clara did not answer Sister Consuelo's question on whether that monster had invaded the abbey."

"As far as I know, he is not here."

"But if he is here, we are all in danger!" Rafaela's speech was quick. "Maybe the Momos can look for him."

"Rafaela, El Sombrerón will not attack us."

"But he already killed Sister Sofia," the gardener exclaimed.

"Come with me," Marica beckoned as she escorted Rafaela out of the kitchen toward her own bedroom in the back. Rafaela was silent as she obeyed. The two entered the cell that only had a narrow cot, a little chest of drawers, and a large hanging wooden crucifix. Marica motioned her coworker to sit on the bed. Marica closed the door behind her and sat herself next to Rafaela.

"How long have you been at the abbey, Rafaela?"

"I think maybe seven winters," the gardener responded. "I was recruited from my village after my husband had died.

No, make that nine winters. I'm not sure."

Rafaela was staring curiously into Marica's dark brown eyes, nervously massaging her hands as she did so. Although Marica was several years older, Rafaela's body was already hunched over and her skin was darker from the rigorous work she did outdoors. Her black hair was loose and she had long bangs across her forehead that contrasted with Marica's that was pulled back into a bun. Rafaela's orange apron was soiled; Marica's yellow one was not.

"What do you know about Mother Superior?" Marica questioned. "I mean, what did you know about her? I still can't believe that she is dead."

"Not much," the gardener's eyes squinted as if she was trying to reminisce.

"Let me tell you a story that you may or may not believe," began Marica. "But it is true."

Putting her right hand on Rafaela shoulder, she told her that the abbey many years before had been an orphanage and a novitiate for young girls who wanted to become nuns. As a practical matter, it also became a refuge for young Momo girls who got pregnant without the benefit of marriage.

Rafaela affirmed that she had gathered that much from observing the grounds and overhearing chatter from the nuns made in her presence.

Shifting her position on top of the bed, Marica continued. She confessed that Melissa was her niece's daughter. She didn't mention that Father Rivoli was the father.

"My niece died in childbirth. She was being tended to by Sister Teresa," Marica paused with a heavy sigh. "I don't think that her death was natural."

"What are you saying, Marica! You are speaking blasphemy!" Rafaela began fidgeting.

"Am I? These nuns behave very aggressively when they perceive any type of threat. I believe that Mother Superior eliminated all potential threats to herself. "

"You can't be serious. Like whom?"

"Haven't you noticed that several nuns always seem to die before a new Mother Superior comes into power? Like at the time she became Mother Superior and other nuns were found dead."

"But what about now? Our old Mother Superior who just died was already here safe and sound," Rafaela tried to counter. "No one was menacing her."

"Did you know that the old Mother Superior had a deep and dark secret?" hinted the cook. "During her first years here as a nun, she had a child."

"What! That can't be true, Marica. That's impossible!"

"Well, it's a fact. The child's name was Victorino. He was the only boy in the orphanage. He was tormented by some of the nuns because he was a male and represented everything that they thought was wrong with the world.

"He grew up with his sister here at the orphanage. Actually, she was a half-sister."

Rafaela did not fully comprehend the familial relationship and that the two children shared a common father.

"Victorino was an unruly child. He was mischievous and was always being punished by Sister Teresa and Sister Anna. He liked to play with the other children and always liked to braid his sister's hair. The nuns used to spank him for this. Nevertheless, he would continue to do it. He loved his sister and always wanted to be with her."

"What happened to him?" Rafaela was now intrigued with the story.

"Somehow, I really don't the actual story. They say that

he started a fire at the orphanage. That building behind us was burned to the ground. Fortunately, no one was killed. The boy suffered a burned face and the loss of an eye. Mother Superior banished him from the abbey. He was sent to live in one of our Momo villages."

"You're not talking about El Sombrerón?" Rafaela cried out.

"Unfortunately, yes," Marica took in another breath. "The story goes, that when he reached adolescence the Momos could no longer control him. He began changing into a creature that was half man and half bee. His fingernails were said to have grown into stingers and he killed several Momos in fits of rage."

"That's impossible!" Rafaela said outraged.

Marica held up her hand. "Victorino keeps trying to see his sister at the abbey, but as you know, has not succeeded. He hates the nuns, especially those he feels mistreated him and wronged him."

"But how could Mother Superior have abandoned this boy if he was her child?" There was a puzzled look on the gardener's face.

"I'm not sure," Marica admitted. "It could have been because of her growing hatred for Father Rivoli, or simply because she had no use for a boy child."

"What does he look like?" inquired the gardener.

"Didn't you see him when Sister Sofia was killed?"

"Not really. I just saw the back of a short person wearing baggy pants. I think maybe a red belt and for sure, big black boots," Rafaela tried to recall. "He had a big, wide brimmed black hat that covered his long hair. I didn't see his face. I was too far away."

"Don't be afraid," Marica looked pointedly at Rafaela. "I

don't think that he would hurt us, you and me. We are not the nuns who tormented him."

"But who killed Mother Superior and Sister Agatha?"

"Well, all we know is that Mother Superior died in the fire," Marica looked into Rafaela's face and said in a very serious manner. "But it seems to me that Sister Clara is suggesting that Alejandro is responsible for Sister Agatha's death also."

"What! That is impossible!" Rafaela was animated and the little bed shook.

"I agree." Marica then recounted to her the conversation that she had overheard the previous night between Sister Agatha and Sister Clara about the succession to the role of Mother Superior.

"Well, I understand that, but how do you know that Alejandro was not the one who killed her?"

"Because I helped Alejandro and Melissa escape from this cursed place yesterday afternoon."

CHAPTER 43

DILEMMA

"Alejandro!"

He could see that two Momos were restraining Melissa's arms. He himself was bobbing upside down from a sycamore tree. He had been caught in a snare and was now helplessly watching two more Momos approaching him.

"Let her go!" he groaned weakly.

The two natives separated in front of him. He was surprised to see their accomplice appear before him.

"My son, you have behaved very badly."

Alejandro looked at the nun.

"My son, you have killed several of our sisters," Sister Beatriz continued. "We treated you so well. And now look how you repaid us."

He kept silent. The three in front of him were blocking his view of Melissa.

"You have to make amends," she continued with bravado.

"Let us go!" Alejandro demanded. "We don't want to be part of your perversions. Just let us go."

"Unfortunately, our Mother Superior is dead because of you," her tone became calmer. "We cannot save our Order without you. We cannot reproduce without you. You must help us survive."

"She tried to have sex with me! It was gross!" he screamed out defiantly. "She turned into a hideous creature! She was slimy! It was her own fault that she died! Please, just let us go."

"Well, my son, it is not that simple," she said softly but in a stern tone as she approached him. She looked him in the eye and tugged on his reddish brown beard.

"You can't make me do anything I don't want to do," he tried to challenge her.

"My son, your fate is already sealed. You will help our Order reproduce," she maintained her matter of fact tone. "But you can decide to save the girl. You really don't have much choice."

"What? What do you mean?" he demanded with ire.

"We know that you and Melissa engaged in carnal knowledge. That is a mortal sin. She should be severely punished. But you can prevent that."

His mind raced. His lust and passion for Melissa had endangered her physical being. Who knows what monstrosities these creatures would inflict upon her?

"How? What do I have to do?"

"Just promise to come back to the abbey obediently."

"And if I don't?"

"Take a look at her. It might be the last time that you will ever see her."

What was Sister Beatriz threatening to do to Melissa? Banish her from the abbey? That might not be too bad. She would be free of these nuns. But what if it was incarceration? Like they did with Father Rivoli! They could even kill her and no one would know. Sister Beatriz is right. I don't have a choice. I'm totally screwed.

He began struggling with his breathing. Alejandro was hyperventilating. More images floated through his mind. They could shave Melissa's head. They could subject her to one hundred lashes. They could leave her out in the open without food or water. I need to save her!

"If I do as you ask, what will happen to Melissa?"

"I will send her back with the Momos to their village. No harm will come to her. This is the only mercy that I can offer. We have to protect the Order."

He tried to peer through his captors to catch a glimpse of Melissa, but was not successful. His head was getting dizzy and he felt nauseous.

Alejandro struggled to think. He wondered if he was willing to give up everything for this young woman. *All this has been my fault. I seduced her. I really f__ked up! I should have behaved. On the other hand, they probably would never have let me leave the abbey anyway. I'm being punished for my wicked ways and for being stupid! I'll never see my family.* Tears welled up in his eyes and trickled down his forehead.

"Okay, Sister," his voice was shaky, "I'll do it."

Sister Beatriz gave some instructions to the two natives. The taller one cut him down while the other supported Alejandro's body as it slumped to the ground.

Alejandro caught a peek of Melissa as she was being restrained by the other Momos. He was distressed.

"Melissa!"

"Alejandro!"

CHAPTER 44

ATTACK

The last thing Alejandro saw was Melissa being dragged away by the Momos. She was screaming all the way. He had promised to take care of her.

"Alejandro!" She was begging Alejandro to save her.

His heart was breaking. A tear trailed down his cheek. He felt so helpless.

"Are you ready to proceed, my son?"

His head moved up and down.

"I don't need to remind you what you promised?"

He nodded "no" slowly.

Sister Beatriz gave instructions to the two Momos in Spanish. One of them left in a run. The other picked up a walking stick and a type of machete and began trekking through the narrow path.

Alejandro followed him from several meters behind. Sister Beatriz brought up the rear. He realized that they were returning the same way that he and Melissa had traveled the night before. He saw the broken boughs and the bent grass. Then he realized that he had made it so easy for the Momos to track him. *Smart lawyer? No, I am such a frigging idiot!*

Within a few minutes, they reached the main trail. It was muddy and washed out in places. The trek back to the abbey would be slow. They had walked only a short distance when they halted. Sister Beatriz was holding her own, but she was getting noticeably winded.

They rested. No one was carrying any water. They would have to endure the trek back under less than ideal conditions.

Sister Beatriz called the lone Momo over to her and they talked. Alejandro heard her issue some sort of instruction. The native unwound a thin hemp cord from around his waist. He took the nun's right wrist and bound it.

Alejandro went into a meditative state. He was in no mood to pay much attention to this action. He was bemoaning his new destiny. He couldn't think of a solution to save him. I'm a lawyer. How come I'm so frigging dumb?

Suddenly, he felt a strong hand grab his left wrist. Instinctively, he jerked it back. Alejandro had come to full attention.

"My son, it is for our own safety," Sister Beatriz said with a calming voice. She was taking no chances with him.

Reluctantly, he put out his wrist. The Momo tethered him to Sister Beatriz with the other end of the cord. *Now, I am really f__ked! I can't escape even if I wanted to!*

The trio resumed their way back to the abbey at a very slow pace, avoiding big puddles. The distance between Sister Beatriz and Alejandro was only about a meter. That made it awkward for them to walk together without difficulties. The trio had to take a few detours, the Momo slashing at wet foliage to clear a passage.

They came to rest on a greenish limestone rock at Sister Beatriz's insistence. Alejandro's wrist was welting up from the constant tension of the bond between him and the nun.

After a brief respite, they proceeded onward. Sister Beatriz's garb was soaked at the bottom and weighted her down. As she and Alejandro were negotiating a downward slope through wet grass, she slipped, almost bringing him down with her.

The Momo increased the distance between himself and the pair to about fifteen or twenty paces.

Carefully, the nun and Alejandro crossed a tiny rain runoff, only to find it very difficult to maneuver uphill. They tried to grab onto rocks, but they were very slippery.

"Ayyyyyyy!" came a shriek from Sister Beatriz as she fell backwards taking Alejandro with her. They slid down the incline.

Clumsily, Sister Beatriz tried to right herself. Her face was muddied. Alejandro kept silent. His arm hurt from being yanked.

"We have a long way to go. We must have patience," she huffed trying to convince herself.

The Momo was up above them. The two zigzagged slowly up the slope. Finally, they reached the top where they rested on wet grass. Alejandro let out a sigh. He was fatigued.

"Sister, your wet clothing is hampering us."

"I know, my son, but I have taken the vows of chastity and obedience. I must comply with them. Life is about duty."

Alejandro was unsure how to respond, but he exclaimed, "Am I going to be imprisoned like Father Rivoli?"

"I don't know, my son."

"That's not fair!"

"Life is not fair," Sister Beatriz retorted coolly. "It has always been the fault of man since the times of the Garden of Eden. Adam sinned. And we must pay for his sins."

Alejandro sulked in his thoughts. *I don't understand why I have to suffer for Adam's disobedience. And what about Eve? She sinned too! Life is shit!*

He and Sister Beatriz kept trudging through the mud and washed-out paths.

Alejandro's mind went back to being catatonic. He eyes

stared directly in front of him. His subconscious was fixated on the perilous fate of Melissa as they approached a large obstacle in front of them. A very tall cottonwood tree had been uprooted and was strewn across their path. Its branches made the passage very difficult along with the mud puddles that inundated the grounds in front of them. The pair sat down on a little mound of wet grass near by.

The Momo advised Sister Beatriz that he was going to detour around the tree and have a look up ahead.

The pair waited for about ten minutes. The Momo did not return.

"Let's go," she barked. Sister Beatriz had decided to follow the native's trail.

The nun and Alejandro stood up and attempted to circumnavigate the fallen tree. She dragged Alejandro along.

As they trudged forward, Alejandro started to think about Melissa again. *What is happening to the poor girl? I promised to protect her. What is happening to her?*

"Ayyyyyyyy!" came the high-pitched scream from Sister Beatriz. She had inadvertently tripped on something. Alejandro saw what it was. It was the severed head of their Momo guide. Blood was oozing from it. The body was missing.

Then they suddenly heard something ahead of them. They saw a black form on the other side of the fallen tree trunk about forty meters in front of them.

Alejandro's heart was racing. His legs were like lead weights. He was only energized by adrenaline. The two started to chase the figure, sloshing through the mud.

The dark figure was thrashing through the bushes in front of them.

"Hey!" cried Alejandro. He had shouted out of instinct.

He wanted to know who this person was. He really wanted to know what had happened to their guide.

The form turned around and started to circle his way back toward them. It had the appearance of a smallish man in baggy black clothes. He was wearing a very large black hat that obscured his face.

The figure closed the distance between himself and the pair. It was now only thirty paces away. Alejandro could not get a good look at the face, but it looked like he was wearing an eye patch.

Alejandro and Sister Beatriz had stopped in their tracks. They were bewildered. They noticed that the stranger was clasping something.

It looked like a thick tree limb. No, it was an arm. A human arm!

Alejandro was sickened by what he saw. This was the demonic creature that had mutilated the Momo!

This must be El Sombrerón! The f__king murderer! The same one who killed Sister Sophia!

"Run, my son," shrieked Sister Beatriz. She panicked and started to run back, dragging Alejandro with her. They got entangled at first but finally broke loose.

Their frantic attempt to escape was clumsy. They almost stumbled several times. Some times Alejandro led the way, while at other times the nun tried to take the lead. Their chests were heaving and their mouths were gasping for breath.

The creature was quick and closed the distance from the fleeing pair. Five meters separated them. Now three! Now one! El Sombrerón sprang forward. Miraculously, the two barely sidestepped the charge and they veered toward the remnants of the path. They all of a sudden stopped from exhaustion and resignation.

The creature halted and directly faced Sister Beatriz as he surged forward again.

Sister Beatriz braced herself. She was breathless as the foreboding figure pounced on her. The nun staggered but amazingly maintained her balance.

Alejandro tried to grab El Sombrerón, but the creature escaped his grasp. Instead, Alejandro was struck behind the ear by El Sombrerón with the Momo's severed arm. He fell to one knee and tried to protect himself. He was trying not to be frightened. He realized that his fate was literally tied to Sister Beatriz.

El Sombrerón feigned to strike the nun again. Sister Beatriz prepared herself to fend off the blow. Instead El Sombrerón turned away and seemed to withdraw. Alejandro regained his balance and stood up next to the nun in a defensive posture.

The nun was tired and could not maintain her guard. Suddenly without warning El Sombrerón pounced on her, knocking her down. She plunged sideways into the blackberry vines, dragging Alejandro down with her. Instinctively, he tried to release himself from the nun. However, he was still bound to Sister Beatriz. El Sombrerón now sprang on top of him.

Alejandro felt a thousand thorns pricking his back and arms. He howled. Sister Beatriz who was trying to escape painfully extended his left arm.

El Sombrerón arose from between his two fallen victims. There was an earsplitting, diabolical laugh that emanated from the beast.

Alejandro tried to get up, but he couldn't. His pants were pinned to the brambles. It was like he was lying on a bed of broken glass.

El Sombrerón glared intensely at them. The creature's right hand went to his left hip. He extracted a large machete. The blade was double sided and reflected the sun's light.

Alejandro felt the tension from the bonds between him and Sister Beatriz.

El Sombrerón came at Alejandro with the machete raised above his head.

Alejandro readied himself. Sister Beatriz was still trying to crawl away, dragging him with her.

El Sombrerón's arm came down. He was powerful. Alejandro felt the tension between himself and Sister Beatriz dissolve.

Warm liquid was oozing from Alejandro's body. He lost consciousness. His mouth went dry.

He could no longer hold on. His eyes closed.

There was a bright light.

There was a silence.

The blood flowed onto the berries and darkened the clayish earth.

CHAPTER 45

LAVENDER

Tuesday, June 25, 1974, Mexico City.

"Alejandro!" a soft feminine voice cooed.

There was a buzzing sound. Actually, it sounded more like a humming.

The dull tones transformed themselves into indiscernible voices.

Alejandro could not open his eyes, but he sensed some external brightness. His mind was still semi-comatose. His thoughts were floating aimlessly in his head. His body was numb. He couldn't feel anything. Not his fingers. Not his legs. Nothing.

There was a perceived movement to his left. His mental synapses slowly began to connect.

He felt the warmth of a hand on his forehead. It really wasn't a feeling sensation. It was more like a weight that put pressure on his brow.

What did he smell? Was it the scent of lavender?

The moments passed slowly. His eyelids started to slightly part. Everything was blurry. The bright light hurt his eyes.

He craned his neck slowly to the left. Alejandro's eyes opened wider.

He saw a figure dressed in black and white. It was out of focus. He tried to concentrate. It was a nun.

Was it Sister Beatriz? Oh, shit! Am I back at the abbey?

Alejandro felt a starchy garment on his body.

Where am I? How did I get here?

"He's regaining consciousness."

"Blessed be the Holy Mother."

His eyes closed. He slid back into a lethargic dreaminess.

A few hours passed.

Alejandro sensed his limbs tingling. Something was resting on top of his right shoulder. There was something pinching his right arm. His body felt hot and sweaty.

He was slowly awakening from a deep sleep. He peered around. The room was bright.

He could now definitely smell the scent of lavender. Subconsciously, he smiled.

A figure approached him.

"How are you, my son?"

He couldn't swallow. His mouth felt like cotton.

"Thirsty," he whispered in his semi-conscious state. "I'm thirsty."

Another figure approached.

"I'll fix him some tea," said the first.

"Thank you, Sister," replied the second. "Alejandro, thank the Holy Mother, you're alive." She bent over and touched his cheek.

In slow motion, he turned toward her.

"Mom," he mouthed softly. He was in a daze. He couldn't collect his faculties.

"My son, we've been so worried. We've been praying for you for days."

"Mom, where . . ." *A thousand thoughts were beginning to race through his mind.*

"Don't try to talk, Alejandro. Just rest," she continued to caress his cheek as she looked lovingly into his glazed eyes. "I need to call your father. He'll bring Ricardo and Lupe. And

Inocente. Everyone has been worried to death about you. We're so happy that the Holy Mother has brought you back to us."

The nun returned with some hot tea. She came over and raised his head. She carefully held the ceramic cup to his mouth. Instinctively, he sipped the hot beverage.

It only whetted his thirst. It was warm in his mouth. It tasted refreshing. It was slightly sweet.

"It's cinnamon tea with a little bit of honey."

"Sister, excuse me, I'm going to call my husband."

"Of course, Señora Rubí."

His mother departed from the room.

Alejandro had only drunk about a third of the cup of tea. The nun returned to her seat in the corner.

A few minutes later his mother returned and sat in a chair to the left of the bed.

"They are on their way," she told him with a loving smile. Her eyes were bloodshot like she hadn't slept for weeks. Her makeup was long gone, but she was animated.

Alejandro's stomach started to feel bloated. His esophagus felt acerbic. He started to experience nausea. He lurched forward, as if to vomit.

"Sister, come quickly!"

The nun rushed over and snatched a large towel. She positioned it up to Alejandro's mouth, but nothing happened.

Alejandro's stomach was convulsing. He groaned.

"What's wrong, Sister?" implored the concerned mother.

"I don't know. I've rung for the doctor."

Alejandro's stomach churned. Its juices were gurgling. This was climaxed by a gigantic belch.

The doctor rushed in. Alejandro's mother and the nun made way for the physician. He examined Alejandro in a routine manner. The doctor felt his brow for a moment and then asked Alejandro to open up his mouth. The physician turned his head for a brief moment to avoid the foul breath.

He then asked the nun a few routine questions. She answered what he had consumed and how long he had been unconscious.

"This young man will be fine," the doctor announced. "Sometimes what is sweet in the mouth is bitter in the stomach. Give him some bicarbonate and water."

The doctor excused himself and left the room.

Alejandro's mother moved back next to her son. She had a worried look. Alejandro seemed to go back into a catatonic state. He stared upwards. He was immobilized.

More hours passed.

He was aroused by a conversation in the room. His parents were talking. He was now awake. He blinked his eyes a few times. For some reason Alejandro thought it was now nighttime.

In front of him stood his parents and siblings and their maid. Everyone was dressed up as if for a funeral.

His mother noticed that he had awoken.

"Alejandro!"

His father came over to Alejandro's side.

"How are you, my son?"

"Fine, father."

"You gave us quite a scare. Your mother has been beside herself."

"I'm sorry, father."

"No, Alejandro, it was not your fault. We are just glad that you are back. Your mother and Inocente have already started their novenas for your safe return. We are thankful that you have survived."

"Father, there is so much to tell. I don't know where to begin."

"Not now, Alejandro, you must recuperate first."

"How did I get here?" his son persisted.

"Rest, Alejandro." Señor Rubí softly placed his hand on Alejandro's cheek. "The details are very sketchy. It seems that your vehicle ran off the road a several weeks ago. This was when you were driving back home to us.

"Some natives found you. You were half-dead. You had deep gashes from the crash. Your left arm was mangled. You had a big bump on your head. And it looked like you had fallen into a hornets' nest. You were stung all over your body. You were totally naked when they found you.

"It took them a few days, but natives brought you to the local authorities who had already discovered the wreckage. The police notified us. They transferred you here to this hospital.

"We are just grateful that you are back, safe and sound. You have been in a coma since you were found. For the last few weeks, you have been surviving on intravenous medication."

Alejandro gazed to his right. Indeed, there was an IV line stuck into his right wrist.

That's what is pinching me.

Suddenly, his father's words sunk in. *Could I have been in this hospital that long? The time frame is all wrong. I think that I was at the abbey for at least two weeks. Maybe three.*

"What about Melissa?"

"Who?"

"Melissa. What happened to her?"

"We don't know anything about any Melissa."

Señora Rubí came forward and looked over to her husband. "I think that was the name he kept calling out when he was brought here. We thought that he was just delirious with fever." She looked so heavyhearted. She was filled with powerlessness at seeing her son helplessly lying there. Tears rolled down her cheek as she looked at him. His left arm was no longer. It had to be amputated because of the fear of gangrene. Obviously, he was in physical pain. The morphine had given him hallucinations. However, she knew that his suffering went way beyond. It was emotional. Maybe even spiritual. She saw sadness in her son's soul.

Tears welled up in Alejandro's eyes. His head turned away from his parents.

"Let's let him rest. This has been traumatic for him."

"Mom, we want to give him the presents," cried out Lupe and Ricardo. They approached their parents.

Señora Rubí gave them an admonishing glare, but Inocente joined the two youngsters in their pleas.

"Oh, mom, please," they pleaded.

"Okay, children," the mother giving a displeased glance at Inocente.

Alejandro rotated his body toward his family. His mouth strained to give a faint smile.

"Alejandro, here. I brought you some cookies. Inocente helped me bake them." Lupe placed the cookies on Alejandro's bed stand.

"Thank you, little sister," he attempted to put on a brave face.

"I hope you like this book I bought you," his brother came forward. "I bought it with my own money. Didn't I, father?"

"Yes, son."

"Thank you. Thank you all."

Alejandro was trying to appear cheerful. He was grateful

to his family, but his heart ached for Melissa.

Another nun entered the room.

"Visiting hours are now over. You may come back tomorrow."

Alejandro's family said their good-byes and promised to return the following day.

"I have to change this dressing. It won't hurt," the nun raised his sheet.

The nun then came around to his left side and cut open the bandages on the stump where his left arm had been. There were little spots of red blood and pus. She wiped the area with alcohol.

It was then that Alejandro noticed a large wilted bouquet of lavender on his nightstand.

"Who brought me these?"

"Oh, they found you in the jungle clasping them. You never let go of them."

The nun finished replacing the bandages and then left the room.

Alejandro shut his eyes. He inhaled deeply. A weak smile appeared on his face as he thought about Melissa and the lavender.

CHAPTER 46

LONG LIVE THE QUEEN!

August, 1974, Somewhere in the Jungles of Guatemala.
"Alejandro!" she cried out.

"There, there, there," the old woman rubbed the girl's forehead. "You are having another nightmare. You're all right, my dear."

"Auntie," Melissa opened up her eyes. "I dreamt that Alejandro was being tortured by the nuns."

"Melissa, as we keep telling you, the white people picked him up in my cousin's village several weeks ago. I was told that he was badly injured, but I'm sure he is alright now"

"I want to see him."

"That is not possible," Marica said softly, trying to sooth her. "He has gone far, far away."

"I miss him. I'm still afraid for him."

Marica nodded her head in an understanding fashion. There was nothing for Melissa to fear from the nuns. Marica knew that none of the nuns at the abbey had survived. Their food had been poisoned. Yes, Marica had needed to protect Melissa from the vengeance of Sister Clara. Rafaela and Marica had been forced to leave the abbey and find refuge in one of the Momo villages. It was there that they finally found Melissa and retrieved her from the Momos who held her in custody.

"Here, drink this," she handed Melissa a gourd of a sweet, white liquid. "Rafaela found this in the outskirts of the village just for you. The Momos here make a special drink. It will sooth your nausea."

Melissa nodded her head in appreciation.

"You must continue to eat all of your food, especially the jelly," Marica placed some toast and condiments in front of the girl. The old cook patted the girl's belly. "It will keep you and the baby healthy."

Melissa thought that her great aunt was talking about fruit marmalade, but Marica and Rafaela had been feeding her royal jelly from the abbey since they had left the abbey two months prior with the assistance of their Momo relatives.

Her aunt brushed the girl's hair with her hand while Melissa ate.

Thereafter, Marica picked up the dirty dishes and returned to another hut in the village. Rafaela was there by a small wooden table.

Rafaela held up two gourds. They were filled with mead nectar. She handed one over to Marica.

They clashed the hard shells together.

"Long live the queen!" they toasted.

༑

ABOUT THE AUTHOR

Rocky Barilla lives in the San Francisco Bay Area with his wife, Dolores, and the dozens of feathered friends who visit the bird feeder daily. He was formally educated at the University of Southern California and Stanford University. He spent two academic quarters in Vienna, Austria.

His passions are 19th Century French literary fiction, Mexican history, global traveling, and cooking. He is a bad golfer.

Rocky has been actively involved in human rights issues, especially involving Latinos and other people of color.

His mantra is "Life is Good."